THE HOUSEKEEPER

THE HOUSEKEEPER

LEONA GRACE

*Dedicated, as always, to the friend who set me on this course
and to all who have given me support and encouragement.*

CHAPTER 1

Peter Sinclair held his breath, praying he had misread the diagrams. Any mistake at this stage would be disastrous and he spread the sheet out and ran his finger along lines, calculating weights and lengths and hoping it was his own tiredness rather than any error on Deborah's part that made the plans look flawed. But it wasn't.

She had failed to allow for the terrace gardens on the fifth floor. Not in itself a disaster, but if the plans were not amended before tomorrow they would not pass building regulations and the firm would lose a major contract. It was tempting to walk away; as the longer serving architect, he'd requested the job only to be turned down in favour of Deborah, and right now she was nowhere to be found. He didn't blame her – everyone at Foster and Hamilton worked hard enough – but he had no way to contact her before the Christmas Dinner Dance tonight. And it might be too late by then.

He spread the sheet out again. It would take him the rest of the day to re-do the calculations and drawings but there was no other option. The only thing he could do was to make the alterations on a second copy and let Deborah update her file first thing tomorrow.

Jacket slung over the back of his chair, he pulled off his tie, undid the top two buttons of his shirt and started work, measuring and redrawing, looking beyond the lines to imagine how it would appear in reality.

It was close to seven by the time he finished and even then he was uneasy. The design would pass inspection, but that was all. He would have opened out the atrium and made a feature of the columns, cut out the terraces which were impractical and costly. But it was not his design, and he rolled up the paper and put it aside.

Tomorrow the board would be holding their annual meeting. The rumours round the office were of promotions and expansion and bonuses. And he'd done good work in his time here – brought new clients into the company, delivered everything on time and well inside budgets, even had a couple of articles in one of the national journals. His work was faultless, his designs popular, his costings accurate.

It had been enough to get him appointed as one of the senior architects before the collapse of his brief marriage. The divorce had been quick and crushing and he had walked away with nothing other than a stammer made progressively worse by the stress. It was easier to remain single now, avoid the embarrassment of finding himself unable to speak, the humiliation of someone ending his sentences for him or rolling their eyes with exasperation at his clumsy efforts to converse.

Since then there had been nothing but hard work and little joy. The dull 'bread and butter' tasks no one else wanted, the crushing disappointment when they passed him over for promotion and brought Deborah in to join the team. At the age of thirty-two he was too realistic to get his hopes up again.

Most of the other buildings around the square were in darkness, the solicitors and accountants and graphic designers all gone home, and he leaned on the windowsill, staring out at the park. There would be no pleasure in the evening ahead. Given the choice he would willingly forgo the annual Dinner Dance but his absence would be noted, and after recent rumours he would be a fool not to attend even if the food was unpalatable.

The temperature had dropped while he worked on the corrections and even from here he could see the glitter of ice on windscreens. A long night ahead but at least he'd brought his clothes to work: dinner jacket hanging on the back of his door, dress shirt and bow tie in their plastic covers, overcoat draped over one of the chairs.

The men's cloakroom was empty, the acrid smell of disinfectant and cleaning fluid hanging in the air and he ran the hot tap, lifting a double handful of water and lowering his face into its welcome heat. The outer door squeaked a warning and he fumbled for the paper towels, grabbing a handful and dabbing water from damp cheeks and forehead.

"Still here, Peter? Thought you'd be the first one there. You know. Checking out the dance floor, eyeing up the ladies?" A smirk of cruelty in the voice. Hamilton.

He should have been used to it by now. As one of the senior partners, Eric Hamilton was a man too full of his own importance to care about offending anyone else and

Peter had become accustomed to the sly taunts. Easier to let them slide over him, like the memories of his past.

"I had…" He took a breath. Calmed himself. This was Hamilton, playing games with him. "I… had… something to f… finish."

"Well, you'd better get your skates on. Don't want to miss the fun and games do you?" Another twist of the thin lips. "You know how important tonight is to the future of the company. The one chance each year to show our face to the competition, forge new contacts, polite words in the right ears, that sort of thing. Reminds me, rumour has it Snagaxa's put a bid in for the Council contract Deborah's been working on. You worked with Johnson before he moved to the planning department didn't you?"

He nodded.

"Good. It's all a bit last minute and there's no one else around so I'm having to leave it in your hands. See what you can find out, let him know we can make it worth his while to put a good word in for us. And I'll do the same for you with the board if you can come up with the goods. Do you get what I mean?"

Water dripped from the tap and gurgled down the pipes behind the sinks, the air vent rattled behind him, someone walked along the corridor, whistling. He kept his eyes fixed on Hamilton, the unspoken words hanging in the pine-scented air of the cloakroom.

Do this or else.

He'd been the recipient of a few of Hamilton's 'last minute jobs' before – the nightmare project in Edinburgh, where the owner wanted costs pared to the bone despite everyone's objections, the awkward week in Carlisle where he ended up redesigning one entire floor of a renovation, the building firm who threatened tools down and a total strike if he didn't stop one of the hoteliers demands for last minute alterations.

"Yes." Single words were a little easier. He despised his inability to tell Hamilton where he could stuff his contract. He stared down at the floor, the thin swirls of water left by the cleaner's mop.

Hamilton paused for a moment. "Don't let the firm down, Sinclair."

The cloakroom door swung shut and he threw the wadded paper towels in the bin. He would have kicked the unfortunate container but for the fact that Hamilton was no doubt waiting outside.

He made his way back to the office, locked the door and unfastened his shirt, losing a button as he struggled with his anger. A quick check in the mirror, a pale ghost on the other side of the glass, a tall and solitary figure, light brown hair and eyes that held little joy.

The last time he'd worn the suit was before the divorce. Now the jacket hung loose on his shoulders, the shirt a touch too wide round his neck, his tie fastened in a perfect bow. The invitation lay on his desk, a rectangle of cream card, the firm logo embossed at the top and the wording formal and quite definite. His presence required.

The main car park was full by the time he arrived, and he was forced to use the overspill a hundred yards away. Heavy clouds obscured the moon but at least it was warmer, and the threat of frost fading. Johnson's sleek saloon was parked near the entrance and the bar was bright and loud, full of men in dinner jackets and women in outfits of every style and colour. He ordered an orange juice and wandered into the dining room to look for Johnson. Better to get it done before the meal if possible.

"Sinclair?"

He turned round. A breath of relief at seeing a friendly face. "Waterman? I thought you were in Dubai until Monday."

"Got a new job in Sydney, starting the end of February. I handed my notice in last week." He gave a quick smile. "Helen's family are all out there and with our oldest starting school next September, it seemed the right time to make a move. There's nothing keeping us here and she's expecting again, so…"

It was easy to talk to Waterman. They'd worked together on a joint project and got along well. "So, how many children is that now? Five?"

Waterman rewarded him with a jovial thump on the shoulder. "Idiot. Three. Well, four counting the one on its way. Helen's in her element but she was too tired to come out tonight so I thought I'd use the invite to catch up on the news." Waterman held up his glass. "Champagne. The one thing I missed out there. So tell me, what's been happening in Fosters? You in line for a management role yet?"

"Mm…" He shook his head with frustration and took another drink, wanting a decent whisky instead of orange juice. But the last thing he needed right now was to be pulled over on the way home and breathalysed. "Maybe… next year." The conversation had become awkward, his throat closing at the thought of having to interrogate Johnson later.

"They're fools, you know. If they're not careful they'll lose you to someone who appreciates your style. You should think about applying for my job. You'd fit in fine at Coupersons and they're looking to expand, set up a new office in Aberdeen for starters." The toastmaster called them to their tables and Waterman held out his hand. "It's not like Foster's – nothing but offices and warehouses. They like their staff to use their imagination and you'd fit in there. To be honest, I'm sorry to be leaving them but moving to Sydney was going to happen sooner or later. Think about it and let me know after Christmas. I'll be happy to put in a good word for you."

Chris Waterman headed off to meet the rest of his party leaving Peter to make his way to the firm's table in the centre of the room.

The meal dragged by: dull conversation about work and cars and holidays abroad, long speeches and toasts, coffee and mints. And then it was over and he dropped his napkin on the table and pushed his chair back before anyone could trap him in conversation. Deborah was already talking to Hamilton and he found a quiet corner and sat, waiting for Johnson to appear.

"Congratulations, Debs! Great news." A familiar voice, one of the chartered surveyors from a firm in the same building. They had not seen him behind the fretwork that concealed his refuge. "When did Eric tell you?"

Eric Hamilton. He listened.

"A few minutes ago."

"Who else was in the running? Anyone I know?"

Deborah's laugh cracked the air. "I'm not supposed to tell anyone, but if you promise…" She leaned forward, whispering.

"No! Really?" A softer laugh. "I've heard about Sinclair. The man's got talent, I have to admit, but I can't see him as project manager, let alone making the grade as department head. He's not got the right character. You need to be cutthroat in this business if you want to survive."

He closed his eyes. There would be no promotion this year, or the next. Probably never if Eric Hamilton had his way with the other board members. He stood there, hiding like a common thief, until the women wandered away, still talking about work and only then did he manage to slip out, avoiding the doorman and the small group of smokers sheltering under a canopy. Hamilton could do his own dirty work for once.

The rain had started again while he had been inside the hotel, drenching him to the bone before he was halfway across the rough gravel. The perfect end to his day. He started the engine and drove away, the wet cotton of his shirt sticking to his skin and his feet numb with cold.

His flatmate had gone out for the night, leaving no indication of when he would be back, but that wasn't anything unusual. Andrew was as much a stranger to him as anyone else in the city, a bank clerk who liked the high life and was more often than not out until the early hours. They shared an apartment and that was all. In the silence of the empty flat, he stripped off his wet clothes and wrapped himself in his bathrobe.

Deborah. He recalled the satisfaction in her voice, imagined the sly pleasure she would get from telling him, oh so politely, how she was heading for a junior partnership in a couple of years. And he knew the reason why; his stammer, made worse by stress or tiredness, was enough to condemn him. Tomorrow would be difficult at best.

Rain battered the windows, rattling against the glass

and pouring down to obliterate any view of the city. Glasgow at its worst. Wet and cold and thoroughly miserable. He poured himself a whisky and sat on one of the sofas, the tv on to catch the late news while he finished his drink and thought about his future.

CHAPTER 2

The night brought no easing of the rain. It spattered like hailstones on the window and drummed on the road outside, muting the sounds of traffic, and he was still awake and restless when his flatmate returned long after the clubs had closed. The all too familiar sounds of the front door slamming shut, the toilet flushing, a woman's voice giggly and drunk. The smell of toast from the kitchen and more laughter, quickly stifled. Footsteps on the laminate floor as they went into the adjoining bedroom.

He thumped a pillow and rolled over, tugged the duvet round his shoulders. The flats were cheap and poorly insulated and he was only here because after the divorce he was too numb to care where he lived. Come February, when the lease was up, he would move out. Sharing a flat was fine for students and struggling juniors or a man newly divorced and homeless, but he had enough money saved up to afford a place of his own now. One further away from the noise of the city.

By five o'clock he had given up trying to sleep. Hamilton's scorn and Deborah's voice echoed in his mind and however much he tried, it was impossible to silence them. There was only one thing to do, and he dressed in his threadbare jeans, found the grey sweatshirt and old trainers and picked up his gym bag.

When the leisure centre doors opened, he was first in line, tapping his membership card at the turnstile and heading for the changing rooms. This early in the day the pool was quiet and he dived in, legs kicking him onward before he breached the surface and began swimming. Length after length, each turn pushing himself harder, his mind counting each touch: sixty, sixty-one, sixty-two. Feet pushed against the wall, outstretched arms cleaved through the water, kick and kick again, shoulders aching with the strain... until he touched the far end with the final count of 'seventy' and clung there gasping, while his breathing eased. And then he turned round and began a half-mile of breaststroke.

The pool was getting busy by the time he finished and he climbed out to swipe water from arms and legs before heading for the shower. It was temporary relief at best, but he would be able to face the day with more determination, the tension driven out of his muscles, his frustration left behind with each push against the walls of the pool.

His flatmate was still asleep when he got back, the bedroom door closed and no sign that anyone had ventured out. He put his damp kit on the towel rail to dry and, heedless of his damp hair, went through to the kitchen, desperate for a drink and something to eat. A slice of toast slathered with a thick layer of dark orange marmalade, taking a large bite and swallowing it down with a mouthful of coffee hot enough to hide the taste of instant granules.

The kitchen door opened and he spun round, aware of his dishevelled appearance, his tousled hair and damp sweatshirt, the slice of still-hot toast in his hand with a bite taken out of one edge and marmalade about to drip from the corner. Heat flushed his face. His flatmate's latest conquest. Ash blonde and slender, bare arms protruding from the sleeves of one of Andrew's t-shirts, her lips wide and expressive and she stared at him with a half-smile and he turned away from her, embarrassed to be thought looking.

"You must be Peter?" She gave him a wide smile. "Andrew mentioned you last night. Nice to meet you." She leaned against the worktop for a moment as if to get her balance and then hitched herself up to sit on it. "Is that coffee you're drinking? Be a darling, and make me one, will you? And is there any more toast?"

He made another coffee – one sugar, just a splash of milk – and put bread in the toaster, sliding the butter and marmalade closer. He would have stayed to talk, but the bedroom door opened and Andrew appeared, yawning and still in his boxers and Peter retreated to his room.

It was still too soon to go into work and he had no idea what he was going to do when he got there, other than hide in his office and keep his head down until it was time to leave. And he had the holiday to face. The curt letter from the oldest of his brothers was still on his desk, reminding him of the family gathering on Christmas Eve.

Three days in the company of Derek and Susan was more of an endurance than a holiday but he'd booked the train tickets and bought presents for his hosts and his parents: a cashmere scarf from one of the designer shops in the city for his sister-in-law, a first edition leather-bound volume of World War 1 poetry for his brother, a couple of the larger Lego sets for Maxim. Not that he knew much about the boy, but Lego was a safe enough bet for a boy aged thirteen, especially one as precocious as Derek's only child. If Maxim didn't like the gifts, he would keep them for himself. His parents were more difficult and in the end he settled for a rare malt whisky for his father together with an early 19th century hip flask in hallmarked silver, and a heavier cashmere shawl in autumnal shades of gold and copper and russet for his mother.

But today he had to slink back into his office and sit at his desk, pretend everything was alright and keep himself hidden, not that anyone would care.

Enough. Today it was going to end, once and for all. There was nothing keeping him here. If Hamilton or one of the others needed a last-minute alteration or a site survey, they could find someone else. By his last reckoning he had three weeks leave still owing and more than a week in overtime. He had two choices – go into work and keep his head down and try to ignore the looks of pity or throw away everything he'd spent the last few years working towards. Whatever happened today, on Tuesday he would have to pack his bags and catch the train south to Chatham and Christmas with the family. All his deficiencies laid bare for their inspection: his disastrous marriage, the lack of progress in his career, his inability to speak for himself.

It was still early but the office would be open for the

morning cleaners and he knew the senior security officer well enough to get inside without too many awkward questions. With luck he might have thirty minutes before the first admin staff arrived and they wouldn't bother him. The rest would dribble in any time before ten, hungover from last night and not in any mood to work.

A quick shower, a careful shave, dressing in work clothes: charcoal suit, white shirt and striped tie. And then he was in the car and driving, hands tight on the steering wheel so by the time he pulled into the empty car park his shoulders ached. Low clouds filled the air with more drizzle and he made a quick dash across the car park to the entrance where the security manager was already opening the door.

"An early start, Mr Sinclair. Everything alright?"

The man was quiet and calm and patient. Sinclair brushed the worst of the rain from his hair, shrugged and gave a brief smile. "Lots to do, George. If... If I don't see you before I go, have a good Christmas." It was tempting to stay and chat, but he wanted to be done before Hamilton or any of the others arrived and he left George monitoring the entrance and made his way up the staircase.

A sharp smell of air freshener lingered in the empty corridors, no footprints marred the vacuumed carpet. He slipped inside his office and locked the door, closed the blinds to stop anyone seeing him and then he pulled out a sheet of headed notepaper and his fountain pen – a gift to himself after his graduation. An extravagance, but worth every penny. He'd managed for years with cheap roller balls and biros, and this pen, with its left-handed nib, fitted into his hand as if it had been crafted for him. No one else had ever used it. No one in his family had ever seen it for that matter. He took off the cap.

The words flowed without hesitation. Black ink on white paper, the script neat and precise and elegant. His letter of resignation, his term of notice being the required one month and covered by his remaining annual leave and accrued overtime amounting to seven working days. He added the dates and put the pen down to read the lines one last time. It was not too late to change his mind. He could stay on, keep his head down and….

Someone walked past his door, soft footsteps on thick wool, and he waited for the door to open, his hand sliding the paper closer. The footsteps receded and he leaned back and relaxed. He had enough savings now to tide him over for a good few months if he was careful, the rent on the flat was paid until the end of February and he had no other responsibilities. It was time to live a little. The nib slid over the page as he signed his full name, and he folded the paper, slid it inside an envelope and addressed it. Done. His career ended, and yet he could feel nothing but relief.

There were few personal things in the office. The fountain pen and pencil, his diary and leather case with his drawing equipment. Everything fitted inside his brief-case with room to spare. And that was it. Not much for five years' work. Envelope in one hand, briefcase in the other, amended plans from yesterday tucked under one arm and no one watching. He walked along the corridor and made his way downstairs for the last time, not looking back once.

The Reception desk was unattended and he put the letter down on the counter together with the plans, his office pass and keys clattering as he dropped them beside the envelope. And then he paused. He owed them nothing, and he picked up the plans and took them into the men's cloakroom, tearing them into shreds and stuffing them in the waste paper bin where they belonged.

His family would be appalled, but Peter Sinclair didn't give a damn. He was free. It was with a sigh of relief that he got back into the flat, stripped off and changed into his comfortable jeans and sweatshirt from earlier.

A couple of minutes on the laptop found a hotel four hours' drive away with views over the Moray Firth, and far enough from Glasgow to forget about work. His overnight bag was large enough for a change of clothes, spare shirt and underwear. A holdall took the rest of his things: walking boots and thick socks, woollen hat and scarf, leather gloves, camera, and the battered case with his pencils and sketch pads. He scrawled a note for his flatmate and left it on the kitchen worktop.

On a whim, he added the presents to the pile together with his laptop and drawing equipment. Andrew had a habit of inviting friends back to stay overnight and although he trusted the man, his things would be safer out of the flat. The warm parka used for site inspections was in the boot of the car and he stuffed the parcels into carrier bags and went out into the narrow hallway.

The woman had disappeared but he could hear voices inside Andrew's room and he let himself out, making sure the door was closed behind him even as he struggled with parcels and bags. Fat raindrops spattered on the windscreen as he drove away.

Late morning traffic made progress slow, the rain lashing down and the spray from lorries and tankers making it impossible to see any real distance ahead so it was with a sense of inevitability that, thirty minutes later, he found himself caught in a slow-moving queue of cars and a mass of blue and red lights some distance ahead. The queue came to a stop, cars falling silent as drivers turned off engines and sat there, waiting.

Ambulance sirens in the distance, getting louder and then the shock of one coming past on the hard shoulder and racing ahead. A fumble in the glove box for a packet of mints, a bar of chocolate, anything. Someone climbed out of the lorry behind him and ran up the embankment into the cluster of trees at the peak, returning a minute later still fastening his trousers and shaking rain from his hair. A car horn blared.

The rain fell, hard and fast, blurring the view ahead, not that he wanted to see what was happening. He tapped his fingers on the steering wheel, turned the radio to local news and tried not to think about last night or this morning. Or what he was going to do next.

The rain eased, disappearing in a final flurry of droplets and the traffic began moving again, a slow inching forward at first, until he was in second gear, and everyone slowing down again as they drove past crumpled vehicles on the hard shoulder, the barrier bent out of shape and men in yellow hazard jackets clearing away debris and he looked ahead, not wanting to share in someone else's distress.

Once the queues eased driving was easier – mile after mile of monotonous dual carriageway until he was crossing the river and heading into Aberdeen. A quick stop for petrol, the sat-nav leading him slowly through the centre of the city before spitting him out the other side. On reflection, he had been a fool to book a hotel such a distance away but it was too late to change his mind, and anyway, the hotel boasted undisturbed sea views. He hoped there would be a chance to walk along the coast.

A few miles outside the city he spotted a busy roadside café in a layby and stopped to stretch his legs and buy a drink. The tea was fresh and strong and the pasty hot and peppery and filling. He bought another and ate that as well. Crumbs littered the front of his parka and despite the weather he took it off and slung it back in the boot on top of the presents and bags. And then he was back behind the wheel, the roads quiet and narrow, the villages sparse.

Still a long way to go. A second stop in a deserted layby sheltered from the road by a line of bushes, a look around before relieving himself against the crumbling stone wall. Dusk would be in another hour, the visibility poor and the skies promising more rain. The seductive voice of the sat-nav took him further into the hinterland, heading north and wondering why he was gallivanting around the Scottish countryside in late December, especially in this weather.

The sun set and still he drove, refusing to turn back yet by now hopelessly confused having travelled for miles along an unmarked road scarcely wide enough for two cars. No lighting or cat's eyes, deep ditches on either side to stop animals wandering onto the worn tarmac and only a few hamlets along the way. With each mile his hopes of finding the hotel – any hotel for that matter – receded. The road was endless, the landscape nothing but a series of gentle rises and falls. He was high above sea level, the distant sea a darker stain in the deep dusk. The rain eased, but the road was perilous with run-off water and floods and he edged his way through, hoping not to flood the engine.

Mile after slow mile, fingers numb on the steering wheel, until the school-teacher voice of the sat-nav – in the middle of telling him to turn round – stopped mid-sentence and the display went dead. Tapping the screen did nothing, and he decided to drive on in the hope of finding a signpost.

He had gone a hundred yards when a dog appeared from nowhere. A huge animal, tall and gaunt, bounding across the road to stand right in the middle of the narrow band of tarmac, dark eyes shining in his headlights. It was instinct that had him slamming on the brakes and turning the wheel towards the other side of the road, but it was too late. A sickening thud, a long howl of pain and he saw the dark shape limping away down a narrow road half-hidden behind a cluster of stunted trees until he could no longer see it.

The lane was single-track, its edges crumbling, the tarmac rutted and pot-holed. Weeds grew tall and thick down the centre, a faded sign stood on one side of the track, the letters 'Private Road. Fitzwilliam Hall' peeling and nigh on illegible, but he ignored it, turning his head-lights to full beam and following the dog down towards the distant, moonlit sea.

CHAPTER 3

"Mr Wilson?" Fiona Cameron held out her hand to the man. A firm handshake before she turned to the woman standing beside him. "And Mrs Wilson? Welcome to the Hall. We haven't met before, I'm afraid. I'm Fiona Cameron, Tom's daughter. My father retired in May so I've been running the business until things are sorted out here. You didn't have any trouble finding us, I hope? Sat-nav is hopelessly unreliable round here and in the dark it's easy to miss the turn-off."

She hoped they didn't ask about what she'd been doing before returning here to run a dying business. She was not the first woman to be fooled by a man, and she wouldn't be the last, but over the last few months the peace and solitude of the Hall had done more to help her recover than anything else. Before coming back, she'd forgotten the tranquillity and beauty of the estate, even though she'd grown up here. There again, when she was a child and living in the Hall, she longed for the bustle of towns and cities, the delight of shops and proper libraries and cinemas. Now her heart ached at the thought of leaving here for good.

The woman shook her head. "We've been several times before. Never at Christmas – work was usually too busy and Jon and I were on call a lot of the time – but we both retired this year and decided to treat ourselves to a quiet Christmas together for once. No unexpected visitors to entertain or being 'on call'. Bliss." She turned to her husband and linked her arm in his. "It was his idea to come back here one last time, before it closes for good."

"Well, I'm glad you're here. I'm sorry the weather isn't so good, but if it stops raining long enough we might get some snow."

Jon Wilson pulled his wife into a close hug. "Sounds as if you might get exactly what you wanted – a white Christmas. You might even be able to make a snowman." He turned to Fiona and smiled. "Don't worry about the weather. We've come prepared for anything: snow, wind, hail – we can cope with it. As long as there's still a corkscrew and bottle opener in the cabin we'll be fine."

Fiona grinned and passed a set of keys across. "There is. I checked it myself. Now, you're at the far end in Number 1. None of the other cabins are occupied, so you have the place to yourself for once. I've seen to the hot tub, but I'd give it another hour to get to the right temperature. The heating's on and there's a bottle of wine and chocolates in the fridge, and I've laid the fire ready for you. Duncan stocked up the log pile this morning so you'll have plenty for the next few days and he'll be round later in the week to see if you need more. I'll be checking the tub each morning around nine but other than that, you'll be left in peace. Just come to the Hall if you need anything or there's a problem."

She watched them drive away, their car jolting over the rough track leading down to the cabin at the far end of the bay. A nice enough couple, a few years younger than her parents from the looks of them, and not expecting anything from the cabin that she couldn't provide. There'd been that dreadful couple in September who'd expected housekeeping and clean towels every day and had left Number 3 a total shambles when she'd gone to clean up afterwards. The Wilsons didn't look the sort of couple who would be much trouble and with any luck she would have a few days to get a few things done before she left.

A last look round, a few photographs, maybe even light a fire in the Great Room as a final farewell. She turned back to her work. There were two more cabins to clean and empty, although there seemed little point now. But first, she needed to get the dirty laundry out from the boot of her car and get it in the machine before it got too late.

She could see the Wilsons unloading their car, hauling bags and suitcases and boxes through the front door of the cabin. Enough for a siege from the looks of it, but the nearest good-sized shop was over ten miles away and no supermarket did deliveries out here. It was the only thing she missed about York – the convenience of having shops so nearby and a decent transport service. And reliable Wi-Fi. And the salary that went with her career as a web designer.

With more force than usual she shoved the washing into the machine, switched it on and set about sorting through the unused clean linens: pillowcases and duvet covers, bath towels and robes, napkins and tea-towels. It would have been quicker to simply stuff everything into bin liners, but she couldn't bring herself to throw them away even though none would be used again. A waste of time really, folding sheets and making sure everything was put back in its proper place. Richard's nephews would dispose of everything left here but she had no use for them either.

One of the duvet covers slipped back into her arms and she shook her head. Of course. Duncan might be glad of spare towels and sheets now that Blu was likely to be staying with him for a while. An unusual pairing – the estate's gamekeeper turned handyman and his unlikely great-nephew.

She'd caught one brief glimpse of the boy since his arrival earlier this week in the Royal Mail van, having been given an illegal lift from the village some six miles away. The lad looked more than a little nervous, squeezed into the space beside the stern red-haired highlander who delivered the mail each day, but the postie was a good-hearted man for all his dour mannerisms.

Duncan's unexpected visitor, once he had untangled himself from the parcels and letters and shopping that filled every nook in the van, turned out to be a skinny and angular teenager, all elbows and elongated legs and with a sullenness that spoke more of neglect than adolescent hormones. Silent and a little cowed, as if he was afraid Duncan might turn on him. And he was too thin by far: scruffy hair that cried out to be washed, bony wrists sticking out from the sleeves of a thin coat, his neck reddened by the wind and his nose raw with cold. She'd gone round the next day with a couple of jumpers and a winter coat her stepbrother had left behind on his last visit a couple of years ago. They were too big round the chest, but long enough to fit a lad of his height.

Since then she'd seen nothing of the boy and precious little of Duncan, but that was nothing new. The man could move through the woods as silent as sunlight and was perfectly capable of feeding himself: grouse, partridge, rabbit, fish caught off the headland, even the occasional deer culled to keep the local herd healthy. But caring for a teenager wasn't an easy matter, especially for a man fast approaching his seventieth birthday. Those few youths who lived nearby were renowned for getting into trouble and there was enough danger round here without looking for it. The rocky foreshore had twisted many an ankle over the years, and careless beachcombers were wont to find themselves trapped in the caves, or on the cliffs when the tide raced in. There'd been a close call last summer when one couple ignored all the warnings and went to explore along the coastline when the tide was on its way back. An uncomfortable few hours for everyone. And the coastguards had been less than impressed.

Two of the bath robes were new stock and she put them aside to take to Duncan's and stood, arching her back to ease the ache. Too much work for one person and yet the solicitors refused to employ anyone else to help with the cleaning. It had been different when her parents were here – they'd had a couple of women from the village to help out on change-over day, and after her mother's death Richard arranged for Abby to come each day to help keep the house clean. Three years later her father and Abby finally saw sense and realised they were in love. She envied them – a second chance at happiness was not something that came to many people.

Now it was Fiona responsible for managing the cabins and Duncan helping out with the heavy jobs as he called them: replenishing the wood supplies, clearing the foreshore of debris after the winter storms and repairing any damage. Compared to her previous life in York it was a somewhat lonely existence: eating meals by herself, checking the echoing and empty rooms of the Hall when she had time and it was still daylight, sleeping in her old room as if she had reverted to her pre-university years. The double bed with its faded covers and worn rug. The heavy curtains and dated colour scheme. Redecorating had been the last thing on her mind when she arrived back late on that dreadful May evening exhausted from the drive. Instead she'd dug out her bedlinen from the flat in York, and her favourite blanket to brighten up the room, not that she spent much time there. It was just somewhere to sleep.

The kitchen was warm if a little untidy, and she slid the kettle across to the hot plate on the Aga to bring it to the boil. Clean mug, tea-bag, boiling water. No sugar. She'd stopped taking sugar last May, stopped a lot of things like eating properly and sleeping and looking after herself, but she was over that now. Next year, she swore to herself. Next year will be a new beginning.

But she was lying to herself. On the sixth of January the legal records would declare Richard Fitzwilliam dead. There would be no grand funeral or memorial service to recall the shy and reclusive laird of the Hall, no dram of good malt whisky raised in his memory in the Great Room as the ancient tradition declared. The only event would be the arrival of his two nephews coming to lay claim to their inheritance, but she would not be there to greet them.

The solicitor's letter still lay on the table from when the postie delivered it three days ago along with Duncan's lad, and she smoothed it out with her fingers, reading the words again, the clinical phrases demanding she vacate the premises by six pm on Sunday the fifth of January or legal action would be taken to recoup any expenses incurred.

A single sheet of paper, not even a legible signature at the bottom, the words cold and legal and impassive and utterly uncaring that she might have nowhere else to go or that she had spent her childhood here until she left the Hall some eight years ago and made a career and a life for herself in York. The attached sheet had listed in precise detail what she was expected to do with the cabins: see to the removal of all rubbish, clean the interiors and leave the keys on the table in the kitchen. Not even a formal hand-over. They wanted nothing else to do with her.

Richard would have been mortified. Fiona could imagine his reaction at the letter: his quiet voice stuttering with anger, those long and elegant fingers holding the page, his once-tall figure stooped with the weight of years as he had been the last time she had seen him. He would be more stooped now, if he was alive, but that was unlikely.

The disappearance of Richard Edward George Fitzwilliam seven years ago had never been resolved. No body, no note, nothing but an empty house and unanswered questions and, come the fifth of next month, she would have no rights here at all. She hadn't told her father yet. There was no reason to distress him with her coming eviction, though he had warned her not to burn her bridges.

She had been so confident the new owners would keep the estate running as it had done for decades: the farmlands and managed forests, the neat line of four holiday cabins that brought tourists and money to this isolated corner of the coastline. But her hopes had been dashed four months ago when their petition was successful, forcing her to stand back and watch as the website was archived, deposits for bookings next year refunded, the contracts with advertisers cancelled.

Had there been no couple staying in one of the cabins, she would have been packed already and on her way and bugger the inventory. Let the new owners take care of that. The furniture in the apartment was part of the estate and had to be left behind: the Welsh dresser, the sideboard where her mother used to keep her tablecloths, the chest of drawers and huge dark wardrobe in her bedroom that she hated as a child and now loved. The personal stuff was waiting to be boxed up and collected after Christmas. An arduous task, sorting through her mother's few remaining belongings and her own childhood possessions. Thank heavens her father and Abby had been brutal in their decluttering before they headed abroad and there was little of theirs left.

It was fine for Duncan. Tenancy laws kept him safe from any threat of eviction unless they found him suitable accommodation, and that was unlikely – the retired gamekeeper was a man set in his ways and nothing would tear him from the home he'd lived in for his whole life. But it was a waste of time thinking about Richard. If he'd been alive, he would have returned by now and sorted out this whole awful mess. Seven years and not one sighting, let alone a postcard or letter. Sometimes it was hard not to hate him for abandoning not only the estate but everyone who cared about him.

Once the Wilsons drove away she would pack the last of her things and say goodbye.. She'd seen the two beneficiaries once when she was waiting outside the courtroom and overheard their plans: the dated cabins to be replaced by a dozen or more new ones, crammed together with barely space to walk between, the Hall stripped of everything saleable including lead flashings and pipework, and then left to fall into total ruin if they didn't get Council permission to demolish it straight away. They would sell the trees for timber and culvert the streams and build a landscaped golf course with hotel and conference centre and helicopter pad to attract wealthy clients. The rugged wilds of Scotland's east coast, caged and tamed.

Two more weeks and she would be gone. There would be nothing tying her to this decaying old building with its neglected rooms and peeling wallpaper and ghosts of the past. No reason to get up early in the mornings to watch otters playing on the rocky foreshore or seals wallowing in the shallows. The end of the Fitzwilliam estate.

Duncan had refilled her wood store yesterday and she went through and put another log on the fire. The last of the lamb stew simmered on the hotplate and she ladled it out and went through to eat in the solace of the sitting room in front of the welcoming flames.

She had only taken a spoonful when the rattle of an approaching car disturbed the silence, and she put her bowl down and went to the window, pulling back the heavy curtains to see who was coming down the lane. Evening visitors to the house were as rare as hens' teeth and she thought about going into the courtyard to close the gates. But then the vehicle stopped down at the bottom outside the gatehouse, and she watched as someone got out and went up to Duncan's door. One of the local farmers probably, come for a drink and a chance to talk. It was no business of hers and she went back to finish her meal by the warmth of the fire.

CHAPTER 4

The sun had set an hour ago with the boy still not returned from his wanderings. Duncan Grant checked the small bedroom again, but nothing had changed: the bed unmade, the lad's few clothes strewn across the floor, the morning's mug of tea left to go cold on the bedside table. Any other man might have slammed the door shut, but his years working first as ghillie and then gamekeeper on the Fitzwilliam estate had taught Duncan the value of staying calm. Patience, he told himself, the boy would return when his hunger got too much.

And hungry the lad was – too hungry for a scrawny teenager. There was a hopeless look in the boy's eyes at times, a look worse than fear in Duncan's opinion. Fear could be overcome, but when all hope was gone, then the journey back was much harder. He swore under his breath, cursing his feckless, feral niece who'd dumped her only child miles away with nothing but a ten pound note and Duncan's address written on a scrap of paper. Had it not been for the postie, Blu might still be lost out there. The Hall was not the easiest of places to find for a stranger.

The click of the door as it shut was enough to rouse Sock from his warm bed by the fire.

"Hush. No need to fret, laddie. The boy'll come back soon enough." At least Duncan hoped he would. There was no telling with a lad like his great-nephew, not that he'd had much to do with the boy since his birth fourteen years ago. Just the occasional visit before his mother took him down south ago in search of a better life, and then it was letters and postcards, most of them asking for money. And, fool that he'd been, he'd sent it. More money than he liked to count, and for what? Being taken for a muggins. He stumped in to the kitchen, face fixed in a scowl and Sock raised his head, listening to the clatter of plates, the hiss of the kettle and the gurgle of water pouring into a mug, the chink of a spoon as it stirred. The creak of the door opening again as the man came back into the warmth.

The small creature settled down again, curling his lithe body, nose now tucked beneath his dark tail, black eyes still watching the man as he carried the tray across and placed it on the footstool in front of the fire: a mug of tea, a pot of butter and a well-used Willow pattern plate with a small stack of crumpets for toasting. The ferret sat up, eyes bright with expectancy.

"Here." He plunked down a saucer with a few pieces of raw chicken. "No more after this. And where's your brother, then?" The man paused, tilting his head to one side. "Ah. There you are. I should have guessed." He opened the cupboard that filled the alcove on one side of

32

the fireplace. "Mitt? I thought you'd learned your lesson?"

The second ferret leaped out to join his brother, wriggling in delight at the prospect of the treat and the gamekeeper left them with their food and picked up the long toasting fork that hung in the companion set along with a blackened poker and pair of tongs.

Toasting crumpets for afternoon tea in front of the glowing peat fire was a task that needed some level of concentration if he was not to end up with burnt offerings or even worse, an empty toasting fork. But tonight he found himself thinking about the boy and it was only when a hard nose nudged his knee that he realised the crumpet was nearly burned. He pulled it off the end of the fork and dropped it onto the plate with a muffled curse, pushing the ferret away from his knee before starting again. By the time he had finished eating, licking butter from his fingers and letting the two ferrets clean any drips from the plate, the boy had not returned and he pushed himself out of the armchair with a frown.

"Come along then. Back in your cage while I go and find the lad." The soup was simmering on the hob and would take no harm for an hour or so. Any longer and he would have to ask Fiona for help and the lass had enough on her plate as it was right now.

The rain had stopped some time before, but the wind was picking up. A foul night ahead with snow on its way in the next day or so. By the time he'd pulled on his boots and fastened his coat, wrapped an old hand-knitted scarf round his neck and found his hat, the ferrets were chasing each other through the maze of pipes in their cage, unconcerned at being abandoned.

The Hall was in darkness, the single occupied cabin out of sight along the narrow track that edged the bay. Fiona would have finished for the day and he would not disturb her tonight, not unless the boy didn't come back in good time. He was too old for this responsibility, or perhaps he didn't want to be tied down caring for a teenager who hardly ever spoke and certainly had no real desire to be here at 'the end of the world' as the boy had described the estate in a voice full of contempt.

The lack of anything resembling a reliable Wi-Fi signal had been another thing to complain about as well as the poor television reception. But that was the appeal of being here – the quiet and the peace and the way the world outside didn't intrude. The cabins had been a great success when they were first advertised for holidays: newly built with expensive fittings and hot tubs, and free run of the estate. But since the laird's disappearance, nothing had been done other than keep them clean and replace linens and so on. They were shabby now, showing their age despite the fresh coat of varnish on the cladding last year.

"Blu?" His voice was drowned by waves crashing against the sea wall but he persevered, calling to the boy until he had walked the length of the gravel track in front of the line of cabins. No sign of the boy, and more worried now than angry, he turned back. There were the grounds of the House to search and then, if needs be, the shoreline as a last resort.

A dark figure appeared ahead of him, hunched and bedraggled and stumbling a little, heading towards the gatehouse from the other direction.

"Blu? That you, lad?"

It was – the boy soaked to the skin and shivering and even then unwilling to say where he had been for the last few hours. Duncan hurried him back to the gatehouse, stripping the lad of his sodden, useless anorak, the zip broken and its seams giving way. The sweatshirt underneath was soaked through and he thrust the boy in the direction of the stairs with a gentle but firm hand. "I want you under the shower to get warm, and no messing about. I'll find you some dry clothes and leave them here, outside the door? Ten minutes. Understand?"

The boy was too cold to put up a fight. The door slammed shut and Duncan pulled out a heavy saucepan and the milk and set to, heating the milk and adding cocoa and a generous spoonful of whisky from the bottle kept in the sideboard. Blu was underage but no stranger to alcohol as far as Duncan could see, and the whisky would do more than warm him through, it might help the boy sleep soundly tonight.

Half an hour later, Blu was finishing his second bowl of chicken broth, devoured with an appetite of desperate hunger. And then, although the lad was not a child anymore, Duncan insisted on tucking him into bed with a hot water bottle, a blanket and a couple of slices of home-made gingerbread. When he opened the door some twenty minutes later to check, only crumbs remained on the plate and the lad was curled up half-asleep, tousled hair a dark shadow on the white pillowcase. He closed the door with a gentleness that would have surprised many people and went back to the fireside to sit and think.

The house quietened. Sock and Mitt curled together in their cage and the fire collapsed in on itself, ready for the night. He poured a dram and sipped it, staring out of the window at the sea in the distance. A storm coming. Not today, or tomorrow, but soon enough. The unexpected knock at the door had the tentative sound of someone fearful of his welcome.

Blu had been the same, standing there with his hand still raised as if to knock again, Fiona close behind him, looking worried.

"Mr Grant?" A long pause, the voice hopeless. "You don't remember me, do you. I'm Sky's son. Blu. She gave me your address and said you'd look after me until...."

Blu. His sister's only grandchild. "Best come in then, lad."

But it wasn't Blu at the door this time. He undid the bolts – an unnecessary precaution for a man on his own, but he had the child to consider now. The heavy door opened without a sound. "Yes?"

The man looked ashen with cold. Shivering and trying to speak, but the words not coming out.

A pause. The man swallowed, and again. "I ... I hit your..." He shook his head. "Your dog. A ... black one."

Duncan frowned and tilted his head sideways to stare past the man into the darkness beyond.

"A dog you say? A black one?" He stepped back, held the door wide open. "You'd best be coming in then."

CHAPTER 5

Peter had been five when one of the Labradors at home had a litter of eight pups and when he saw them for the first time they were a week away from leaving their dam. Seven fat black wriggling bundles, each one destined for a wealthy home elsewhere. As any small child would have been, he was enchanted, spending every moment with the puppies and pleading for one of his own until, to stop his pestering, he was given a toy dog, plush and furry and cuddly. It was not as good as the real thing, but he slept with it in his bed every night until he went to boarding school two years later and his father refused to let him take it. It was not on his bed when he came home for the holidays and he never saw it again.

And now he had hurt a dog, had hit it with his car causing who knew what injuries. A broken leg, internal bleeding? He didn't think his wheel had gone over the animal, but he had only caught that one glimpse before it limped away down the narrow track.

His search for the hotel could wait.

The lane was single track and even that description was generous: the tarmac crumbling away at the edges, treacherous potholes so full of water he had no idea of their depth and the thought of being stuck out here with a flat tyre or broken suspension was enough to make him sweat. But the dog was still there, a dark shadow ahead, stopping to turn round and look at him every couple of hundred yards, its eyes shining with an eerie green glow in the headlights. He caught a glimpse of long legs and tail, dark shaggy fur and then the dog was gone again, leading him further down.

Shadows darkened the deep gorge running alongside the road on his right. Trees filled the chasm their branches empty of leaves, a neglected drystone wall providing a thin barrier between road and yawning gap beyond. The road seemed to drop away beneath his wheels, and he put the car into second gear then slowed even more as he realised the severity of the gradient. He hadn't driven down a road as steep as this for years, and that had been in a four-by-four, not an everyday saloon car. It was going to be a nightmare getting back up to the main road but he had committed himself and even if he hadn't there was nowhere to turn round.

The dog limped on, over the brow of a narrow bridge – little more than an ancient stone arch – which crossed a stream brimming with flood water heading for the sea. Even in the dark he could see how close the flood was to the bottom of the arch but there was nowhere else for him to go and he drove over, half-expecting the span to collapse under the weight of his car and throw him into the water below. But his fears were unfounded, the bridge proving solid enough, and he followed the dog, the road levelling out after a few hundred yards.

Ahead of him the dark sea stretched to the horizon and on his left, on the other side of the stream, the outline of something far bigger than he expected out here in the empty land – a tall building a few hundred yards away on the headland. The road widened and in his headlights he saw a second bridge – steel struts and sturdy wooden deck – crossing back over the stream again and leading away into the darkness concealing the building.

He expected the dog to make its way there, but he was mistaken. Instead the beast turned away from this newer bridge and made its way towards a second, much smaller building on his right – a two-storey house surrounded by a stone wall. A light shone in one of the downstairs windows and it was to this house the dog limped, disappearing behind the wall and no doubt making for the door.

The track widened enough for him to turn the car around and he pulled to a halt, switched off the engine and stepped out to peer at the house: a gatehouse from the late 18th century, two rooms downstairs and two up, one of which would have been divided to make a bathroom. In his time as an intern he'd done more than a few redevelopments for old dwellings such as this one.

The bitter wind took his breath away even before he had taken three steps and by the time he was at the stone wall he was chilled to the bone. Too late now to go back and get his parka from the boot – the dog was somewhere nearby. The gate swung easily when he pushed it open, the path was smooth underfoot and he stepped up to the painted door and knocked.

The man who opened the door could have been his paternal grandfather, not that he remembered much about the old man, but he'd seen his portrait in the library at home: tall and stern, the wiry strength of sinew and tendon and bone rather than bulky muscle, the expressionless face scored with age and experience, grey eyes that had could see into a man's soul and, standing there on the worn stone step, his courage deserted him. He had been an utter fool to come here in the dark and alone.

"Yes?"

The voice was softer than he anticipated. The cultured lilt of Edinburgh with all its refinements. And the gentle, half-pleased, half-concerned smile was unexpected. He paused, trying to force the words out past his frozen tongue, swallowing his failure down before trying again. "I… I hit your…" He shook his head with frustration. "Your dog. A…b… black one."

The old man frowned, peering past him into the darkness beyond as if searching for the animal. "A dog you say? A black one?" Peter waited for an outburst of anger, but the man stepped back and held the door wide open. "You'd best be coming in then."

CHAPTER 6

Despite the chill outside the room was unbearably warm or perhaps it was the pounding in his chest making him dizzy, his vision blurring and his legs shaking and then a pair of strong hands took hold of his arms and he found himself slumped on a sofa, head held down between his knees and that gentle voice talking to him as if he was a child.

"And breathe. And again. That's grand. Now, when I let go, lean back slowly. Don't try to rush yourself."

He waited for a patronising 'well-done' or a pat on the back but there was nothing, apart from cool, strong hands lifting from the back of his neck and then footsteps moving away across the floor. The chink of glass, a quick gurgle of liquid and the voice again, soft beside him.

"A black dog you said? Are you sure, now? A big beast was it?"

Somehow it was easier to speak when he had his head down and he was too ashamed of his weakness to make himself sit up and face the man. "Bigger than a Labrador. Like a lurcher, but taller." And limping.

"Could it have been a wolfhound?" The man was sitting beside him on the sofa and holding a thick glass in one hand. The fingers were worn with age, the knuckles white beneath the skin but this was a hand that had worked hard and was battered and scarred and still strong. So unlike his father's hands with their manicured nails and expensive signet ring and even more expensive watch.

"I think so. Maybe. I mean… yes. That's what it was. I'm so sorry." The stranger pressed a glass into his own fingers and without even thinking about it, he took a drink. Whisky. A highland malt from the taste of it, peaty and earthy with a hint of smoke. Another sip, his heart steadying and his breathing easier. "I couldn't drive away and leave him."

"Her. She's a bitch. And no, you did the right thing coming here." A hand touched his shoulder. "She'll not come indoors so you stay here while I go out and see to her. And don't you worry. I've known her for a long time and she's a tough old girl. She'll be fine, trust me."

He nodded, mute with misery at the thought of the dog out there in the cold. Christ, he was tired. A tiredness nothing to do with work or long hours or the drive here. The fire crackled in the hearth as a log slipped, throwing out a flurry of sparks, and he could do nothing but sip his drink and wait.

The sofa was deep and soft and he eased himself back onto the cushions, letting the weariness wash over him, the warmth of whisky in his throat as he looked around the small room. Oak floorboards and a thick rug in front of the fireplace with a well-used leather armchair closer to the warmth. Firewood and peat bricks were stacked on one side of the slate hearth and he could see a poker and a toasting fork with long curved tines. Dark beams crossed the low ceiling. A desk in one corner and, on the other side, a large cage hidden in the shadows and half covered by a blanket. The whole room had a sense of calm, of peace and safety and he leaned back and took another mouthful, his eyes closing despite his determination to stay awake.

The click of the door opening roused him from his doze and he pushed himself up, the soft cushions of the sofa enveloping him in their embrace, his glass empty, though he could not recall finishing the drink. "Did you find her? Is she...?"

"She's fine. Not a scratch on her and you'll be glad to know she's back home, safe and sound where she belongs."

The release of tension was too much and he found himself shaking, not from cold or dizziness, but with the humiliation of finding himself close to tears. A grown man, crying over a bloody dog. His father would have mocked him for such weakness.

A hand pressed on his shoulder. "Here. Drink this." A second glass of whisky, this one with a splash of water to soften the potency. He gulped it down as if it was lemonade. A shameful waste of a decent malt, but he could have emptied the bottle without caring right at that moment. "When did you last eat?"

"I don't know. A few hours. I've been..." He could feel the emptiness in his stomach, the whisky doing little to ease the ache.

"Hungry? You look like you need something inside you and not just more of my whisky. That's twelve year old Balfour you were drinking."

"I'm…"

The man laughed. A sound like cool water on his face, clear and refreshing and washing away any guilt. "Don't fret yourself. I drink enough of it as it is." He held out a hand. "My name's Duncan Grant. I'm – well, I was – the gamekeeper here on the estate. Now? Now I keep my head down and do what needs doing. And you?"

"Me?" Peter blinked. The hand was still extended and with a blush of embarrassment, he took hold. "Peter Sinclair. From Glasgow."

"Not born there. Not with that accent."

"I work there. I drove up, set off this morning." It seemed a lifetime ago and a world away from here.

"A long journey. Did you mean to come here, to the Hall, I mean?"

Peter gave a brief laugh. "The Hall? To be honest, I've no idea where I am. The sat-nav died on me not far from here but even then I was lost. I'd been driving for hours and I was about to turn round and find somewhere I could ask directions but then the dog came out of nowhere and…" He shuddered, his hands clasped together, knuckles standing out white against his pale skin. "I was sure she was hurt so I … followed the road down and hoped I'd find it before…" And he still had to find the hotel. A miserable prospect given the fact that he could feel the whisky taking effect, his limbs weakening, his alertness fading.

"Chicken soup. No, not for the soul, Mr Sinclair, though there are those that say my chicken broth is the best thing for any man's soul. I have some waiting to be warmed up, with fresh bread, home-made this morning. Would you share a meal with me?"

"I should be going. I can't…"

"Drive? I wouldn't let you drive away from here even if you were well-fed and rested. No man who's got two of my whiskies inside him is fit to drive, especially on these roads in the dark. You left your car unlocked, Mr Sinclair and I have your keys." He smiled and patted his pocket, but his face made it clear there would be no driving tonight. "So. You'll do me the honour of eating with me and then I'll find you a bed for the night. And in the morning? Well, we'll see what tomorrow brings. Now, go upstairs and wash your hands. Don't be too long, supper will be on the table in five minutes."

The bathroom was austere to say the least. Basin, toilet, a simple shower, but it was also spotless apart from a pile of wet clothes in one corner. Jeans and a sweatshirt, mismatched socks, a pair of boxers. He studied them for a moment, wondering who had left them, but it was not his concern and, mindful of his host he busied himself. Cold water on his face and the back of his neck, hot water to clean his hands – the bright yellow coal-tar soap another reminder of his childhood – and he went downstairs into the spacious kitchen with a renewed sense of calm.

"Just in time. Take a seat." Duncan Grant gestured to one of the chairs. The table was oak and old and beautiful and he would have liked to inspect it more closely, but the soup was waiting and he ate hungrily, mopping up the final scrapings with a crust of bread. The family house-keeper used to give him soup, but never anything as rich or as satisfying, the seasoning perfect, the stock having the unmistakable taste of being simmered for hours and he put down his spoon with a sigh of contentment.

The effect of the whisky had worn off and he was awake once more. "I should be going. I've already caused you enough disruption tonight." The words flowed with no hesitation in his voice. Had the man opposite him been his father or Hamilton, he would be sitting there tongue-tied. "You've been more than kind and the meal –"

"Sit down, man." The voice had the same sharp tenor as one of his teachers at school and he sat down again, a little shocked at hearing such a stern voice from a man who had been so gentle earlier. "I already said you're staying here tonight. I'd let you sleep in the spare room but it's being used, so you'll have to make do with the attic. It's warm and dry and there's a bed of sorts, but better than nothing. You brought any spare clothes with you?"

"In… in the car." He hoped the hesitation would go unnoticed. "I'll n… need…" If he had his keys he could drive away, find somewhere to sleep – a layby maybe, until morning.

"I left it unlocked." Duncan pushed back his chair and started to clear the bowls and plates. "Away and get your things while I see to my two in there."

The car was parked at an awkward angle, but he could do nothing about that. It was raining again, a heavy drizzle that clung to his sweatshirt and had drenched his face by the time he retrieved his bag from the boot and slammed the lid down. It seemed wrong to leave the vehicle unlocked, and then he shook his head. They were miles off the main road and he could not imagine any car thief making his way down here in the dark on the off-chance of finding an unlocked vehicle, especially such a drab one as his. A second-hand purchase, over sixty on the clock and rust eating into the edge of one door. But it was a car, though his family would have regarded it with scorn. Another reason for getting the train down to Chatham for Christmas. He hurried back, head down to avoid the worst of the rain.

"Here." Duncan handed him a towel and he put the bags down and dried his hair and face before toeing off the wet trainers. The fire was blazing in the grate, a couple of logs added to the flames and he went over to warm his hands, only to find two dark, sleek bodies tussling with each other on the thick rug.

"Ferrets. You have ferrets." He could hardly contain his surprise, or his delight. The gardener at home had kept a few for hunting rabbits and rats – untamed and intractable creatures with a wicked tendency to bite anyone wary enough to poke them, but he had sneaked down to their cage as often as possible. "Do they bite?"

"Not if you're gentle. They're well trained. The one with white paws is Mitt, the other one's Sock." Grant bent down and picked Sock up. "Here. Hold him firmly, he'll wriggle away otherwise."

The sable fur was softer than he'd imagined, the slight body supple and strong, the accompanying smell much fainter than he remembered from those childhood days. But these small creatures were gentle and inquisitive.

"Blu doesn't like them." Duncan shrugged. "I keep them in their cage when he's around, unless I'm here with them."

A peculiar thought, that someone could be frightened

of such small creatures, but there again, he disliked spiders and small spaces. "Blue?"

"The boy who's staying with me, my niece's son. She called him Blu. Like the colour only without the 'e' at the end. It's no name for a lad who's just turned fourteen, or for any child in fact. He turned up a few days ago after his mother did her usual disappearing act. He's bright enough as far as I can tell, but he doesn't talk much, not to me at any rate."

He knew the feeling. At times it was easier to stay silent than try to speak and make a fool of oneself. The ferret made a lunge to escape and he lowered it to the rug. "You're willing to let me stay here, a total stranger, even though you've got a child in your house?"

"Aye, well…" Duncan shrugged. "I have my reasons and anyway, something tells me you are a trustworthy and honest man and not someone likely to murder me in my bed. Am I right, Peter Sinclair? Anyway, come with me." He led the way up to the landing where a loft ladder went up to an open trapdoor. "No one will disturb you up there tonight. The bed's an old one but it's clean and there's a sleeping bag and a couple of pillows and blankets so you'll be warm enough."

Even so he hesitated. "But…"

"If it makes you feel any better, I'll be across the way, here." The man pointed to one of the two doors on the corridor. "I'll have my door open and I'm a light sleeper. But as I said. I trust you. Leave it at that, Mr Sinclair."

～

Duncan Grant listened to the silence inside his house. The boy – he could hardly bring himself to think of him as 'Blu' – was sound asleep, not even waking when Sinclair climbed up the ladder to the loft room. And his unexpected guest asleep as well. Duncan had given him a half hour before making a cautious climb up the ladder to check the man was settled. Sinclair was not what he expected. Quiet and nervous like an ill-treated dog for all his education and manners. Duncan had no idea why the man was here, but it was not his business. Not yet.

His own bed was waiting for him, but first he had to make sure. The front door creaked slightly, not enough to wake either of his guests, but enough to alert his companions. A quick squeak of interest came from the cage.

"Not now. You be quiet, d'you hear me?" The ferrets subsided and he pulled the door wide open and walked down the path, slow patient strides, letting his vision adapt to the darkness.

The dog was sitting next to Sinclair's car, a dark shadow against the mud-spattered paint. A great black wolfhound, tongue hanging out of her mouth, her eyes watching as he opened the gate and took a couple of steps towards her. Not close enough to touch her – she would only fade away if he tried. "It's been a long time, Bess. Are you sure about this? He doesn't seem to have…"

The wolfhound stood, stretching her long forelegs and arching her back like a dog waking from sleep. A single swipe of her tail before she raised her head to sniff at the air. In the distance, far away, young children were laughing and calling out and before he could take another step, the dog was loping away into the night, paws soundless on the rough gravel. He watched her disappear and a moment later came a child's cry of delight and a gentle 'woof' before the sounds faded, leaving him to retrace his steps and close the door behind him.

There had never been any need to lock doors here, not even when the cabins were all occupied, but he had care of the boy as well as Peter Sinclair. The little-used key turned with some effort, and he pulled it out and put it in his pocket and went through to his bedroom to open the small safe and retrieve another key, this one for the gun cabinet concealed in his wardrobe.

A quick inspection of the shotgun to make sure it was empty, and a second check. Unloaded, as he knew – he was meticulous about keeping it safe, but that was no reason to take risks. The leather cartridge bag was hidden behind toilet rolls in the bathroom, but the gun itself was enough of a deterrent. The ferrets were sleeping and the living room warm, but he went upstairs and checked the boy's room again.

His own bed welcomed him and he undressed and lay down, the gun close at hand should it be needed, but he had faith in the black dog who had guarded this land for over two hundred years and after a few minutes he relaxed enough to fall asleep.

CHAPTER 7

The house was quiet, only the faintest scratching sounds and the occasional squeak from downstairs, and Peter imagined the ferrets playing in their cage. Georgia, his ex-wife, had refused to let any animal into the house, not even a cat, and once he was on his own, keeping a dog was impossible in the small flat. He envied Duncan Grant.

A surprisingly good night's sleep considering the embarrassing state he'd got himself into. His phone was dead and he had no idea of the time, other than it was still dark outside. There was no rush anyway. Once he was up and had said his goodbyes he would... what? Find his way to the hotel? All thoughts of spending a few days walking had disappeared late yesterday when he ended up here. For some reason he had been guided to this isolated stretch of coastline and found an unexpected welcome, but it would be best to leave before he became accustomed to Duncan Grant's kindness. The thud of footsteps downstairs warned him it was time to get up.

A few minutes spent putting on jeans and clean socks, sweatshirt, trainers and he was making his way down the ladder. The door to the boy's room was closed and he headed for the bathroom first and then down to the kitchen.

"You slept well?" Duncan was breaking eggs into a bowl. "That was my bedroom when I was a boy. My sister had the small bedroom, but I liked the attic. There was no proper window back then, just panes of glass instead of slates in a couple of places, but it was quiet and no one bothered me once I was there. The laird had the proper window and the loft ladder put in when the cabins were built some fifteen years ago." He picked up a fork and began whisking the eggs.

"Cabins?"

"Four of them. The laird's idea. And a great success. They were booked out most years until this last year." Grant put the bowl down and reached for a long-bladed, heavy knife. "Can you chop the herbs for me?"

For a moment he thought he'd misheard, then Grant held the knife out, handle first, and gestured to a small heap of dried leaves on a thick wooden board. Sage, thyme, parsley.

He took the knife and set to, knife in one hand, the fingers of the other holding the blade in place as he sliced down in rapid movements. The leaves were fragrant and he scraped them into a neat pile, turned the board and continued chopping. A companionable silence apart from the thud of steel on wood and the rattle of the fork in the white earthenware bowl.

Duncan glanced back at him. "Put those in the eggs

when you're done. You do eat eggs? I never thought to ask."

He nodded. "It's very kind of you to do this. I don't know how I can repay you."

"Enough about repaying. I was only doing what any decent man would do. You weren't thinking of leaving this morning? Surely there's no rush to get back to Glasgow, or have you got someone waiting for you?"

A long pause. The knife rattled against the board. "N... No. There's..." He shook his head in frustration, his mind going blank as he struggled to say the right words.

Duncan Grant put the bowl down on the worktop and pulled a frying pan out of the cupboard. "Well then. It's going to be a fine morning though the weathermen would tell you otherwise. A brisk wind but nothing that'll hurt if you wrap up warm. You should have a look around while you have the chance. You can't go in the main part of the Hall, but it's worth seeing from outside. Mind the housekeeper, though. Miss Cameron's a little wary of strangers right now."

He'd only seen the vaguest outline of the Hall last night, little more than a dark shape against the night sky, but it was worth a look. Miss Cameron was another matter altogether. He had no wish to upset or annoy an elderly housekeeper. He would have a quick look and then set off to find the hotel.

"How old is it? The Hall, I mean?"

Duncan shrugged his shoulders. "There was a tower house here long before anyone remembers. Miss Cameron's the one to ask. Where the cabins are..." He waved a hand at the foreshore. "There were twenty or more stone cottages along there, or so they say, crammed

53

together on the narrow ledge between cliff and water. A hard life, making a living from the sea and the smugglers only made it harder."

"Smugglers?"

"Gin, brandy, tea, tobacco. You name it, they brought it through here. Some old tales say they hid their cargo in caves along the headland but it would have been a perilous place to store anything valuable, and others say they used a secret passage. That way they could come and go without being seen by anyone."

Dungeons and smugglers. The sort of story he had dreamed about as a child. Revenue men creeping through the night, silent men hiding in caves and secret rooms. His fingers gripped the knife tighter.

"Eggs ready?" Duncan's amused voice brought him back to the bright warmth of the kitchen and the knife still in one hand.

The question caught him off-guard. "N..." A final chop, the herbs scraped together into one neat pile. "There." The quiet pleasure at a job done well. He stirred the herbs into the eggs, handed the bowl across, to where Duncan was melting butter in the pan. "What about your lad? Is he awake?"

"He doesn't stir until mid-morning." The note of disapproval was surprising for a man who had shown such compassion last night. "He'll get up when he's ready. And then... well, no doubt he'll disappear until it's time for something to eat. Lord knows what he does with himself outside all day long."

Probably the same as Peter had done at school – find somewhere quiet where no one could find him, and then hunker down until it was time to go back. He didn't envy the boy. "I can go up to the house by myself. There's no need for you to take me, is there?" It would give him the opportunity to take a real look at the building as well. "You could take your lad fishing maybe?"

Duncan shook his head. "I offered yesterday but he wasn't of a mind. Though perhaps I should take him out with me today. With all the rain we've had there's more than a few ditches need checking, and there'll be flood water coming down off the hills in the next few days. I could take the quad bike if he might prefer that."

But there was a note of hesitancy in the man's voice. Peter sighed with memories of long days at home. "When I was a lad, I'd've jumped at the chance to do something like that. He might complain – teenagers do – but I bet he'll love it, even if he doesn't tell you."

"You think so? Did you ever do that, when you were a lad?"

Another shrug of his shoulders. "I didn't really get to do much when I was a boy. It was mostly school and then keeping myself to myself when I was home for the holidays."

"I understand, I think." Duncan finished the omelette, sliding one half onto a plate for Peter and the other onto his own. "The quad bike it is then. I'll wake him when we're done here. Now eat up, Mr Sinclair, before it gets cold." He gave a quick smile before turning his attention to his breakfast.

It was close on nine o'clock before the boy wandered into the living room where Peter was sitting on the floor, playing with the ferrets. "Who the fuck are you?"

The words were still high-pitched though Peter could hear a distinct crack. The start of manhood. A confusing time for any boy, let alone a teenager dropped out in the wilds with no parental support. He'd had little enough of his own when puberty began.

"Peter Sinclair. I got lost on the roads and your uncle was good enough to let me stay here last night." Sock wriggled his way under his sweatshirt and peeked out, wary of the boy. "In the attic, in case you're wondering."

A monosyllabic grunt, a scowl of disapproval or perhaps wariness before the boy slouched into the kitchen, slamming the door behind him. Angry words echoed from the other room, Duncan's voice low and stern and patient, the boy not bothering to mute his replies. Sock was silent and still in the protection of his sweatshirt, but Peter lifted him out and put him back in the cage with his brother.

It was time to go. He'd caused enough of a ruckus already and even though it was tempting to stay longer, it was clear he was not welcome, at least by the boy. His bag was already downstairs and he found his car keys on the windowsill and went through to the kitchen. The lad was standing beside the heavy oak table, his thin frame tight with anger, fists clenched, legs trembling, shoulders stiff with tension.

Peter ignored him and held out his hand to the man. "I've come to say thank you. I should be on my way. You've done enough for me, already." He looked at the lad, seeing more than anger. There was some other emotion there as well – shame? Or maybe fear. And not fear of him, nor of Duncan. The lad would not have slept so well had he been frightened of the old man. Something else was scaring the boy. "I'll put my stuff in the car and have a walk round before I head off, if that's alright?"

Duncan nodded, his eyes fixed on the boy. "Have a safe journey. And if you're passing again, come in and see Sock. He seems to have taken a shine to you."

The boy ignored him.

"I will, and... thank you." For once it was not raining and he walked down the path to the car, slinging his bag into the boot. From where he was standing he could see the neat line of cabins looking out over the Firth, but it was the Hall standing on the headland that intrigued him the most and he grabbed his camera and turned to face the tall building a couple of hundred yards away on the other side of the wooden bridge he had seen last night.

The style was familiar, a classic tower house extended over the years into an L-shape and now four storeys high with a steeply pitched roof. The stair turret at the nearest corner was topped with a cap-house which added to its charm, as did the row of windows under the eaves and at the top of the gable ends on either side of the chimneys. An iron-studded oak door stood between stone arches, another arch was set in the wall enclosing the courtyard. But the Hall had been neglected for some time.

Even from this distance he could see weeds flourishing between the stones. Ivy had colonised one of the walls and several plants had taken root in the shelter of the chimney stacks where mortar had rotted. A thing of beauty for all its neglect and slow decay. He stepped back to take photographs as a battered Land Rover drove out of the gateway, down the slope and over the bridge with its steel struts and sturdy wooden deck, the thick planks rumbling as it crossed and then it was coming towards him, bouncing on the rough surface of the gravelled track that edged the small harbour.

CHAPTER 8

The daily check of hot tubs was a tedious task, especially in bad weather, but from talking to the Wilsons yesterday Fiona was confident there would be no problems. She was tired enough after yesterday and worrying about Duncan's lad, and emptying and refilling a tub was the last thing she needed right now.

For the first time in what seemed like months the sky was clear, but that was little relief. The whole area was saturated by rain and the weather broadcasts warned of severe flooding inland in the next day or so. There was no time to worry now – the Wilsons would be waiting for her to arrive and check the tub and she grabbed the test kit and the bag of sheets and bath robes for Duncan and went out into the courtyard where the Land Rover was parked at the far end.

The car from last night was still outside the gatehouse, and a man standing next to it. For one heart-stopping moment she thought it was Richard returned from the past, a portrait come to life. The same height, the same stooped posture, but then he straightened his spine and the weak sun shone on light brown hair, not silver, and the face was that of a man who bore little resemblance to the missing laird other than in his height and the way he carried himself. The closeness was all in her mind, nothing more than wishful thinking in an attempt to save the house before it was too late. Even then it was hard not to hope for a miracle – the stranger turning out to be a long-lost son arriving in time to disinherit the nephews and bring new life back to the estate.

She pulled up alongside the car – nearly as old as her Land Rover – and jumped out, boots splashing in one of the numerous puddles. "Is Duncan still home?"

He stared at her. "I…" A shake of his head, his throat bobbing as he swallowed. Fingers ran through his hair and he seemed to shiver. "Duncan. Yes."

Shyness? Or something else. He looked uneasy and yet those eyes had a look of keen awareness. He glanced away, revealing the curl of one ear, the strong line of an unbroken nose, firm lips and a chin with the slightest of clefts. Pale skin stretched over a perfectly shaped skull. Her breath caught in her own throat. How could she have thought him anything like Richard? Golden stubble cast a faint shadow on cheeks and chin and throat, the handsome face unmarked by age, but there was an austerity to his expression that spoke of a lack of joy, a man who had not seen much happiness in his life so far. It was hard not to step forward and give him a hug.

She was staring like some love-struck teenager. "I'm sorry, that was rude of me. I'm Fiona Cameron. The housekeeper here." She held out her hand. His fingers were cold, his eyes not quite meeting hers. "Did you spend the night with Duncan? I mean... I'm sorry, that sounded..."

She got a quick glimpse of a smile, eyes crinkling as his lips twitched and his shoulders relaxed. "It's a long story. I turned up at his house in a bit of a state last night and very sensibly he refused to let me drive. I ended up sleeping in his attic bedroom." He arched his back as if to ease some lingering stiffness. "I wonder. Would you mind if I have a look at the outside of the Hall and maybe take some photographs? I have a passion for historic buildings."

"Give me a few minutes and I'll show you round the outside if you'd like. First I've got to drop these off for Duncan and have a word with him about..." She was gabbling. He would think her an utter idiot. She tugged her waxed jacket into place and grabbed the bin liner from the passenger seat. "Look, walk up and wait in the courtyard for me will you? I won't be long."

The bag was heavier than she thought and, as she lifted it out, it split, linens and towelling spilling out towards the muddy gravel. And then he was reaching down, scooping up the tumble of white cloth and black plastic before it touched the ground, his grey sweatshirt stretching to reveal surprisingly broad shoulders for someone who looked so drawn.

Another smile, broader this time and more confident. "Don't worry, I've got it. You go ahead and open the gate."

Duncan was at the door, watching. "Fiona. I see you've met Mr Sinclair."

Mr Sinclair. No first name and no mention of why the man had arrived last night. "I've brought some spare sheets and stuff, if you can use them? It's stupid to throw them away." She bit her lip, aware of the stigma of being thought a charity case, but Duncan nodded.

"Thank you. I'm sure I'll find a good use for them. Put them inside will you, Peter? On the table, if you don't mind?"

She watched Sinclair edge into the house, a sideways shuffle though the doorway with his arms full.

Duncan turned to face her, lowering his voice and looking serious. "Mr Sinclair stayed here last night. I thought you should know."

"He told me. It's nothing to do with me who stays here. It's your home, Duncan."

A shake of the head. "I know, but with the way things are at the moment you're right to be wary of any strangers. You need to know something else." He put his hand on her forearm. "Bess brought him here. Last night. He thought he'd hit a dog on the top road and he followed her down to my house."

"Oh god." She put her hand over her mouth. "Was she...?"

"Angry? No. Far from it. She was waiting outside when I went to check on her."

"And?" She didn't want to know, but at the same time she was desperate.

"I heard the children laughing and she looked at me and wagged her tail and went off to join them, like she always does." His hand squeezed her arm, gently. "She brought him here, Fiona. I don't know why. I let him stay last night because I thought if he left we'd never see him again."

The creak of the door alerted her to Sinclair's reappearance, the boy standing behind and scowling.

She leaned closer to the old man. "So I should trust him, is that what you're saying?"

He let go of her arm. "I'm not saying anything. All I know is that Bess wanted him here. The only times she's failed anyone was when Richard disappeared, and no one knows what happened to him. He might have gone in the sea for all we know." He looked up as the man and boy approached. "Blu? You're coming out with me today. I've got ditches to check before the flood waters get too high and you can help out. If we get it all done in time, I'll give you your first quad bike lesson. Might as well learn to drive one if you're staying here for any length of time."

Fiona hid her smile at the look on the boy's face – the guarded dismay at having to help clear ditches and the equally guarded delight at the prospect of driving the quad bike. A boy with his own secrets. She wondered what his life had been like before he arrived here, and what it would be like when his mother came back for him. "Have a good day, Blu. And Duncan? Let me know if you find any problems on the estate. I don't want the new owners to accuse me of keeping secrets." She shook her head, thinking of the unpleasant days ahead of her and the work she still had to do. There were better things to be doing with her time than showing a perfect stranger round the grounds of the Hall, but it seemed she had little choice now.

"I will, lass. Don't worry."

She turned to the man standing there. "The courtyard, Mr Sinclair. Give me five minutes; I have a hot tub to sort out first.'

The Wilsons were finishing breakfast when she pulled the Land Rover to a halt and clambered out again, test kit in hand. At least she could see them inside the cabin instead of turning the corner and surprising them in the tub. The most annoying thing about having the tubs on the site was that she never had a chance to enjoy one but now was her chance. The two cabins nearest to the Hall were waiting to be shut down: the power still connected and the rooms untouched. She could come down later and fill one of the tubs ready for a long dip tonight. No one would know, or care.

The lid was heavy and wet from the night's rain and difficult to lift. It was one of the few tasks she loathed and even more when there was a problem and the system had to be drained and refilled and re-heated. It took her a minute to get the sampling flask and the test paper and check the levels, and then she was done, dropping the lid back down and fastening it. The wind was getting up, crashing waves against the edge of the foreshore, flinging spray into the air and coating her face with tiny droplets. The test kit landed on the passenger seat and she drove off, gears grinding and wheels jolting on the rough surface.

Sinclair was waiting for her under the arch, wrapped in a waterproof parka and thick scarf, walking boots and gloves. Her father's work coat was too large, her bare hands cold and her hair already coming out of its messy plait. She hadn't even bothered with make-up. Fiona Cameron, who last year owned a dozen lipsticks and more eyeshadows than she could possibly use and who had her hair trimmed every six weeks. It needed cutting now, the plait reaching half-way down to her waist. The old Fiona Cameron insisted on designer clothes and a perfect manicure. Now she was content with high-street jeans and jumpers and a borrowed jacket past its best ten years ago. Matthew would have been appalled.

The thought hit her like a slap to the face. He had no part in her life now, but even so it was hard to shrug off the memory. The wind stung her eyes and she rubbed them, wishing she'd thought to pull on a scarf and hat before coming out.

"Ready?" She slammed the car door shut, regretting her haste in offering to show him round. The airstream was straight from the north, bitter-cold and arctic, the sort of wind that worked its way through even the thickest windproof coat. An icy draught chilled her spine.

"Do you mind letting me have a look?" He hunched his shoulders, stooping as if the wind was beating him down.

She waved a hand at the house. "It's no bother. You're not seeing it at its best though. The house and gardens used to be magnificent, but it's been neglected for years." She looked up at him. "It probably won't be here next time you come."

"Unsafe? It looks sound enough to me."

Her nose was cold and starting to run and she fumbled in her pockets for a handkerchief. "New owners. Next month. They have plans for the estate." Her fingers found cotton and she pulled out the handkerchief, relieved to see it was cleaner than some others she owned. "Excuse me..." She turned away, embarrassed, her cheeks getting colder, her fingers numb as she stuffed the handkerchief in her pocket and turned back to face him.

"Here." A sudden warmth of wool filled her hands and from more than the material itself. He had taken off his scarf to give to her, and she snuggled into the comfort.

"Sorry, but you look absolutely frozen. I should let you get back inside where it's warm."

The scarf was long enough to wrap round a second time, her words now muffled as she answered him. "No need. I'll grab a hat and gloves." She led him across the courtyard and down a short flight of steps to a weathered oak door. "This is the housekeeper's apartment, where I live. The rest of the house isn't occupied. Come inside." She saw the momentary pause as he stood in the entrance and looked around. Despite the room being on the lower ground floor, one side window looked out over the bay and two taller windows straddled the doorway, letting daylight flood in. "Hurry up. You're letting all the heat out." And he smiled and stepped inside, closing the door behind him and pulling off his gloves.

"Mrs Sullivan used to say that. I'd forgotten until now."

"Mrs Sullivan?" Her gloves and scarf were on the rail by the Aga, woollen bobble hat hanging from one of the door knobs. She unwrapped his scarf and handed it back with some regret.

"The family housekeeper when I was young. She used to get cross if I left a door open." He was holding his hands out in front of the Aga. "She'd have given her eye teeth for one of these in the kitchen."

"I couldn't manage without it. Not that I'm much of a cook, but it keeps the kitchen warm whatever the weather outside. Richard wanted to replace it with a modern oven but my mother threatened if he got rid of it she'd never make him another chocolate cake ever again." She tugged the bobble hat on, tucking her thick plait out of sight. Scarf next and gloves. "Right. Where do you want to start?

The remains of the original tower house? The best place is over in the far corner."

"If that's alright? Who was Richard? Your father?"

"Good God, no," she said and instantly regretted it. "I'm sorry, I thought Duncan would have told you. Richard Fitzwilliam, is – at least until the sixth of January – the laird of the Hall and this entire estate."

She opened the door for him, her hands and face warmer now, but that would not last for long. With any luck Mr Sinclair would be satisfied with a quick tour of the exterior and she could get back to the warmth of the kitchen. By the time she had closed her front door and made sure it was latched, he was at the top of the steps and looking around the courtyard, the wind less vicious here within the protection of the high walls. His breath crackled in the chill air. "And what happens on the sixth?"

It hurt to say the words. "The court grants a decree confirming his death and his nephews inherit: Hall, estate, everything." She tugged the scarf tighter. "He went missing seven years ago. They never found his body."

"I'm sorry. That must have been difficult for everyone. It sounds like you don't approve of his nephews either."

"Richard didn't leave a will. At least none that anyone can find. And yet he was meticulous about that sort of thing. His nephews are the next of kin though they made no effort to see him while he was alive, and they have their own plans for the house I think. And the cabins."

"I don't envy you looking after all this by yourself – the house and the cabins. A lot of work."

Easier than leaving here. She shrugged. "I took over the job in May when my father retired. It was hard going in summer but now there's only one cabin occupied, and the others are mothballed, there's less to do and Duncan helps out a lot. As for the Hall, it was more or less abandoned after Richard's disappearance. The trustees refuse to allow any work to be done inside and I'm not even supposed to go in but I do, as often as I can. If something isn't done soon, the damage will be irreversible." Despite the scarf and hat and gloves, she shivered. "This way. I'll show you the outer storerooms where they kept grain and so on. Those haven't been used for years so you can look inside if you want."

He was staring up at the turret, eyes fixed on the small window as if watching something. "You said the Hall's empty? No one living in it?"

"No one. Not for the last seven years. Why?"

He shook his head but she could see the puzzled look in his eyes. "Nothing. I was… I was wondering about the state of the roof." A frown creased his forehead, but he said nothing else, following her in silence across the courtyard and down steep steps to an open archway.

"There used to be a door here, a long time ago. You can see where the hinges went." She pointed them out, feeling like a tour guide. "The walls in the original parts of the building were over five metres thick in places, but these are thinner – look." The walls were dark with rain, the floor squelchy with mud, but she stepped inside and pulled out her phone to illuminate the darkness. "You can come in, if you want. It's quite safe."

He shook his head again, stepping back a pace to let the light in. "Duncan said there were smugglers here in the past? Did they use these storerooms?"

"I suppose they may have. Some of the old tales talk about pirates landing here and hoarding treasure in the caves, but if they did, there's nothing left. A fairy tale, that's all." She started back up the steps, leading the way out into the courtyard. "It was the serious smugglers who were the real problem. They used the bay as a safe harbour for landing their goods and some stories say there was once a secret passage from the caves up to the Hall but nothing's ever been found from this end and searching the caves is an impossible task. No one bothered with the smugglers until the winter of 1784 when their boats were preventing the local fishermen going out. One of the villagers got angry and brought in the local customs men. The smugglers had pistols and the customs men had knives. You can imagine which group came off worst. And then when it was over, the smugglers took their revenge on the fishermen and their families by burning the cottages and kidnapping the laird's two young daughters. Probably for ransom."

"What happened to them? The children?"

"The story goes that the weather was so bad the smugglers couldn't risk launching the boats to get back to their ship. So they made their way up the cliff path and into the woods to wait for better conditions. The children were found by the family's wolfhound who led them to safety and the smugglers were never seen again. No one knows what happened to them. Some people say they were lured to their deaths by something, and a few people claim to have seen ghostly figures in the woods late at night, but that's probably the drink talking." She waited for the next question, hoping he would not delve too deeply into the story.

"And Richard's the last in the line? No children?"

She brushed mud from her sleeve. "He never married.

There were rumours about a long-lost love when he was younger, but that was all. He always seemed happy here, writing a history of the house and the family. He was a sensitive man, kind and thoughtful and everybody loved him and he cared deeply about the estate and the Hall. It still hurts thinking about what might have happened to him." A seagull flew overhead, its shrieks loud enough to break the peace in the courtyard. "Anyway, I'll show you the remains of the tower house and the window to the dungeon. Not much left to see but it's the bones of the Hall, as Richard used to say. Without that, there wouldn't be much here at all. As it is, the estate is falling apart."

"Old houses like this end often end up derelict. Too expensive to maintain, and no one willing to take on the responsibility." He turned back to stare at the turret. "Are you sure there's no one in the building? A child perhaps?"

His question annoyed her. "I check the Hall nearly every day. There's no one inside and no way anyone could get in without breaking one of the lower windows and they're all barred."

He pointed. "There. Top level, the window near the end. See? There's a... child? No. Two of them, young girls staring at us. They were there before we went into the storeroom, but I thought I was imagining things." He turned to face her. "You can see them, can't you?" The note of urgency in his voice was frightening. She put one hand on his arm. He was shaking and not from the cold.

"Come back inside. Please."

It was like trying to move an oak tree. Unbending, unmoving. He was staring with such concentration she knew it was hopeless. What had Duncan called him? Peter. That was it. "Peter? Peter, come with me. Please."

She tore off one glove, pressing her hand against his cheek to turn his face towards hers. He was bitterly cold. "Peter!"

He blinked. "I... Oh god. What happened?"

"You were looking at something in one of the windows." She took his hand and started leading him back to the apartment. "Duncan said you saw a dog? Last night?"

"She..." He took a breath, tried again. "She ran out in front of me. On the road." It was only her hand on his arm that stopped him stumbling down the steps. "He said she wasn't hurt, and ... I believed him."

An icy wind followed them into the kitchen. He looked ashen, eyes wide with shock, but then he took a deep breath and blinked, his cheeks losing their greyness. "They... they..."

"What happened? Are you alright?" She spoke with a sharpness of real concern, but even so he flinched.

"I don't know." He pressed one gloved hand down on the table. "Do you mind if I sit down? I think..."

"Of course not." And yet, he was a stranger, and Duncan was no doubt out with Blu by now. She fumbled in her pocket for her phone, but the signal was dead as usual.

"I wasn't imagining them. The children." He glanced up at her, a quick grin twisting his lips. "And I promise you I'm not an axe murderer."

The laugh burst from her before she had chance to supress it. "Duncan's the only one with an axe round here, though he prefers a chainsaw most of the time. And from the look of you right now, I could probably give you a run for your money." She dropped her gloves and hat on the table. "I think we both need a hot drink. Tea? Or do you prefer coffee?"

His hands were bare now and clenched together. No wedding ring that she could see, or a watch. Short clean nails. Strong hands unmarked by scars or tattoos or nicotine stains.

"Tea, if... if that's not any trouble."

"It isn't. Besides, I've packed the percolator away and I hate instant."

He tilted his head to look at her. "You're leaving?"

"When the new owners come. They don't want me here." The comforting familiarity of dropping teabags into clean mugs, the search for a teaspoon and getting the milk out of the fridge. The kettle boiled and she poured the water. "Milk and sugar?"

"Just milk, please. And for what it's worth, I'm sorry. I know what it's like to lose your home and your job."

He was speaking easily now, the hesitation barely noticeable but even so, she could see the exact moment when he retreated inside himself. Eyes blinkered and unfocussed and shuttered. The tea was ready and she passed his over and sat down opposite him. It was strange drinking tea in the kitchen with a man she knew nothing about, other than the few things garnered from Duncan earlier. But, the dog had brought Peter Sinclair here last night, and even more worrying, he had seen two small girls standing at one of the upper windows.

Impossible. Someone must have told him the stories, or else he'd done his research, though the history of the house was not widely known outside the area.

"What are you going to do now?" The chocolate digestives from last night were on the table, only one eaten, and she unscrewed the wrapper and held the packet out. He shook his head and she put them to one side, for later.

"Find the hotel I guess, if they've not given my room to someone else. Don't worry, I'll be out from under your feet before lunchtime." He didn't look enthusiastic at the prospect and his face still had the pinched look of someone on the edge of exhaustion. "I wish I'd known about this place a couple of years ago. But it's too late now." He drained his mug and stood. "Thank you for the drink and showing me round and for not..." He shrugged. "Well, for not making me feel even more of a fool."

"Stay." Had she said that aloud? From the look on his face she must have done. She pushed her mug to one side. "I mean, there's no reason why you have to go is there?"

"Duncan did enough for me last night and I don't want to be a burden. Best if I head off, and the sooner the better."

"There's a cabin. I should've emptied it out yesterday, but all it needs is a quick clean and a change of bedding and so on and you can have it for as long as you need."

She could see the look of utter delight flash across his face and disappear. "It's kind of you, but..." He held out his hands. "I don't have any food or..."

"No problem at all." She stood up. "Follow me."

CHAPTER 9

The room was a few paces down the hallway and cold enough to be unpleasant. Peter stood in the doorway, trying to take it all in and failing: five-litre bottles of water crowding the corners, deep shelving full of cartons of UHT milk, tins of soup and tuna and corned beef. Packets of tea and sugar and flour, dried peas, rice, lentils. Two chest freezers lined up along the far side. Candles and matches and toilet rolls. He'd never seen anything like it. Not even at home where the pantries were always well-stocked.

"This is…"

She waved a hand. "Welcome to Scotland in winter. We've been cut off before now for over a fortnight so having a good storeroom is vital. I could feed an army for a fortnight with what's in here. There are paraffin lamps and a fully stocked first aid kit as well, though I'm no nurse." She picked up a packet of biscuits and fiddled with it, turning it over in her fingers before putting it back on the shelf. "Look. There's no way I'm leaving any of this for the new owners so you're welcome to help yourself to whatever you like. There's bread and butter and cakes in the smaller freezer, pizza, fish and ready meals in the other. Pretty much anything you might need including eggs so you can have a proper fry-up for breakfast if you want?" She turned to face him. "What do you think?"

It was a more than generous offer. He could spend the time rethinking his future before driving back to Glasgow on Tuesday in time for the last train south. "I'm... I'm grateful. Thankyou."

"However there's something I'd like you to do, if you don't mind."

It was Hamilton all over again. His throat tightened. The flagstones on the floor were uneven and dusty, one of the bottles of water was losing its label. He swallowed. "Wh... what do you need?"

She shrugged, her face reddening enough to bring a flush of colour to her pale cheeks. "I could do with some help clearing out the other cabin once yours is done. Would you mind? Not the furniture, but all the kitchen things and so on."

He nodded, unwilling to risk speaking again. Strange how easily the words had come earlier, when they were sitting in the warmth of the kitchen but now it was as if his mind refused to find the words. Helping her out was the least he could do.

Her hand rested on his arm for a second. "It'll be fine. Trust me. Let me get some things together then we'll take a look at your cabin and you can tell me what you think."

~

Being a passenger in an old Land Rover was a new experience, but it was quicker than walking and he was still shaken by what he had seen in the window, earlier. Not so much the sight of the two children but the unexpected and inexplicable swell of distress and grief and loss that flowed into him as he stood there. It was not his own anguish, but it had been enough to fill him with horror at whatever had caused the emotion. Even now he was hard put to stop his hands trembling and he held onto the seat belt as the vehicle bouncing from one pothole to another until they were juddering to a halt outside Cabin 3.

It was showing its age and, to his eyes, the design more than a little dated. He would have given it huge windows and a vaulted ceiling, angled it to take advantage of the view from the living room, made the patio wider and replaced the ugly wooden balustrades with glass. But for all its inelegance, it was far better than many he'd seen and with the nearest occupied cabin a good hundred yards away, he was unlikely to be disturbed.

He clambered out of the vehicle, his spine wondering if it would ever recover from the jolting. "How old were you when they were built?"

"Thirteen. I was a typical young teenager and didn't want anything to do with them. My parents did most of the organising: planning permission, building regs, that sort of thing. From what I remember, it was something of a risky venture, but Richard insisted he had the money, though he never seemed to spend much on the house, or himself." She opened the door of the cabin and led the way inside. "Living room and kitchen area." Another door. "One bedroom with ensuite. Small, but these were only ever intended for couples. No children allowed, not even babies."

There was not much cleaning to do and he set about stripping the bed while she brought in fresh sheets and the bags of food.

"What about the hot tub? Would you use it?"

He frowned. There was a Jacuzzi at the gym, and on a couple of occasions he'd soaked in its heat, but only for a few minutes after a strenuous session. And yet it was selfish to give her the extra work of emptying and refilling it. "Yes, I probably would. But it's more for you to do."

"Not really. It's a faff having to empty and refill it, but with two of us it'll be a lot easier. Finish in here and I'll put this lot away for you." She headed into the kitchen and he tugged the sheet into place and started on the duvet cover.

The hot tub, once emptied and refilled, looked more tempting than at first sight. Tucked in one corner of the patio, it looked out over the bay and he would be able to sit in it and watch the stars. A rare luxury and there had been few enough of those for the past couple of years. Maybe it was time he did something for himself.

"There. It'll be ready to use this evening." She put down the last bag and handed him the set of keys. "I'm pleased you're staying. It's awful seeing the cabins left empty and waiting to be pulled down. I'm glad I won't be around when it happens."

"Where are you going to go?" He tucked the keys in his pocket and followed her to the Land Rover to start on the next cabin.

"Not sure yet. I've a couple of friends who still live

locally but until last March I was renting a flat in York and working as a graphic web designer with my future all planned out. Then my father had a heart attack and I took extended leave to help run this place until he recovered."

"And you decided to stay? It takes courage to give up a career like that."

She shrugged. "Not my decision in the end. Turned out the firm didn't need me after all. Two weeks later they decided I was surplus to requirements and then my fiancé decided he didn't need me either. So, two rejections within three days. As you can probably guess, it wasn't a good week. I drove down, packed up all my stuff and came back here until I could work out what I was going to do next."

"That must have been a rough time for you." She looked fragile and uneasy, the mere mention of her fiancé or work enough to open the wounds. Scars like those took a long time to heal.

"It wasn't the best of times, I have to admit. And then I took over running this place when Dad was told to retire. Still not sure what I'm going to do now, but, I'll find something. There's always contract work, but for that I need a reliable Wi-Fi connection and a place of my own." She slammed the driver's door shut. "Sorry. Not your fault. Far from it. I should have known Matthew wasn't to be trusted."

"Your fiancé?"

"Ex." She started the engine and let the handbrake off.

"I'm sorry."

"No need. It's in the past now. He was a social climber – found someone with more money and contacts in all the right places."

"I know the feeling." He turned towards her. "So you took over the reins when your father retired? Where is he now?"

"He and my stepmother are in America, believe it or not. The cardiologist said he needed to have less stress in his life so they set off to tour Florida in one of those huge campervan things. They write often – no point in relying on Skype out here – and from the sounds of it they're having a great time."

"Are they coming back for Christmas?" It would be pushing it and he hadn't seen any signs of Christmas in the house.

"My step-brother teaches at the university in Gainesville so they're spending the holiday with him and his family. It's going to be my first Christmas here for a long time. I just hadn't expected to be alone."

The Land Rover pulled to a halt outside the cabin with a jolt. "I don't think any of us ever expects to be alone. As for owning a home? Join the club. I don't own one either." He put his hands on his thighs and stared ahead. "I… I was married for a short while. We divorced two years ago and she took the house and everything else. It was a small price to pay, really."

"That must have been painful."

"It wasn't the easiest of times." He stared out of the window, wondering how much to say. "I started stammering when I went to boarding school. Stress makes it worse." Or being caught in the middle of a divorce or a family meal or an argument with his boss. But not in the middle of nowhere while sitting in a battered Land Rover next to a stranger. Even the shock of the seeing two imaginary children inside the house had not reduced him to his usual painful silence.

"It isn't obvious. I wouldn't have known if you hadn't told me."

"Perhaps it's the quietness here. The slowness. Life seems to have its own speed somehow."

"Dead slow you mean? I used to hate living here when I was a child. I mean, my parents were great and Richard let us have the run of most of the Hall but I wanted more. A cinema and a McDonalds and a swimming pool. The sea here's okay for swimming so long as you watch the currents, but it's not the same as a heated pool. All the fresh fish you could want out there in the ocean and all I craved was a Big Mac or KFC. A typical hormonal teenager. What about you?"

Her hair was coming undone, a shining rope of auburn silk. He wondered how long it would be when it was loose and what it might feel like in his fingers. She was waiting for an answer. "Me? I was either at school, or home for the holidays. I was born sixteen years after everyone thought the family was complete. My parents didn't know what to do with me, and I was something of a changeling which didn't help either."

She twisted round to face him. "You didn't fulfil your parent's expectations?"

"Got it in one." It was hard to keep the bitterness from his voice, and from the way she lowered her head, some of his anger had seeped out. He softened his tone. "I'm sorry. My family… well, let's say it has a military tradition that goes back over two hundred years. And I broke it. They've never forgotten or forgiven me."

"Good for you. Were you a troublemaker at school as well?"

He couldn't stop the bark of laughter. "Me? I was the smallest in the year and I had a stutter and baby-blond curls. Boys like me didn't become troublemakers, we were fodder for the bullies."

"Blond curls?" A slight giggle.

"Don't you dare laugh or I won't give you any more help." He risked a smile. "Thank god it changed as I got older and I had a serious growth spurt. I ended up towering over everyone else in the school. That finally stopped the bullies. As for the curls, if I keep it cut short they don't show."

She shook her head. "When I was young I used to think going to boarding school would be wonderful – all those exciting things you read about in those old children's stories: Midnight feasts in the dormitory, sneaking out to swim in the ocean, that sort of thing."

"It was probably fine for a lot of boys, but I..." He shook his head and opened the door. "Shall we get started? I'm sure you have enough to do as it is."

The cabin was identical to the other one and he set to work, clearing the kitchen drawers of utensils and oddments, getting plates and dishes out of the cupboards. Everything put in boxes in the back of the Land Rover for disposal later on. Conversation to a minimum, avoiding her glances, keeping himself occupied and all the while fighting down the memories.

He started clearing out the small utility room, listening to Fiona humming as she stripped the bed and stuffed linens into bin bags. By the time they were finished it was well past noon, his stomach rumbling as he took the last bag out to the vehicle and stuffed it on top of everything else.

Fiona closed the rear door before any bags tumbled out. "That's it. Done. And thank you. I would have asked Duncan to help, but he's got enough on his mind right now." She gave him a smile. "And I don't know about you, but I'm starving. Would you like to come back to the Hall for a sandwich or soup or both? I've got more than enough food to spare."

The sun was shining, the sea looked glorious and the wind had eased enough to make a walk along the fore-shore possible, even enjoyable, but more tempting was the thought of sitting at the table and sharing a meal.

"That'd be great. And afterwards, if you want, I'll give you a hand unloading."

She gave him a quick smirk.

"Why else did you think I was offering? Come on, hop in."

CHAPTER 10

The soup was out of a tin, but there were thick slices of toast and butter, a wedge of strong cheese and a jar of quince jelly and the cold wind had given him an appetite. They polished off the best part of a loaf before they started unloading the bags from her vehicle and storing everything in one of the outbuildings.

"What happens to all this?" He waved a hand at the piles of bags and the shelves full of unwanted items. Saucepans and baking trays, mugs and sugar bowls, untidy heaps of cutlery. Everything necessary to furnish a holiday retreat. "And all that food in your pantry?"

She dropped a bin liner into one corner. "This stuff's not my problem. As for the food, I'll empty the freezers next week and take as much as I can to Duncan's – assuming he's got space. And he's having everything that's not perishable as well. If there's anything he can't use, or hasn't got space for, I'll either leave it here, or take it into the village. They've got a community shop there, so they're welcome to whatever they want. But if there's anything you need, just let me know."

"That's generous of you." He handed her another box. "Careful, I think the bottom's dropping out of this one."

Her fingers tangled with his. The finest dusting of salt sparkled on her cheek. He caught a hint of her perfume, or perhaps shampoo? Something fresh and clean and lively, like her. He loosened his grip bit by bit, not wanting it to slip.

"Got it. Thanks."

He let go with some reluctance. "That's the last so I'll be off now. Thanks for lunch and for the loan of the cabin."

She stepped away from him, turning her back to put the box on one of the shelves. "Remember, I'm here if you need anything. Have a good evening."

His car was still parked askew outside Duncan's, and he paused, watching as the quad bike puttered slowly down the track. Blu was in the front seat, hands clutching the bars, rigid with determination, clothes and face and even his hair filthy with mud and slutch. The quad bike was muddier. And from the look on the boy's face, the trip had been both exhilarating and gruelling. The bike slowed down and stopped with a grating judder.

"You'll soon get the hang of it, lad." Duncan dismounted and Peter saw the thick mud coating his waterproof jacket and overtrousers. "Another lesson tomorrow I think. You can start first thing. Take those shoes off in the kitchen before you go upstairs to shower, mind you. I don't want mud trailed through the house."

The boy clambered off, stiff and ungainly and wincing, before trudging away to leave the men alone. Duncan shook his head before turning. "Still here, Peter? I thought you were in a hurry to be off?" But there was pleasure in the voice.

He waved a hand at the cabin. "Fiona said I could stay in Number 3 for a couple of nights." Even now he found it hard to believe.

"Will you come and have a drink with me later then?"

The idea was tempting, but the man had his own responsibilities and entertaining a stranger was not one of them. "I think your lad might prefer your company tonight. Looks like you've had a busy few hours from the state of your clothes."

Duncan laughed. "That we did. He found himself going arse over tip in the deep end of one of the ditches. Looked a right mess when he crawled out, but it taught him a lesson. Next time he'll be a bit more careful."

"So I take it he enjoyed himself?"

"I think so. He didn't say much, but he did a good job. I'll see what happens tomorrow, but I expect I'll be buying him a set of decent waterproofs come the New Year." He climbed back on the bike and started the engine. "If you change your mind, come round about seven. Blu prefers to spend the evenings in his own room so you're more than welcome. And I've an old Speyside malt you might like and a ferret who'd be pleased to see you again."

It was strange opening the cabin door knowing he was going to be staying here for the next couple of nights. He dumped his bag on the floor and went back for the rest of his things, leaving the Christmas presents in the boot. Then it was time to settle in: hanging his coat and scarf on the wooden pegs in the hallway, unlacing his boots and putting them in the utility room, flicking on the kettle.

The day had stayed dry for once and there was still an hour before sunset.

He took the drink outside onto the patio, sipping hot tea and staring out across the bay until the cold air had him fleeing back to the living room to strike a match and light the fire laid in the log burner. The childish pleasure of watching flames take hold, the hiss and pop and crackle, heat spreading outwards. There was no real need – the cabin had central heating and the radiators were efficient – but he'd always loved an open fire.

The place mats and small vase on the dining table found a new home on the kitchen worktop and, with the surface clear, he reached for his sketch pad and pencils and began drawing: the headland and Hall, the bay and its cabins, the gatehouse. Nothing serious, a few rough outlines, but enough to give him a baseline for more detailed work. This was the real challenge as far as he was concerned: letting the landscape speak for itself. The shape of the hills, the lines and curves and gradients, trees and rocks and water.

He couldn't remember the last time he'd designed anything without thought of costs and limitations, the ideas coming so fast it was hard to get them down in time. Page after page, sheets torn from the pad and scattered across the table, one or two crumpled and thrown on the floor to be disposed of later. This was what he loved doing, allowing his imagination to run wild before settling down to the more practical designs, no-one looking over his shoulder and telling him to rein in his fanciful ideas and do things on the cheap.

The result was a series of individual cabins, each planned to make the best of their location: one set into the cliff face behind, one perched right on the edge of the drop down to the foreshore, another on two levels to take advantage of the slope at the far end. Even a stubby light-house with small viewing room on top in place of a lamp.

There were others as well. Ideas so outrageous they would never be viable without enormous expense, but who was bothered about cost when a building appeared to float above the sea, or fade into the background until only the keenest of eyes could perceive it. It was later than he realised when he finished the last sketch and he put the papers back in their case and stood at the window, watching the ocean in the moonlight, the water rippling in the wind.

Fiona had left a generous stack of ready meals in the freezer but it was too early to eat and he settled for a biscuit, distracted by the ideas still flooding through his mind. It was too late to start on the proper designs – for that he needed daylight and to walk along the track and the foreshore and get a feel for the land and take photographs. This tiny harbour with its view over the wide expanse of the Firth deserved better than a row of mass-produced cabins with no soul, and although he knew it was a waste of time and effort, it was his time to waste. He would ask Fiona for permission to use the work in his portfolio.

The tide was turning again by the time he was ready to leave, and he grabbed parka and scarf and made his way along the wide gravelled track to the gatehouse. Duncan opened the door, Sock's dark face and tiny bright eyes peering out from behind his shoulder.

"Peter. I was hoping you'd come. I could do with some advice." He scooped the ferret off his neck and handed it across. "Take this beastie into the living room and I'll fetch us both a dram."

Holding the ferret was as tricky as last time, the animal squirming in his hands until he let go and allowed it to find its way to the hood of his sweatshirt. A surprisingly heavy weight given its small stature, and he was somewhat relieved when it curled up and stayed there. The Scotsman came back with two whisky tumblers, each holding a scant half-inch of dark amber spirit.

"Try this. A small local distillery re-opened a while back. This is their fifteen-year-old. I'd like to know what you think about it."

He took a sniff. "That's…" And another. His father would have sold some of the family silver for a glass of this whisky, let alone a bottle.

"Go on lad. First of all, what can you smell?" Duncan took a sip of his own and sat there, impassive, unreadable.

A test then. He swirled the burnished liquid in his glass and watched the beading cling to the side. A more thoughtful sniff this time, his eyes closed, the weight of the ferret at his neck, the room warm and peaceful. "Peat. Not a lot, just a touch. And…" He paused and breathed in again, inhaling the aroma. "Yes. Oil. Sort of oily smoke if that makes any sense?"

"It does. Now. Taste." The man sat back, arms folded.

He let it touch his lips, cold at first, then a slow warmth on his tongue, heat at the back of his mouth and throat. A tingling numbing of lips and tongue and the taste of … "Treacle? No, wait. Toffee. That's it. Treacle toffee."

"And?"

Another sip – holding it on his tongue for longer. He'd

sat through enough of his father's lectures about whisky to know what was expected here. And no lying either. Duncan Grant deserved an honest answer. He took his time, and a second sip. "A definite sweetness with a hint of spices at the end?" He opened his eyes. "How did I do?"

Duncan held out the bottle. "You have an excellent nose for a good whisky, Mr Sinclair. Now, let me top up your glass and this time you can relax. The exam is over and you passed." He poured a generous measure into each glass and pushed the cork back into the neck. "Sit back and enjoy. How did you like the Hall? Did Miss Cameron show you inside?"

"The Hall? No, just her kitchen and storeroom. It must be hard on her living there by herself."

"You see her as a weak little woman? I thought better of you. She's proved herself enough times these past few months. Not an easy thing for a single woman to take on the management of the cabins. I'm surprised she's still here, to be honest. Had she not come back though, there'd have been no one to look after the Hall. I couldn't have taken on the job, I've enough to do as it is, keeping an eye on the land but Miss Cameron doesn't need your pity, or mine."

He shook his head. "I didn't... I mean, she's intelligent and hardworking and probably a darned sight more capable than I would be in her situation. But she's by herself in that house. It gets lonely after a while, eating meals alone and having no one to talk to." The whisky burned down his throat and he coughed, waking the ferret still curled up in his hood. He put one hand up to calm the small creature back to sleep.

"She never said much about what happened to bring

her back here and I'm not one to ask. If she'd wanted me to know she'd have told me, but I think I have the right of it. A man, and an untrustworthy one at that."

A small nose touched the back of his ear and he put his whisky tumbler down and reached up to pluck the ferret from its hiding place and put it on his knee. A small body under his fingers, soft fur and strength, the thrill of having a living creature place its trust in him. "And she's going to lose her home shortly. That seems unfair."

"Life is unfair, Mr Sinclair, and the sooner you learn that, the easier it gets. Something Blu's mother never accepted, more's the pity."

"Where is he? Blu?"

Duncan shook his head. "In his bedroom reading. Or asleep after the day he's had. He prefers his own company in the evenings, especially if I have a guest. I don't mind, but there's more to the lad than meets the eye." He picked up the bottle. "Another, before I put it away?"

He shook his head. "Better not. I'm going to try out the hot tub later."

"And I don't want the boy imagining I'm a drunk. He's seen enough of that already."

"His father?"

"Mother – not that she's much of a parent. No idea who his father is." He pushed the cork back into the bottle and slid it out of reach. "My sister Elaine was twelve years younger than me and we were never that close. She fell pregnant with her daughter, Skye, when I was thirty and assistant gamekeeper here. Elaine married the father but it didn't take long before she upped and left him for someone else. She always had a touch of wanderlust about her I suppose, never settled in one place for any length of time, even with a baby to look after." He stared into the fire, turning the tumbler round in his fingers. "Skye was born in '78, but I didn't get to see much of her or her mother for a good twenty years." He gulped the last of his drink and put the tumbler down.

"That must have been difficult for your parents." It was hard to know what else to say.

"Aye. It was. They died when Blu was a toddler. A good age both of them, but I think they'd have liked to have known him better."

The question had to be asked. "And you? Did you marry?"

His impertinence was rewarded by a deep chuckle. "Marriage never interested me, lad. I've no intention of being tied down to one woman. Too set in my ways and I enjoy my independence too much." He ran one finger round the rim of the glass and gave Peter a wink. "I'm not without my comforts though. There's four of us who go fishing together off the headland every chance we get and as for…" He took a drink and ran his tongue over his lips. "Well, there's a couple of widows in the village who are always pleased to see me come up their path and who keep me well supplied with all the comforts a man could want."

"Just a couple?" It difficult to hide his amusement and his envy. Duncan was everything Peter had aspired to be when he was a child: content with his life and with enough friends to be sure of a welcome. And living away from the clamour and rush of the city. A man at peace with himself and confident enough to stand his ground.

"That would be telling, now. But don't think of me as someone lonely, Mr Sinclair, or to be pitied. If anything,

I'm the selfish one. I have everything I want right here, and no one can take it away from me. Not even the new owners of the Hall. Unlike Fiona."

"She told me she was having to leave. I wish there was some way to help."

"There's nothing anyone can do, more's the pity. I blame the laird. It was his responsibility to make his will, but he didn't and now the whole place is going to fall apart. Who knows, I might end up throwing myself on the mercy of one of the widows, if things get bad here."

A cast-away remark, a touch of jollity to ease the sombre topic but Peter could hear the worry in the man's voice. The ferret had made its way back to the warmth of his hood and he scooped the creature out again and handed it across. "You wanted some advice? About Fiona?"

The older man shook his head. "No, not about her. It's Blu I'm concerned about. There's something bothering the lad, and I'm not sure how to tackle him about it."

"It can't be easy on him. Didn't you say his mother had disappeared?" A child abandoned by his mother. He knew the feeling only too well. "Have you heard anything from her?"

"Her?" The scorn in Duncan's voice was sharp. "She'd sooner forget all about the boy. Last time she came here, he was about four years old, thin and scrawny and too scared to speak. Richard gave her a job cleaning in the Hall, but it didn't last longer than a week. She was never one for hard work. She hung around for a while longer and then one day the two of them were gone. I've not seen her since." He picked up the poker and gave one of the logs a fierce jab. "I'd have him here to live, but with the way things are at the moment it's no place for a boy. And I'm not getting any younger. What young lad wants to live with someone who's nearly seventy? I can't give him what he needs."

"What does any young teenager need? Someone who cares about them, who bothers to take them out and teach them how to drive a quad bike. Someone who doesn't send them hundreds of miles away to boarding school. You're here for him, and that's all that matters."

"Ah. That was what happened to you? How old were you, if you don't mind me asking?"

He swallowed, hoping his voice would not fail him this time. "S… seven. I didn't go home again for close on four months." It was easier than he thought to utter the words. Perhaps because of the alcohol, or more likely that, unlike his father, Duncan Grant was not a man to judge anyone on how they spoke.

"Christ almighty. That young? What sort of bastards would do something like that to a bairn?"

He ignored the outburst and looked at the whisky tumbler, wondering if it would be rude to ask for another, but there was no need. Duncan was already twisting the cork out of the bottle and gesturing at his glass. "I couldn't do that to any child of mine. I'm sorry, Peter. You had a harder childhood than I imagined. But, putting that aside. Blu. As a man who remembers his teenage years better than me, whether they were good years or not, what do you think I should do?"

"Honestly? I'd do nothing if I were you. He'll tell you when he's ready and there's no point trying to force it out of him – he'll only clam up and get angry. I'd ignore what-ever it is, keep him busy, get him involved in what you're doing. Take him out on the quad again. He enjoyed that didn't he?" He allowed the other man to pour another dram, a splash this time.

"Apart from the mud, he did. But he did well. Did you do much with your father?"

The drink was not as pleasant this time round, or maybe it was the memories that burned.

"He was usually too busy. He didn't need a small boy under his feet, or a teenager. I'd have done anything to have my father give me a driving lesson when I was Blu's age, but he wasn't interested. Ever." The whisky was gone, an acid burn in his gut to remind him. "I'd better be going before the lad thinks I'm staying for the night. Thanks for the whisky, I'm sorry I can't offer you any in return."

The man waved aside his apology.

"No need. I have friends who keep me well supplied in return for a cut of venison when I'm called on to cull the herd, or a few brace when shooting starts. And I'll do as you say with regard to the boy."

CHAPTER 11

Despite the sharp bite of frost, it was pleasant walking back to the cabin knowing that for the next couple of nights it was his alone. No flat-mate bringing a stranger back, no one surprising him in the kitchen in the morning. The hot tub was waiting and he quickened his pace, aware of his stomach rumbling. There was a lasagne in the freezer – a meal for two, but he could have left-overs tomorrow – and he put it in the oven and found a garlic bread to go with it. Thirty minutes until it was ready. Plenty of time for a long soak.

The sky was still clear and it took him less than a minute to strip and wrap the bath towel round his hips, then he turned off the main lights and stepped outside.

The breath-taking shock of cold air on naked skin, slate paving stones icy under bare feet, the first tentative step into deep water, the long sigh as heat surged through his body. Nothing had prepared him for the sheer indulgence of soaking in hot water, and he leaned back as the jets soothed his aches.

Stars spattered the sky and although he had never studied the stars or constellations in any great depth, Orion's unmistakable shape loomed over him, huge in the sky. And there... a wide ribbon of what could only be the Milky Way. He lost himself in the beauty of it, the galaxy stretching across the sky and it was only when someone called to him that he realised Fiona Cameron was walking along the patio. Too late to reach for the towel and make his escape, too late to do anything other than set the jets to 'high' and sit there hoping she didn't come any closer.

"I'm sorry. I didn't think..." She took another step forward. "I remembered you didn't have a bottle of wine and there's supposed to be one in each cabin so I brought it. I hope white's okay?"

"It's... fine. You can put it inside if you like." The towel was behind him on the upright lid. Whatever he did, she would realise. His nakedness was not something he was ashamed of, but to find himself in this situation with no recourse and trapped in the frothing water, made him aware of his vulnerability. Had his visitor been Duncan, he would have told the man to get them both a drink and then join him in the water. It would have done the Scotsman good to relax for a while.

"Oh. You're..." She took another step and then stopped.

He could hear the amusement in her voice and also the envy. "I didn't bring my swimming trunks; didn't think I'd need any."

"You don't." She was at the end of the tub now, the bottle still in one hand. "I was hoping to have final dip before I leave, but I can't see it happening."

To hell with it. He lifted one arm out, resting it along

the rim and spreading out his hand. "Then join me; there's plenty of room in here. There's the bathrobe inside and I bet you've gone swimming in your underwear before now. I promise not to look until you're in." Even in the shadows he could see the blush darkening her cheeks.

"I can't. Really. It wouldn't be…"

"What? Indecent? Improper? I'm here as your guest and I'm pretty sure you trust me. And I'm the one at a disadvantage right now." He splashed water at her. "It's hot and I've been watching the stars and you're getting cold standing there. Go on. Why not take the chance while you can."

"You promise?"

"Not to watch?" He grinned. "I promise. Now hurry up and bring us both some wine."

She was back in less time than he expected, bathrobe belted tight round her waist, a glass in each hand. "I hope you don't mind plastic. We don't like people using breakables in the tub."

He took his glass and twisted sideways to offer her more privacy, though it was tempting to sneak a quick glance. The splash of her stepping in, the sigh of delight, the water level rising around him a little. "Decent?"

"Decent. Oh my, I'd forgotten how good this was. I can see why the Wilsons use theirs so much."

Her foot touched his knee, a gentle nudge and quite accidental he was sure, and he pulled his legs back, tucking them as far under as possible. It was difficult to lean back and watch the stars without stretching his body out and floating up from where he sat across from her, and so he sipped his wine and tried to avoid staring. It was difficult. The strap of her bra had slipped from her shoulder. White lace against pale skin.

"The Wilsons?" He sat up a little straighter, his shoulders exposed to the bitter air.

She lifted her arm and pointed, the curve of one breast emerging from the water. "In the cabin at the far end. They'd been in and out several times since they arrived. I'll have to top the water level up tomorrow." She shook her head at him. "Look – stretch out properly, you're going to freeze like that. You're quite safe with me, I promise not to do anything and anyway, I've left my axe back in the kitchen. The chemicals in here dull the blade and it takes ages to get the edge sharp again."

He couldn't stop the laugh escaping and then it was easy to slide down a little and warm his shoulders and turn the jets to a lower setting so they could talk without the extra noise. The darkness was a little overpowering and he turned on the tub lights to see her face. "I don't know much about the stars. I recognised Orion above us, but that's about all."

"I haven't seen the sky like this since I went away to university. And after I came back there wasn't the time to stargaze." She was leaning back as well, the line of her throat and curl of her collarbone, the curves of her body blurred by bubbles. Her leg touched his again, and this time he did not pull back. His ex-wife would have despised this – sitting outside a run-down cabin in the middle of nowhere – but right now Peter Sinclair could not think of anywhere else he would rather be. He let the water take his weight, let the jets massage away his worries until he was left with nothing but the stars above and the heat around him.

The wind dropped, the crash of waves diminishing to a low rumble as the tide continued its retreat. He closed his eyes and let the warmth of the water lull his senses. A seagull called out with a delicate cry. Not a seagull. "Children. I can hear children singing. Listen."

She was watching him. An intent gaze, her eyes fixed on his face as he sat there, trying to make sense of the sounds. There were no children here, he knew that much, but it didn't seem to worry Fiona. And then the quite distinct sound of a dog. Not a bark of anger, more a sound of joy. Fiona had heard as well – he saw her relax and sink deeper into the water as if she had been waiting.

It was none of his business, though it heightened his curiosity. From what he had learned so far, the Hall and its people had their own secrets and he would not break their trust by asking unwanted questions. Fiona would tell him in due course if she thought it was necessary. He leaned back again, the stars disappearing now behind a thin veil of cloud and his glass near empty, the water losing its heat, and he sat up and finished his wine. "I think it's time we got out. I've got lasagne in the oven and it'll be ready soon. Would you like some? I just need to put the garlic bread in, but that'll only take a few minutes."

She drained her glass and put it on the edge and he had no time to turn away before she was standing, water shimmering down her body as she flicked her plait back over her shoulder and reached, almost casually, for the bathrobe without bothering to wrap it around herself. The curve of her hips in the light from the water, the tantalising roundness of breasts visible through wet lace. He could sense her watching him, gauging his reactions as she sat on the edge and swung those long, wet legs round to jump down to the slate paving, before reaching out to collect both glasses. And then she was gone, a dark trail of footprints on the stone path, leading inside the cabin to where he had left the log burner waiting to warm him.

He sank down, submerging his shoulders beneath the foam one last time before he sprang upwards, pushing himself out of the water and grabbing the towel. By the time he'd closed the lid and fastened it securely against any wind, he was shivering and the bath towel damp and clinging. She'd closed the patio door and he pushed it open, unsure of what he would find.

The log-burner was open to warm the room and Fiona, wrapped in the white bathrobe, was sitting on the sofa, legs tucked alongside her. Her hair had come out of its plait and she was running her fingers through it. In the flickering light of the flames it shone like burnished copper and it was all he could do not to bend down and kiss the nape of her neck. He stood there, watching a single drop of water slip down her cheek.

She let the damp strands fall, a tumble of auburn strands dark against the white material that sheltered her. "I put the bread in the oven."

"Great. I'll…" He saw her watching him. "I'll get dressed."

"I should have, but I hadn't realised how comfortable these are." She plucked at the collar of the bathrobe. "And its warm in here." Another glance at him. "Do you mind?"

"Mind?"

"If I stay for something to eat? I feel a bit cheeky, foisting myself on you like this."

"No. It's your food after all, and it'll be good to have

company. I eat alone a lot of the time." He shook his head. "That sounds pathetic. I didn't mean it like that."

"I'm the same. It very quiet round here sometimes, and there aren't any pubs nearby where I can go and have a meal either." She started plaiting her hair, and he stood and watched her fingers twisting the thick strands with delicate precision and wrapping a band round the end. "Go and get dressed. I'll get the food out, so don't be long or it'll go cold."

The bathroom had a second towel and he scrubbed himself dry before dressing. Jeans and the sweatshirt, no socks or shoes. The aroma of garlic filled the living room. She had divided the lasagne between two warm plates and refilled the wine glasses and he sat down across the table from her and took a slice of hot bread. The food was better than he expected: rich and flavoursome, a generous amount of tender meat, the cheese sauce bubbling with heat and he took a forkful, blowing out to cool his mouth. "This is really good. Better than any pub meal."

"There's a farmer's market every month in the village. One of the local women makes these and cottage pies and so on. I bought a batch from her a few months ago. This was the last in the freezer." She dabbed at her lips, the neck of the robe gaping open to reveal white lace beneath. The sleeves were too long for her arms and she pushed them up.

"And you let me have it?" The garlic bread glistened with butter and herbs and he tore off another slice. "I feel selfish now."

"Don't. I've had enough of them in the past, and it would've been a shame to waste this one." She fiddled with the stem of her glass, her eyes watching him.

"I appreciate it. And the wine. You've been very generous."

"You've just come at the right time – empty cabins and a load of food to use up. And you've more than earned a few good meals today. I'd never have managed to clear the cabin without you helping me." She shrugged and pushed the glass aside. "Anyway, enough talking about food. What have you done this afternoon? There's not much to do round here this time of year."

The drawings were tucked away out of sight and he was not ready to show anyone or even talk about his ideas. It was easier to tell her about his visit to Duncan, the whisky and the ferret and the man's concern about the lad, and by the time he had told her everything, their plates were empty. It was only natural that he should pick up the wine bottle and go to sit on the sofa and she joined him, legs drawn up again, bare feet poking out from beneath the white robe.

He added more logs to the fire, aware of her closeness, her silence as if she was waiting for something. She had not moved, and he went back to the sofa and sat, stretching his legs out to let the heat warm his feet. She was staring into the flames, her eyes suspiciously bright and he ached to take her in his arms and hold her close. Her feet were pale, though the heat from the stove was enough to warm anyone sitting nearby and he reached out and tucked the end of the robe under them and she started, as if waking from sleep.

"I'm sorry. I should leave you in peace and go home." She rubbed her arms and stared into the fire. "God knows what you must think of me. I think I've made a fool of myself, sitting here like this."

It was his turn now. "No. You haven't. I've enjoyed your company and there's no need for you to leave yet." He let his hand rest on her shoulder, feeling the coldness, the subtle tremor under his fingers. "I don't like to think of you going back to the Hall by yourself, certainly not right now. Sit here for a while? We can finish the wine and watch the fire and you can tell me about the Hall and Richard. I'd like to know more about him. And you, if you feel like talking? But first, why don't you get dressed?"

She blushed. "I'm embarrassing you, aren't I? I'm sorry."

"Don't be." He reached out to let his hand rest on her knee. "And no, you're not embarrassing me. If it was summer, I'd probably be sitting here in nothing but a towel given how private this cabin is, but your feet are cold. Go on. I'll top up the wine."

She was back in less than a minute, her face still pale, shoulders hunched in the thick woollen sweater, hair falling forward to curtain her face from view. She curled up in the corner of the sofa. "So, what do you want to know? There's not much to tell about me. Other than the fact I have a habit of making an idiot of myself."

"With me? Or in general?"

"Does it matter?"

"If anyone's the idiot, it's me. Yesterday at work I handed in my notice and ran away before anyone could stop me. Booked a hotel room, threw a few clothes in a bag and set off with virtually no idea where I was heading other than somewhere on the coast. Less than a week to Christmas and right now I have no idea exactly where I am. And I don't care." He stretched out his legs. "Even if I had someone I wanted to contact, I can't get a signal on my phone."

"No one? Not even your family?"

"What do they call it? Dysfunctional? That's the Sinclair family." He rubbed the back of his neck with one hand, rolling his shoulders to ease his tiredness. "We get together at Christmas and the odd family celebration, but that's about it. And even then we're strangers. And the conversations…" He grimaced. "Who's going to get the next promotion or a mention in the honours list, whole hours devoted to military manoeuvres and mess hall gossip. I try to find an excuse to leave early, but most of the time that's not possible."

"I can't imagine anything worse. And do you have to go? You can't make some sort of excuse?"

"It's not worth the aggravation." He allowed himself one smile. "It's always nice when it's over."

"So you drove up here from Glasgow?"

The fire was dying down again and he unfolded himself from the depths of the sofa to push a couple of logs into the burner. "I suppose I was trying to get as far away as I could. I was trying to find the hotel only…" The leather of the sofa was soft against his back, the wine smooth in his throat. "I got side-tracked by a dog and ended up here instead."

He heard her sigh, as if she had come to a difficult decision. "Duncan told me you thought you'd hit her – the dog. She's called Bess. Everyone round here knows her."

"Thumping great beast she is. I was sure I must've hurt her, but Duncan said she was fine. There wasn't a mark on the car, either, not that I could see at any rate. I didn't imagine it though. She really was there." He refilled their glasses. "I've got a bottle of malt whisky if you'd like some? It's a decent one, though I say it myself, and I think even Duncan might be impressed. It's in the car if you want me to get it?"

"Drinking and driving? Not a good idea, Mr Sinclair." She gave him a thin smile and raised her plastic glass. "This is fine, honestly. Unless you want a dram yourself."

She had one arm along the back of the sofa now, her legs no longer a barricade between them. He raised his own arm, the tip of his fingers an inch or so from hers. Such a small distance. "It's an expensive Christmas gift for my father. I don't know why I bother really."

"He doesn't drink whisky? So why buy it for him?"

He sighed, turning away to stare at the fire. "He drinks it, but whatever I get him won't be good enough. I could turn up with the last ever bottle of rare single malt and he'd still look at me as if it was some cheap supermarket brand. The only way I could please him is if I joined the army, but it's far too late for that now and even if it weren't, there's not a cat in hell's chance I'd do that. So as far as he's concerned I sold the family honour for a cushy job in civvy street and that makes me a coward in his eyes." He drained his glass. There was enough in the bottle for a final drink for both of them. "I'll have to look out for this label."

"It was always a toss-up between buying red or white for the cabins but white's more popular." She held up the glass for inspection. "It's not bad. I should have brought two bottles."

"You'd have a hangover in the morning." He took a smaller sip and put the glass down on the on the floor. "So. Tell me about Richard."

She tilted her head back to stare at the ceiling for a moment. "He'd be eighty-three next June. You'd have liked him I think. He was a real gentleman – you know? The sort of man who held a door open for a woman. I never heard him swear once when I was a child."

"You were fond of him, weren't you."

"He was part of the family. Mum's parents adopted her when she was a baby, and they never had any other children. So no aunts or uncles on that side of the family, and Dad was quite a bit older when they got married. All my grandparents had died by the time I was eleven, so it was a bit like having a surrogate grandfather living next door. We were what people call a nuclear family. Just the three of us – and Richard of course. He was always ready to listen when I moaned about how dull it was living here and he never told me how lucky I was like Mum and Dad did. He used to sneak me extra pocket money or sweets, and he let me have the run of the Hall whenever I wanted to get away from things. I'm going to miss it."

He heard the sadness in her voice. "And you miss him?"

"Desperately. When Mum died it was horrendous. It still hurts, but at least we knew. But Richard? No one knows how he died or where and the worst thing is that we've never been able to have a funeral for him. Nothing. And the Hall won't survive more than a year or so once those bastards take over."

"There's nothing you can do to stop them? I mean…"

She shook her head. "They're his next of kin. I'm just the manager, and a temporary one at that. You know what hurts most?"

He waited.

"They don't care what happens to the people or the land. Nothing matters other than making money. Richard spent his whole life here and now its all going to be wiped away as if it never existed." She drained her glass and stared at it, quiet tears spilling down her cheeks and he plucked it from her fingers and put it to one side before it fell. It was only natural to pull her close and wrap one arm around her shoulders. No words, no platitudes, just silence and sympathy. It was more than grief at the loss of a family friend, or the far deeper loss of her mother and he could do nothing to ease her sorrow but hold her.

The logs burned, flames devouring the dry wood until there was nothing left but ash and glowing embers and calmness. She had stopped crying and was watching the fire, her head a warm weight on his chest. It was no hardship to lie there for a while longer – he was comfortable enough and she was calm. He arched his back enough to adjust the cushion in the hollow of his spine and ease his legs along the length of the sofa. There was no rush. No rush at all.

"Ready to walk back?"

She pushed herself up and sat there, shaken. "I'm so sorry." It was hard to keep the embarrassment from her voice.

"Why? I think Richard would be proud of you." He swung his legs over the side and sat up, stretching his arms wide and yawning. "You're tired. We both are. Come on." He pushed himself up. "You did walk didn't you?"

His yawning had set hers off as well, and she shook

her head, hiding her mouth behind one hand. "No need for that. I'm perfectly safe." But the thought of going back, alone, made her shiver.

"I'll get my shoes." The sofa creaked as he stood up, and she sat there, rubbing her face, the air cooler, the logs in the grate reduced to warm grey ash. No point in hanging around – she pushed herself up and out of the depths of the sofa. A quick stretch to loosen the kinks in her neck, fingers running through her hair in a futile effort to make it look tidy, the glasses collected and put on the worktop next to the plates from earlier.

Her jacket was on the back of one of the dining chairs and she struggled into it, the zip sticking as usual and, after a few tugs, she gave up trying and wrapped the sides round herself, for once glad of its generous size. She stood there, waiting. The toilet flushed, the sound of running water, a thud as something dropped to the floor – a shoe from the sound of it. His feet were slender. She'd tried to ignore Matthew's feet with their too-long toes and thick nails. But Peter's were nice. Neat and well-cared for. She bit her lip to stop herself giggling. Did she have a secret foot fetish? There was a bottle of pink nail polish somewhere in her bedroom, unused and too expensive to leave behind when she fled north. She would dig it out and do her toes tomorrow.

The sea was calm for once, a wide swathe shimmering out to the horizon. On any other night she would be curled up in her bed listening to the sounds of the house settling around her, the creak of wood, tiny chunks of mortar falling, the scrabble of birds on the windowsills. It was a rare thing, this chance to stand and look at the ocean without having to wonder about checking hot tubs and cleaning.

In the dim light her surroundings looked forlorn and tired and old. Had there been the money available over the last few years they would have been upgraded: new kitchens and bathrooms, a better shower, a larger television. But it no longer mattered.

The door opened and she turned to face him. "Thank you for doing this, but you don't need to. Really."

He handed her his scarf. "You don't know who's out there, waiting in the dark. Or what."

"The dog, you mean?" The soft wool still held a faint scent, fresh and spicy but not overpowering. A subtle fragrance rather than the heavy overtones with which she was more familiar. "She won't hurt anyone. Trust me."

"Even so, I won't let you walk back by yourself." He held out one hand and she took it. Strong fingers, even in in gloves. She wished she thought to wear hers, but bringing the wine out was meant to be a short walk and nothing more. "Hang on." He pulled the gloves off and passed them across. Too large for her hands, but they were well-worn, the leather pliant and shaped to his own hands. Her fingers encountered warmth and softness. It was like holding his hand.

Gravel crunched underfoot as they walked. It was too late for Duncan to be awake and there was no one else who might see them pass along the edge of the tiny harbour, the cabins spaced out on their left and the old harbour wall on their right. They reached the steps leading down to the shoreline and she paused, looking out over the silt and sand exposed at low tide. It was different standing here with someone next to her, someone who wasn't in a rush to leave and who appreciated the quiet beauty of the ocean at night.

"Do you ever see dolphins here?" His voice was hushed with reverence and she found herself smiling.

"Best time is late July, but they live in the Firth so chances are you can see them all year round." It was hard to realise how complacent she had become over the years, but a childhood spent in this tiny community had hardened her to its real beauty. "There are ospreys and otters if you know where to look. And seals."

"Would you mind showing me? Tomorrow perhaps?"

"If the weather holds. You have to go up on the tops for the best chance and it's a hard slog, and not that safe now." Despite coat and scarf and gloves the cold was creeping through her bones and she shivered. "Come on. You'll be frozen if we don't hurry."

A quiet walk back, his arm round her shoulders, not heavy and possessive like Matthew's hand. It was comforting rather than restrictive and even though she was safe out here in the dark she leaned into his body. She reached the steps down to her door and he withdrew his arm, leaving her cold and alone.

The kitchen was dark but the Aga had kept it warm and once she turned on the lights there was no reason for him to stay any longer.

"Well. Thank you for walking me back." Damn. A feeble way to end the evening. She took a deep breath. "Look, I'm not supposed to let anyone in the Hall itself, but if you'd like I'll give you a tour tomorrow. I try to go round a couple of times each week to check on things so you might as well join me." She pulled off his gloves and dropped them on the table.

"Really? You won't get into trouble?"

"With the heirs? They won't know will they? I certainly won't be telling them." The scarf next, unwinding it from her neck and handing it back with regret.

"I'd love to. If you can spare the time."

A genuine smile, a slight dimple at the corner of his lips, blue eyes crinkling. She wondered what it would be like to kiss those lips. "Good. I've got packing to do here, so afternoon some time? Around two?"

"I'll be here." Gloves, scarf, a quick dip of his head as if he was about to kiss her cheek and thought better of it, and then he was gone, running with quick steps up to the courtyard and out into the darkness. No point in trying to watch him head back – the night was dark enough to hide anyone walking along the quayside and she locked the door and went through to her bedroom, fingers against her throat to capture the lingering warmth of his scarf.

CHAPTER 12

Blu's jeans were still filthy from earlier in the day, stinking of mud and slutch, the denim clammy and foul against his skin, but he had only one other pair and if those got wet, questions would be asked. He could put these in the washing machine first thing tomorrow and no one the wiser. The old man was asleep, snoring worse than his mum's last boyfriend and dead to the world, the ferrets locked away in their cage. The rucksack she'd given him was under his bed and he knelt down and hooked it out. Phone – though he had no credits – torch, bag, anorak. Safer and quieter to carry his trainers downstairs.

Only two more nights and he'd be gone from here. Two nights of a warm bed and good food. Of hot water and quiet evenings and feeling safe.

The ferrets were asleep and he managed to get outside without waking anyone and then he sat on the doorstep, his arse freezing, while he pulled on the ratty trainers.

Maybe she would buy him a decent pair if he did this right.

There was only one way down to the foreshore unless he risked jumping down from the track. The ancient steps were difficult enough in daylight with no handrail, and the uneven treads thick with seaweed and treacherous underfoot, but it was the only way. He fastened the anorak, wishing he'd put on a second jumper or maybe one of the decent ones Miss Cameron had left for him, but it was too late to change his mind.

Heavy clouds obliterated the night sky, not like earlier when he'd sat on the windowsill staring at the stars while he waited for the old man to go to bed. Life before coming here had mostly been in cities and towns where light pollution turned the skies dull orange and made star-gazing close to impossible. He'd thought about asking the old man if he knew anything about the night sky but the moment never arrived and now it would be too late.

The silence was enough to give him the shivers: no cars, no sirens, no one shouting. Just the wash of waves in the distance. He'd forgotten to ask about the tide, but it looked a long way off and with any luck he'd be in and out without anyone knowing. Job done and he'd be on his way home on Monday and settling into a new town the day after with any luck. The thought should have made him happy, but it didn't.

The steps were even more lethal in the dark but he got to the bottom without too many scrapes and then it was a matter of picking his way over the wave-worn rocks and streaks of sludge out towards the tip of the headland. An exhausting trek, even in daylight and he was tired enough after a day clearing ditches and driving the quad. He would miss that. Filthy work but satisfying. Mud and muck and seeing the ditches run clear when he'd removed the debris. It was good to get things working properly, and better for the land as well.

Without the light of the moon he found himself ankle deep in mud or sliding on thick ropes of seaweed, cursing as he slipped on his arse again and skinned his palms when he landed. The headland didn't appear to be getting any closer and he took a breather, plunking down on a rounded rock and hoping this time he'd have more success. It had taken him nearly an hour on Friday evening to work out where he was meant to go, and with the old man watching him every minute, night-time was his only chance.

His backside still ached from the hard saddle of the quad bike, his shoulders stiff from steering, and yet it had been a good day. The old man had not said much, but that didn't matter. They'd got along okay, even shared a laugh when he dropped a piece of his cheese and pickle sand- wich and a seagull swooped in and nicked it like one of the bloody birds on the seafront at Blackpool. One of the crappiest places they'd lived. Dossers and drunks and a string of men living in the flat until she was kicked out for not paying rent and brought him up here to dump him in the back of beyond.

He dug in his pocket for the crumpled packet of ciga- rettes. The last one and he pulled it out and stuck it between his lips. Getting a flame was not so easy – the wind extinguishing every attempt until he was bent double and holding the lighter close to his face. The glow of the tip, his mouth filling with smoke. He breathed it in, waiting for the nicotine to hit, but there was nothing, no buzz from the smoke, no sense of satisfaction. A filthy habit and stupid. Waves rumbled in the distance. He tossed the half-smoked cigarette away, hearing the soft hiss as it landed in a pool of seawater.

Time to be making a move and he pushed himself off the rock and followed the line of the headland, his slight figure hidden in the dark shadows of the steep rocky slope. For a moment he wondered what would happen if he fell or got trapped or lost. Would anyone find him? Would they even care?

She wouldn't. He knew that well enough, but family was family and she was all he had, other than Duncan Grant. An old man. Too old to look after a young lad, especially one with his background. The anorak was useless against the wind and he tugged it closer and trudged on.

By the time he reached the large rock, the waves were creeping forward, soaking his already wet trainers and dragging at the tattered hem of his jeans. He'd miscalculated. A stupid mistake, but there might still be time to get inside and have a quick search.

Barnacles grated his skin and snagged the wet denim of his jeans, the broken shell of a mussel – razor sharp and jagged – pierced the pad of his thumb and he cried out like a child with the shock before pressing his fingers against the cut. Salt spray stinging in his eyes, the smell of seaweed and dead fish and something rotting, cold eating into his body and numbing his face, the sound of waves and the rumble of pebbles. A low growl came from somewhere close behind him and he spun round, terrified.

There was nothing, but it was sufficient to deter him. He would try again tomorrow night. Unless...

Unless there was something in what his mum had told him about the Hall and its history. The way the laird and all the locals called it Black Dog Hall and muttered warnings about the ghost of a wolfhound that searched for lost children and attacked any enemies. The old man hadn't said anything, but even now, standing there in the dark, he could feel something, someone, watching him. Another low growl was enough to make him start running, feet slipping in the muck and wet seaweed and the water rising higher round his calves, pulling at his legs with watery fingers until he was sobbing with fear and horror and childish dread.

He fell more than once, jarring his back and knees, splattering his face in mud that clung to his lips and tasted of death. One of his trainers slipped off and he grabbed it and ran on, his phone soaked and lifeless and his eyes fixed on a beacon ahead – a soft glow of light coming from one of the cabins. and then he saw the door open and he hid behind a rock and listened to them walk by, quiet voices and soft laughter and it was only when he could no longer hear footsteps that he made his move, running bent double towards the steps leading up to the cabins. And then he saw their silhouettes, right at the top of the steps.

He'd been an idiot to come out here at night. Pure and simple. He hunkered down, making himself small and still and silent as he had learned to do over the past years, his teeth chattering and his feet numb. Ages they stood there, until he was close to giving himself up, but then he heard them walk on, their footsteps fading, and he unfolded himself with a hiss of pain.

By the time he reached the top, he was gasping for breath and barely able to walk. He stuffed his bare foot back into the trainer, and limped on, wanting nothing more than a bowl of chicken soup and to sit by the fire and get warm. Fat chance. If the old man discovered why he was here, there'd be no more warm beds or quad bike lessons. It would be Blackpool again. Or emergency housing. A stinking single room with a mattress on the floor for him. Bile rose in his throat.

No one had noticed his absence – the ferrets curled together in their cage and the old man bundled under his duvet. Blu stood in the doorway breathing in the smell of soap and a hint of cologne. A clean smell, like the man himself. A kind man as well, unlike most of his mother's transient boyfriends. There was nothing unpleasant about Duncan Grant despite his years and his stern look.

Tomorrow was Sunday, and he was supposed to be having another lesson on the quad bike. He went into the bathroom and stripped out of the filthy clothes, grimacing as the sodden denim rubbed the scrapes on knees and ankles. He wanted a shower but it would wake the old man and he had to content himself with a sinkful of hot water and one of the flannels kept in a pile on the windowsill. It was enough to remove the worst of the muck though not sufficient to warm him, and he added the flannel to the pile of clothes and padded back to his own room. His own room. No need share with anyone else, no need to worry about some stranger sneaking in and stealing the small amount of money he'd managed to hoard without her finding it.

Perhaps Duncan might let him return next summer and help out. It was unlikely. She'd be coming back for him on Monday evening and if he wasn't waiting there, then he'd be on his own.

His bedroom was warm and he slid between clean sheets and lay there, wondering if the rumours were true and the ghost of a dog had been lying in wait for him. A deep, gruff sound came from the old man's bedroom, wind whistled against the window and Blu Capson curled up in his bed and shivered.

CHAPTER 13

The rattle of the Land Rover's engine was enough to wake Peter from his dreams and he lay still, listening as the vehicle pulled up outside the Wilson's cabin, the slam of the door as Fiona got out, gravel crunching as she went to check the hot tub. The curtains were open, the window covered with intricate frost patterns and, despite the central heating, the room had a chill that made him snuggle further under the duvet.

He would have stayed there, warm and peaceful, but for the need to use the bathroom and when he came back out, yawning and rubbing his jaw, he heard the rattle of hailstones bouncing on the patio. The noise increased and, heedless of standing naked in front of the window, he watched the hail fall with the fascination and excitement of a small boy.

By the time the storm passed – leaving the sky clear for once – the patio was white and childish delight had him dressing with as much speed as possible and finding his walking boots. Wind had driven the hail into drifts, softening the harsh lines of the wooden balustrades and obscuring the flagstones and he hesitated for a moment before taking his first step, the crunch of boots crushing down, the silence in the air as if the whole world was holding its breath.

On an impulse, he hurried back inside, grabbing camera and hat before making his way along the quayside to the far end and working his way back, taking more photographs in one hour than he had taken all year so far: hailstone decorated cabins, icicles hanging from eaves, the footprints of small birds. The Hall black against the sky, weak sunlight glinting on ice crystals, the sea placid and grey. Each click of the shutter took him further away from the drudgery of work until his mind was full of ideas and plans.

He was making his way down the perilous harbour steps – clutching his camera like a favourite teddy bear and hoping for some decent shots from the lower level – when someone called down to him. A crisp greeting, the voice sharp enough to make him flinch.

"Good morning. Looks like it might be a white Christmas after all."

He pressed one hand against the dank stones of the wall, kept his feet still on the treacherous slabs. "I think this was a mistake." The hailstones were slippery and he turned round and made his way back up, step by step, body tensed in anticipation of his feet sliding out from under him. It would be a killing fall. A stupid thing to do, risking injury for the sake of a photograph. He reached the top and leaned against the wall. "Should have known better."

"I thought about going down there first thing. The

wife persuaded me not to. There's thick ice under those hailstones and it's lethal. She told me if I broke a leg she wasn't going to fix it for me. She's the medical one in the family – retired now, thank heavens," the man explained with a shrug of amusement before holding out a hand. "Jon Wilson. Not a doctor I hasten to add. We're in the end cabin. I'm surprised to see anyone else staying here. Fiona said the other cabins were shut?"

Peter tucked his camera back in his pocket. "Peter Sinclair. I got waylaid on my journey and ended up here Friday night. Miss Cameron was good enough to rent me one for a couple of nights."

"Ah. I wondered. Saw the lights yesterday evening and wondered who it might be. You're not from around here, I take it?" Wilson's eyes were busy, gauging everything about him. A quick glance over at his car before resuming his evaluation. "She didn't say anything about you this morning. Are you staying for the week?"

"I'm from Glasgow. Work, that is. But I'll be leaving Tuesday at the latest." For some inexplicable reason it was important to explain himself to the man.

"Christmas Day with the family? We're avoiding that this year. First time we've had a chance to spend the day without the family descending en masse. Brought every-thing with us, apart from a tree, but Fiona said she'd ask Duncan to cut one for us this afternoon. There's not much to beat a real pine tree at Christmas, especially fresh cut."

He hadn't had a Christmas tree since… well, since he walked out on Georgia. There'd never been a need for one after that. He wondered what Fiona was doing – he hadn't seen any signs of decorations when he'd been in her flat, but he'd only been in a small part of what had to be a decent sized apartment. Perhaps she had a tree in the living room, though the Hall itself deserved something better. A Norway spruce perhaps. He imagined it would have been magnificent when the owner was alive. "I'll look forward to seeing it. Just hope the hail doesn't make it any more difficult."

Jon Wilson shook his head. "The forecasts say rain by midday. Anyway. I must head off. The hot tub awaits." He shook his head ruefully. "We must be mad with all the ice on the ground, but there's not much else to do right now other than relax. Exactly what the doctor ordered." A nod of his head and he was walking away, leaving Peter feeling as if he had been through a rather subtle interrogation.

He'd planned to walk up the road as far as the stone bridge and get some photographs before going to look round the Hall but the road was likely to be as treacherous as the steps and his car would never cope with the ice on the road. It might be better to ask Duncan for a ride in the quad bike higher up the road so he could get a better view of the bay. He took one last photograph of the headland and made his way back along the quay to the cabin and a shower.

The hot tub tempted him with its promise of heat but he had other things on his mind and he made toast and coffee, stood at the window to eat while seagulls swooped over the sea and the waves crept forward. High water had been and gone, but the thought of walking along the foreshore was not something he cared to do in these conditions. Even after such a short time here, he'd seen how rapidly the water advanced until it was washing against the harbour wall. No wonder this had been a popular place for smugglers with its tiny, deep harbour that was remote enough, even in this secluded corner of Scotland, to be left alone. A swift tide to get the boats in and hidden from sight.

He cleaned up the kitchen. A simple enough matter: plate and knife and mug, the empty bottle from last night, the two glasses. It seemed wrong that he couldn't return the favour, but he had nothing to give her. And he looked at his sketch pad and pencils. A long time since he'd drawn a detailed picture of an existing building, but he still had the ability even if unpractised.

Midday found him hunched over the table. The rain had started again, reducing the hail to slush, but he had been too busy drawing to notice. Fitzwilliam Hall was coming to life on the paper and he stepped away to get a better perspective before continuing. Something niggled him about the drawing – was it that the turret was slightly too tall or too wide, or maybe it was the windows along the top level that made the drawing seem at odds with the photograph from which he was working. The eraser brushed over the faint lines and dabbed at one awkward corner before he picked up his pencil and carried on. In the end, hunger drove him to search the supplies for something easy to make.

A tuna sandwich was simple enough, with a packet of crisps and a couple of chocolate biscuits, a mug of strong tea to finish and then he was back at the table, eager to finish off the bare bones of the sketch while the light was still good. It was with a sense of real regret that he put it away and began spreading the designs from yesterday out on the table, putting them in order and casting a couple aside as being – now in the cold light of day – too impractical even for his wild imagination.

But the others had possibilities. A range of individually designed lodges for people searching for high-end luxury holidays. A spatter of raindrops against the windows broke his thoughts and he looked at the clock – well past the time he had agreed to meet Fiona and he put the pages in a neat pile on the table and grabbed his car keys.

In the downpour the Hall looked bleak and forlorn, louring clouds adding to its air of neglect and he took a minute to study the way the building fitted into the terrain: the neat courtyard close to the house itself then the sward of sheep-grazed grass stretching to the tip of the headland and the cliffs down to the sea. No sheep dotted the grass today, they would be inland no doubt, sheltering from the winter sleet and rain. A miserable existence.

Fiona must have been waiting for him to arrive – appearing at the top of the steps as he parked his car next to her mud-splattered Land Rover. He kept his head down, hurrying across the paving and down into the tiny lobby, shaking raindrops from his hair and face before stepping inside the familiar warmth of her kitchen.

"I thought you'd forgotten, or…" She looked embarrassed and he could guess her thoughts.

"I'm sorry, I was working on something and didn't realise the time." He started to unfasten his coat but she held up one hand.

"You'll need to keep that on when we go through. It's bitterly cold on the other side." She was getting her own coat and scarf and a heavy iron key. "This way. You've got your camera?"

"Am I allowed to take photographs? They'd only be for me."

A shrug of her shoulders. "It wouldn't matter to me – the Hall's likely to be demolished in a year or two, but for now it's still Richard's home and there's all his personal things still here." She led him out of the kitchen and along the passageway past the pantry and an open door that revealed a sitting room. He could see signs of her presence everywhere: an empty wine glass, a book lying open on the arm of the leather chair, woollen throws on the back of the two sofas. "This is all the housekeeper's residence. Sounds fancy, but it's a little shabby now. I'll still be sorry to leave, though."

More closed doors. She ignored several but paused at one to open it and give him a glimpse of the interior. A long stone-walled cellar with a low barrel-vaulted ceiling. Boxes and random objects littered the floor, cast-off items no one wanted to throw away: an umbrella stand complete with a half dozen walking sticks, a paint-spattered wooden ladder, a tangle of orange ropes that might once have belonged to fishermen. He orientated himself, trying to place this room in his mind. "This is close to the dungeon? That makes it..."

"That's right. One of the internal storerooms. We use them for storage. Anything and everything. Richard didn't like throwing stuff away if it had any use. We're in the oldest part of the building here and this was part of the original tower. Above the kitchen and family area is the later part of the building. The rooms I live in were converted from the newer storerooms underneath the main house." They reached an oak door: iron hinges, studs, a bolt longer than his forearm, a keyhole more fitting for a dungeon than an interior door. She turned to him. "Look. I don't mind you taking photos, but…" She grimaced. "Not anything personal. You'll understand when we go inside."

The key turned, not even the slightest effort needed to unlock the door. She stepped through and he followed.

Cold. A bitter, raw cold that made him gasp. 'Dragon's breath' as the gardener used to call it. Colder than outside. They were in a bleak passageway, stone walls, stone-flagged floor and devoid of any decoration other than a single cast iron radiator. "Do you never put the heating on?"

"It needs three boilers to keep this place warm. The last one stopped working four years ago. This way. I'll show you the kitchen. It's on this floor, but Richard rarely used it. He preferred eating with us when he was home, at least he used to."

He had no idea what to expect, but this wasn't it. A large underground room, the ceiling higher than he expected. An electric oven stood against one wall, next to it a stainless steel sink marked by the slow drip of water from a leaking tap and a row of cupboards with dated Formica worktops extended along the rest of the wall. A pine table with bentwood chairs took up one corner.

The history of the room was evident everywhere he looked: a great open fireplace on the other side with spit and fire dogs still in place, the chimney bar hanging down with a battered iron pot at the end, a brick-built oven in one wall for baking. A dresser with a row of plates and cups and saucers. A brush leaning against one wall, even a tea towel waiting on the dusty steel drainer for the owner who would never pick it up. Salt and pepper pots standing sentry on the table along with a folded newspaper. A film of dust covered everything.

Had he been alone in a stranger's house he might have been tempted to drag his finger across the table to leave a mark, but Fiona was watching him and he realised how difficult this had to be for her. Dirt blurred the glass in the windows, cobwebs filled the corners and hung from the ceiling but the spiders had died years ago. There was no life in here.

He stuffed the camera back in his pocket. Even in this dead room he could sense Richard Fitzwilliam. Not the man's ghost, but those small everyday items waiting for their owner to return and put them away. The rest of the house would be the same, a man's private life laid bare for casual inspection.

Fiona nodded. "There's not much else on this level other than the pantry and buttery and they're empty. We'll miss out the next floor and go up to the family rooms."

More passages before they reached the bottom of a wide staircase. Mildew and damp speckled the carpet, the bannister rail dulled from years of neglect. His hands left traces in the dust, dark footprints marked his passing as he followed her up to a wide landing and along the hall.

Each room was frozen in time: the billiards table in the games room with cue and chalk resting on the baize and the balls scattered as if the players had left the room a few minutes ago, the library where he gazed in awe at the rows of books and where wingback chairs faced each other across a crimson carpet and decanters lined up on an oak sideboard, the drawing room with its stiff formality and rotting curtains and blackened candelabras. Richard's four-poster bed and solid furniture and musty smell of disuse.

Room after room, wallpaper peeling in great sheets from the walls, mould creeping along the upper corners, rain finding an entrance through cracked windows. The cloying smell of damp and mould and rot. It sickened him to see such needless decay.

"How did it get like this? Does no one care?"

The door to the next room was warped. She gave it another push and it yielded with a reluctant scrape. "Richard's estate office. Where he kept tenant records and such. The solicitors deal with all that now. And, yes." She slammed the door shut before he could get more than a quick glance of a heavy Victorian desk, bookcases lining the walls, a printer and desk light. "We all care. But this isn't my house; I'm the caretaker, that's all, and that means little more than making sure no one breaks in. There's no money for anything but the minimum. I used to light a fire occasionally in a couple of the main rooms but the chimneys haven't been swept for years so I stopped doing even that."

"I'm sorry. That was thoughtless of me. You must find it difficult."

She leaned against the wall. "Frankly, it's impossible. Everyone's spent the last seven years hoping he'd turn up again. You know – a magical reappearance after recovering from amnesia. A bang on the head, that sort of thing. We hung on, day after day, leaving things as he left them, just in case. And..."

"He didn't. And now it's too late. And if you move

things now, you'll feel as if you're betraying him and all the things you feared will come true."

"You do understand." She gave a sigh. "There's not many people who realise how difficult it is, looking at things like that newspaper in the kitchen and not being able to throw it away because then I'd be admitting he won't ever come back, and so he won't."

The corridor was cold, his breath sparkling in the frigid air. She looked pinched and miserable and he wanted to take her hands and rub them. "Come on, you've shown me enough. Let's get warm."

"No. No you haven't seen the rest. I'll take you up the turret stairs. It's a bit narrow, but Richard liked using it. It always makes me think of him."

The turret was narrow inside, its ancient walls solid and deep and a tight spiral of steps leading to the top floor. On and on, his legs numb with cold. He paused by one of the square four-paned windows looking out across to where the cabins stood. Rain pelted down on the old glass, a tiny crack in one corner letting water trickle inside. The wood was rotting, the paint bubbling and distorted. The beginning of the end.

"Come on, before I freeze up here."

One finger traced the path of a raindrop before he turned away and headed upwards, holding the thick hemp rope as if his life depended on it. It was a relief to reach the tiny mid-landing and step out into a hallway running the length of the building. The spiral continued upwards to the cap-house and the access to the roof, but there was nothing there to interest him.

The first door was some distance along the corridor and he stepped inside expecting to see servants' quarters only to find a huge room with windows looking out over the courtyard and the ocean beyond. An oak desk faced the view, more bookcases lined one wall, two leather chesterfield sofas stood opposite each other with a coffee table between them. Intricate linen-fold oak panels lined the room, a large fireplace on one wall, the dog grate laid with kindling and a basket of logs close at hand ready to be added when the flames had taken. He turned to face her. There was no need to ask.

"Richard's favourite room. This was his private workspace and library and sitting room where he spent most of his time. It's the main room on this level and he never invited casual visitors up here, only close friends. If you look in the corner, there's a servants' bell. We used to ring it if he had visitors or he was needed. Or he would ring down if he wanted a drink or something, not that he often used it. He'd come down if he was thirsty – the turret stairs lead down to the kitchen – quicker that way he said." She picked up a log that had slipped from the basket and replaced it, ran a hand over the mantelpiece with its ornate crest as if checking for dust.

He went over to the fireplace and bent down to peer up the chimney: a tangle of twigs and leaves, a cluster of pale sticks that formed themselves into the skeleton of a bird. It would have fallen down and died here from thirst or hunger. A cruel death. Little remained but the bones and a few straggly black feathers. The skull was white, the eye sockets empty and he blew away the dust and held it out on his palm. Not a seagull – the beak was thick and black, deep and blunt and sharp. Such a small thing and yet he was in awe of its strength.

"Razorbill." Fiona stroked one finger over the skull.

"Poor thing. I had no idea that was in the chimney but it looks as if it'd been there a while. Its partner will be somewhere out there, waiting for this one to return. They mate for life, you know."

He didn't, but he slipped the skull into his jacket pocket, his fingers stiff and his feet numb.

"Dad made sure this room was always ready. I've tried to do the same. It's stupid I know, but…" She stood there, biting her lip as if she was worried about what he might say. "There used to be a vase of fresh flowers in here every week but once probate was agreed there wasn't any point. Keeping the fire ready was all I could do. I come up here and dust it every couple of weeks, air the room – that sort of thing – more to feel close to him than anything. If he was going to come back anywhere, it would be here."

Three windows looked out over the courtyard and the ocean beyond. A glorious view in summer, but the sun had set and the dark sky was heavy with rain. There would be no star gazing tonight. The faintest smell of polish and lavender floating in the air, heavy velvet curtains hanging at the windows, a thick Persian rug on polished oak boards. Richard's room. Even bereft of its owner the space was welcoming. He touched the edge of the desk with a cautious finger.

"It looks as if he's gone out for a walk. Papers on the desk, his pen…" It was the same make as his. And the propelling pencil as well. A fragile connection to a man probably long dead. He stared at it, his mind seeing the clues. "He was left-handed."

She frowned. "Yes. How on earth did you know?"

"He kept his pen on the left side, same as I do." His fingers itched to pick it up and try using it, see if it was as good as his. Better probably. He'd looked at this model when he was buying his, but the price was well beyond his reach. "What did he do in here? I mean..."

"He was supposed to be writing a history of the Hall but we never found any of his research. There were folders and files and notes all in a heap at one time. Masses of stuff. And all of it handwritten. I know he was planning to get a book published, nothing huge, just for the locals really, and then my mother died and when I came up here to see him after the funeral, the desk was clear and he refused to talk about it. He was upset about something, but I never found out why."

"I remember you saying about your mother. It must have been a difficult time for you all. Do you mind me asking what happened?"

She perched on the edge of the desk, arms folded. "It was one of those stupid things that everyone round here warns you about. She hit a deer on the main road and it went through the windscreen. The coroner said it would have been instantaneous. I was fifteen."

"I'm sorry." Useless words.

"We were devastated. All of us. As a child you grow up thinking your parents are invincible. Dad wanted to give up and move away, but Richard persuaded him to stay on and I helped out as much as I could. It was a terrible time. Duncan was the gamekeeper back then, but he ended up doing more of Dad's work and keeping the cabins running properly until Abby started coming fulltime."

"She married your father?"

"Yes. She and Dad just fell in love. I'm happy for them. It's not the same as having Mum here, but he loves her and that's all that matters. She kept him going when

Richard disappeared. I think if it hadn't been for her, Richard's disappearance would have finished Dad off completely. They used to go fishing together, spend the evening watching football on the telly downstairs. Anyway, this is the main room on this floor. There's a warren of rooms further along, most of them disused servants' quarters or storerooms."

He could see her starting to shiver. "Come on. Let's go down and get warm. Or you could come back to my cabin?"

"Is that an invitation to join you in the hot tub, Mr Sinclair? I wasn't sure you'd want me annoying you again or crying on your shoulder."

"My shoulder is available any time you need it. As is the hot tub. You bring the wine and I'll provide something to eat." He hoped there were pizzas in the freezer.

"You're on. But I haven't shown you the best room in the Hall. Come with me."

She had a glint in her eye that intrigued him and he took one last look at the fountain pen lying there and made his way outside. Soft fur brushed against his hand but that was impossible. It was nothing more than warm air on cold skin.

He paused at the threshold. "Did you hear that?" A bird calling out perhaps, but not exactly a bird. It was the sound a person might make, a sound of sorrow or of loss, rather than a cry of pain or a call for help.

"No. What was it? I hope to god it wasn't another loose tile or the flashings. Not in this weather. That's the last thing we need now."

He shook his head. "It was probably a bird or something." He looked back inside the room, confused and more than a little perturbed. He'd heard a noise – and from inside the room itself. One hand rested on the wall, cold stone and paint, the roughness of a small repair, the slight bubble where damp had lifted the plaster from the wall.

He had imagined it. One last glimpse inside Richard's private apartment. A gentle click as she pulled the door shut, closing off the scene and he followed her down the long corridor to the imposing staircase at the other end deeply aware he had overlooked something important.

CHAPTER 14

"Welcome to the Great Room. By rights it should be called the Great Hall, but Richard thought that sounded rather pretentious considering the Hall itself isn't that big."

"What the –" Words failed him as he stood in the doorway. It surpassed anything he could have imagined in such a relatively small manor house like this. "It's…"

"I think 'welcoming' is the word I'd choose, but yes, it's quite wonderful."

It was. He'd thought the fireplace in the last room was impressive, but this beat it hands-down, even in electric light. An inglenook large enough to stand upright inside, a ceiling rich with plaster mouldings between dark oak beams, a carved wooden screen at one end and a dais at the other leading to other rooms. A long rectangular room, its proportions so perfect nothing seemed unbalanced or off-kilter. Three well-worn leather sofas formed an open square around a low table in front of the fire and a huge faded rug covered the flagstones. He wondered how many times Richard had used this room for entertaining guests, how often the fire had been lit. An architectural masterpiece for all its relative unimportance, its walls bare apart from more carved panelling. A room full of history.

The dining table could seat twenty with ease, a heavy oak carver standing guard at the head. How could anyone walk away and leave something as beautiful, as aesthetically perfect, as this room?

"There's a long-standing tradition that says we salute the death of the laird by drinking a toast to him in here and then sharing a feast together. The chance to forgive those who sought to do us harm, to heal old quarrels and make new friends. It never happened for Richard, and now the tradition will be lost forever, like this hall." She took his hand and squeezed it. "I need to show you the family portraits. Through here."

The long gallery lacked the size of the Hall, but it was as impressive. Oak wainscoting with a row of dark oil paintings above in a line. She let him walk the length by himself and despite the cold he took his time. Men and women, families, a man with his horse, two children... He read the details.

Hannah and Emma Fitzwilliam. 1785.

He put a hand on the wall to steady himself. "The children. These are the ones kidnapped by the smugglers? How old were they when they died?"

"Hannah and Emma? Yes. They were the laird's daughters. Their brother was born a couple of years after this was painted and he inherited the estate. Both daughters went on to marry wealthy landowners and lived until they were well into their nineties I believe. It's a lovely painting, one of my favourites."

Two beautiful children, blonde-haired and blue-eyed, each with a look of confidence and intelligence. They gazed out, watching his every move. He had to have been mistaken. But he wasn't. Yesterday morning he'd seen these two faces staring out from one of the windows of Richard's favourite room. Had experienced that wave of sadness and isolation. But neither of these children looked sad. Far from it.

"Peter? What's wrong?"

He'd been tired and stressed and his eyes must have been playing tricks on him. Best forget it. "N... Nothing. I was thinking. Which one's Richard?"

"He told us he destroyed his portrait when his father died. I think it was an unhappy relationship; he never talked much about his father, just that he was a stern man. You won't find a portrait of his father either, or much else. It's as if Richard wanted to erase any memory of the man." She looked up at the portrait of the children. "There's something magical about this painting. I was hoping they might let me buy it, but everything's going to an auction house by the end of January. Every last thing that might have some value."

The fountain pen and pencil, the books in the library, the desks and the tables and chairs. Even the curtains would be pulled down and sold, leaving the rooms bleak and desolate and decaying. No wonder she didn't want him taking photographs.

She turned away. "Come on, let's go. I've shown you

everything really, other than the boring stuff like bathrooms and so on. There's the lower level storerooms – the ones that aren't accessible from outside, but they aren't that interesting unless you're desperate?"

"I think I can do without seeing them." He rubbed his hands together in a futile attempt to bring some life back to the frozen fingers. A stupid thing, not wearing his gloves, but he hadn't realised how cold the house would be. "How about a coffee? My place or yours?"

It made her laugh and he took her hand, following her back to the Great Room and a small doorway opening onto the turret. A score of steps took them down to a wooden door and he stepped out into the bright warmth of her kitchen.

"I didn't realise…" He'd thought the door was yet another cupboard.

She grinned at him, delighted at his reaction. "The turret's a sort of secret link to the Hall above and the other floors, and also to the roof. Not many people got to use it when the house was in use, but it comes in handy. Tea?"

The sadness of the abandoned house seemed a lifetime away. "Please. So, what are you doing for Christmas?" Had it not been for the necessity of visiting his parents, he would have asked to stay in the cabin until the end of next week, but it was an imposition.

She was busy finding the teabags. "I hadn't thought. There's plenty in the freezer. Duncan might ask me over – he's likely got some venison, or grouse or something. If he doesn't, I'm happy enough by myself."

"No tree? Isn't Duncan getting one for the Wilsons today? You could ask him to pick one for you tomorrow morning and I could help you put it up if you want." The heat in the kitchen made his face hot.

"I don't know. Let me think about it. He has enough to do as it is without me adding to his work. It means him going out again tomorrow."

He took the mug from her hands. Hot and strong and he took a sip relishing the heat in his throat. "I bet Blu would jump at a chance to drive the quad bike again. Good practice for the lad."

"That's mean, Mr Sinclair. Preying on my good nature like that." She sighed. "Very well, but only a small one. Five foot at the most."

"Six. Go on. Live dangerously. I'll even give you a hand decorating it." He hadn't helped decorate a tree since he was a small boy and Mrs Sullivan offered to let him do the tiny one in the kitchen. Needles prickling his fingers and working their way inside his jumper, the baubles glittering in his small hands, the smell of pine and cinnamon and dried oranges. A proper Christmas tree, messy and decorated with enthusiasm and love.

"You're on then. You'll have to help me get the boxes out of the storeroom so I hope you don't mind getting dusty. This way."

The storeroom was eerily cold after the warmth of the kitchen and they set about checking cartons. By the time they'd found two of the boxes, both of them were shivering.

"There's another one, somewhere. Over by the ladder I think, safe out of the way." Fiona had stacked the two boxes on top of each other out in the passageway and was busy opening other cartons. "It's a big one full of Richard's ornaments, but I don't think anyone will mind us using them one last time. Some of them are gorgeous. Hand-blown glass, that sort of thing. They'll only get thrown away I expect."

A sturdy packing case half-hidden under a scrap of tarpaulin caught his eye, and he dragged it away from the dark corner where it had lurked, unnoticed. Metal scraped against stone and he looked down, concerned that the box might have marked the pale stone of the floor. But his fears were unfounded, the large square stone on which it was standing already chipped along its edges and deeply scratched, any mortar holding it in place long rotted away. The box was labelled 'Christmas' but although it was tempting to open it right away, it was heavy and he left it for later. It was an easy matter to scoop up the two lighter ones and carrying them out, leaving Fiona to close the door behind him.

Deep shadows filled the kitchen. "How about a dip in the tub. To get warm?" He shifted one of the boxes a few inches away from the edge. "Might be your last chance." Another shift of the box, careful to avoid her eyes. "If you'd like to, that is."

"I'd love that." She grabbed a bottle of wine and leaned forward to kiss his cheek. A brief contact, warm lips against his cold skin, and then she was still, her face blushing pink and her eyes staring into his. "Peter?"

He took the bottle from her hand and put it on the table. "Yes."

Icy fingers cupped his face. Her voice soft and low and needy. "Kiss me. Please?"

It was so easy. A single step forward, her eager face cupped in his hands, the warmth of her lips against his. Gentle at first. A tentative exploring of lips, her hands on his waist bringing him closer. Boundaries observed, as was only right and proper. She pulled away, reaching up to touch his lips with a cool finger.

A longer kiss this time, tongues breaching the gap between them, breaths shared, her eyes closing in sheer pleasure even as he watched her face. He could see her eagerness, her body pressing against his, the heat of her intensity and his own reaction. A long time since he'd craved such intimacy, but this was not right, not the time or place. And she was lonely. It would be so easy to take advantage. He pulled away, cupping her face in his hands and leaning in to give her one last, gentle kiss. "I should be going."

"You don't want..." She turned away from him, her face red with humiliation and he reached out for her.

"I do, believe me, but this isn't right, Fiona. You're beautiful and I admire you, and you deserve more than this, more than me. I have nothing to offer you right now and..." He paused, leaning forward to cup her face in his hands and kiss her forehead, hating himself. "...I would hate you to wake up tomorrow with regrets. And somehow I think you might. I'm not good enough for someone like you."

She was silent for a long while, biting her lip, her eyes full of tears. "You're wrong, you know. Bess trusts you and so does Duncan. But I'll wait if that's what you want." She leaned forward and kissed him. A gentle kiss that held so much promise. "We're both frozen. I'll get a bottle of wine and we can go and warm up."

He nodded, grateful for her understanding. They hurried to his car, the bitter wind taking their breath away and leaving them both gasping by the time they were inside and the doors shut. A turn of the key, the engine stuttering once before catching and then they were out and rumbling rattling over the wooden slats of the bridge, rattling over the rough gravel in front of the cabins and pulling to a stop outside his temporary home.

A dash to the door. He put the bottle on the table. "I could do with a quick shower first if you don't mind waiting?"

"Hurry up, then." She opened the cupboard and pulled out glasses and he went through to the bedroom and closed the door.

There was a folder next to the bottle and, curious as ever, she opened it. Drawings. Sketches of cabins and lodges and the harbour. New lodges, designed to replace the old ones, this one. She felt cold and betrayed and tarnished. The hot tub was forgotten, the glasses tumbling from her fingers as she picked up the papers and leafed through them. Their plans brought to life.

Her voice came out in a whisper, her throat stifled, choking. "You bastard, Peter Sinclair. You utter, utter bastard." And she flung the papers away, throwing them in a flurry of white pages that flew across the room like birds in flight. Had the log burner been lit, she would have added them to the flames, but her heart ached too much to even think of picking them up now.

He had used her. All her dreams and hopes about love and someone decent who cared about the Hall, all Duncan's promises that Peter Sinclair was to be trusted. All false. She hated him.

The door crashed back as she yanked it open, not caring who might hear the noise. It took all her courage to open the bedroom door – he was gone and she heard the shower running. A minute. That was all she needed and then she was in the living room, dragging on her coat with fingers that refused to obey her. And then he was there, dripping wet, a towel round his waist and his face ashen.

"Fiona? What's –"

"Don't speak to me. Don't you dare speak to me. You're working for them, aren't you?"

"Working? F... f..." He shook his head as if desperate. "I... I don't ..."

She might have forgiven him if it hadn't been for the drawings of over a dozen individual cabins each on the narrow strip of land between cliffs and sea. She'd heard the heirs talking about new holiday lodges but she hadn't anticipated designs quite as wonderful as the ones scattered on the floor. They would look fabulous when they were finished, which made it worse in a way. And even worse was her betrayal of Richard's privacy by letting a stranger look round the house. She stumbled away from him, banging her hip against one corner of the table. A sharp stab of pain and she cried out. His hand touched her, steadying her and she thrust it away with another cry, this time revulsion.

"Them. You're working for them. The ones who want to tear everything down and ruin it forever. Richard's sodding heirs. Don't deny it, I've seen your plans. Twelve lodges? Why don't you go the whole hog and put in twenty? Cram them together and destroy the whole point of coming here."

"Plans?" He had the temerity to look confused. "No. You... you–"

"Don't lie to me. I've seen them. No wonder you were

so keen to look round the Hall. Did you see enough? Manage to make a list of everything valuable so you can report back to them? How many times did you laugh at me?"

He shook his head again, his throat bobbing, lips moving silently, but she was done with being kind and sympathetic.

"Don't bother. I'm still in charge here, for what it's worth, and I want you gone by noon tomorrow. Drop the keys off at Duncan's. I don't ever want to see you again."

The door shook on its hinges as she flung it open. One last retort, hatred and anger and desperation clogging her throat so that the words came out raw and rasping. "You can tell Richard's nephews they won't be successful, whatever they try. Bess will make sure of that."

A slam of the door that shook the whole cabin and doubtless woke the Wilsons. She no longer cared. It had stopped raining, but that was little comfort.

The Hall loomed ahead, her hands and feet freezing and she had no energy to do more than drag herself along the track one step at a time. Somewhere behind her a dog growled and she turned round, hands on her hips in an attempt to look defiant. "Bugger off. You brought him here, so you deal with the consequences."

Moonlight shone on the track and the puddles and the great black dog standing foursquare, head to one side, eyes watching her. Two young girls wearing old-fashioned clothes waited in the background.

"I don't know what you want anymore, Bess. Or you girls, either. You're supposed to be the guardians here. You're supposed to save people, not help destroy everything Richard worked for. Why can't you leave us alone?

Go and haunt Richard's nephews instead." She turned away and walked on, her footsteps loud on the wooden deck of the bridge, her tears silent and unseen until she reached her temporary refuge of the Housekeeper's Apartment.

CHAPTER 15

Sunrise found him awake and packing. Not his own scant possessions – those had taken a couple of minutes to stuff into his bags and drop in the boot of his car on top of the presents – but the cabin had not been emptied and it was the last thing he could do for her. Even now he had no idea what had happened other than she had seen his designs and had somehow thought he was working for the new owners. Her anger had been distressing enough for both of them and all he wanted now was to do as she asked and leave once it was daylight and he'd finished here.

Another cardboard box filled with plates and mugs before he stuffed the gaps with paper towels. The bed already stripped, linens washed and dried during the bleak night hours when sleep was impossible. They were folded away in one of the bin liners along with the duvet and the coverlet.

The hot tub sprang to life, bubbling away beneath its cover as he walked out onto the patio, but he was too heart-sore to be tempted. It would have been easy enough to empty it and one less job for her to do, but he could not bring himself to do it. And anyway, she might yet use it.

The end cabin was still in darkness, the Wilsons enjoying a lie-in, and he could hear no sound from the Gatehouse either. Another box left for collection, each one a reminder of his failure.

Breakfast was basic. A mug of strong coffee to keep him awake on the long drive back, an apple and a banana – the latter a little speckled but still edible. He drank the coffee outside on the patio, took one bite of the apple and threw the rest into the bushes for the birds to eat. The banana followed. Blu was running along the edge of the waterline, a small figure in the distance making for the tip of the headland to explore the shoreline, the waves thundering out at sea.

The tide would be turning at midday, heavy waves pushed by the wind blustering down the coast from the north. A cold wind as well, promising more ice and snow. There would be floods on the high ground. A hard drive back and a harder arrival. He swallowed the final mouthful of bitter coffee and flung the dregs away. A quick rinse of the mug under the tap, a shake to get rid of the excess water and he put it in the last box along with the dishwasher tablets and the unused tea towels. And then he was done.

Three nights. He'd spent three nights here, and yet it was as if he had lived here all his life. Duncan's unquestioning acceptance and friendship, the silence and simple beauty of the ocean, the sense of peace that filled him. The thought of leaving and never coming back was unbearable for some reason and he felt a tear trickle down to catch in the rough stubble on his cheek. He dashed it away with an angry hand.

Two hours before she expected him to leave. It would be easier to go now before she drove past to check the Wilson's tub, but the drawing of the Hall was unfinished and though she might hate him, he wanted to leave it for her. He sat with his back to the window, deaf and blind to anyone outside. It was not the detailed sketch he would have liked, but it was all he could do in the time available.

The picture was finished with time to spare, his initials in one corner, the letters intertwined and as unobtrusive as he could make them. He had no tissue paper to protect it, but a plastic folder would keep it clean. It would be easy enough to give it to Duncan and ask him to pass it on later. But he could not leave it at that – to walk away without saying anything would be wrong and even if she rejected him, he would never forget the taste of her lips and the heat of her body against his. Wanting her as much as she wanted him. The tenderness in her touch.

The fountain pen waited to be put away but he picked it up again and reached for a clean sheet of paper. He might be useless at speaking but he could write. And he did, page after page in the elegant script he'd learned as a child, the pen faltering at times as he tried to explain.

By the time he was done it was coming up to noon and the rain had started again. There would be no final walk. He put the designs in an envelope – he would never be able to use them knowing how much pain he had caused, and she could do with them what she liked. At least she would know the truth. It was little comfort.

The letter went in the envelope along with everything else, and he placed it on the table along with the razorbill skull. She would find them, later. One last check to make sure he had not left anything behind other than his heart, and he locked the door and drove away.

No one answered when he knocked on Duncan's door. The house was silent and empty other than two ferrets peering with button-black eyes from their cage. The keys clattered on the kitchen table. A hollow sound. All that was left was to say a proper goodbye to the man and thank him for his kindness. The coughing rattle of the quad bike echoed down from the hills and he started his engine and drove away.

The stream was overflowing, the water a surging torrent full of mud and debris and he pulled to a halt to watch, both fascinated and more than a little horrified by the sight. Leaves and twigs and small branches tangled together like a giant cat's cradle, plastic bottles and worse bobbed briefly before being submerged in the filthy run-off from the recent rains. The wooden deck was high enough to avoid being flooded but he didn't envy Fiona having to drive across. He shook his head. It was no longer his concern but even so, he was unable to dispel the sense of unease.

The road leading up the narrow valley was as steep as he remembered, and he took his time, wishing the weather was kinder so that he could stop and take one last look. He would never come back. The thought of returning here and seeing the house left to rot, the cabins replaced by cheap monstrosities and the stream culverted, was more than he could bear.

The road was a watercourse now, water pouring down from the hills, the stream swollen and raging. Tyres gouged a path through the rainwater, his wipers struggled to clear the windscreen but he could make out the grey shape of the hump-backed bridge ahead. The car was straining on the steep incline, his hands sweating on the steering wheel. A slip could end up with the car in the ditch or worse.

He was at the ramp to the bridge, slowing to a crawl, when the dog leapt out from nowhere, barring his way. It could only be the same one from Friday evening, a black wolfhound, teeth bared, her eyes blazing with rage, hackles raised. He slammed on the brakes, heart pounding with the shock of encountering the animal again and then he heard the quad bike coming down the road on the other side, Duncan's voice shouting – no, roaring – a warning.

"Get back! For god's sake, get back!"

When he looked back at the bridge, the dog had vanished. The bike skidded on the other side of the hump, Duncan struggling to hold it steady and Peter had barely enough time to throw the car into reverse and jerk it back to the flat ground behind him before the bike was charging at the bridge. And then he saw the danger. A shattered tree trunk, its branches long gone, roots washed bare by the floods, swirling and twisting in the raging water and about to hit the arch of the bridge. Even the strongest mortar could not withstand such an impact.

It struck with a grinding scream of wood against stone, the blocks sliding and twisting and the bridge tearing itself apart even as the tree swung round to slam against the solid masonry walls and shudder to a halt.

The quad bike overturned with a hideous screech of metal, sliding out of sight down the bank and he was scrabbling at his seat belt, throwing open the door and running.

"Duncan?" His own shout louder than the water and the creak of breaking wood. Louder than the brief roar of the quad bike's unfettered engine before it slid into the stream. He slipped in mud and water, fell to his knees in the slutch as ancient masonry toppled into the current a few yards away. "Duncan? For god's sake, where are you?" Rain blinded him, soaked his clothes and his hair. His trainers skidded on wet stones, filthy water splashing into his mouth and still he could not see the man. He would have to go into the water.

"Peter?" A choking cough, a splutter, a groan of pain. "Down here –"

It was Duncan, sprawled on the steep slopes of the stream below the ruins of the bridge and trying to drag himself out of the water. Blood masked his face and for one moment Peter imagined a fractured skull or worse, but then he saw the gash on his forehead.

"Hang on. I've got you." He had to lie flat and reach down to grab hold of the man's outstretched arm. The tree had formed a dam against the remains of the bridge and the water was rising. Not much time before the waters surged over and swept them away. "How bad is it?"

"Cut my hands. And my head, I think. I was lucky. Thought you were going to be on the bridge when the tree hit. You wouldn't have stood a chance."

"I owe you a bottle of good malt." He spat mud and rainwater. Under the dark blood, Duncan's face was grey, the man holding himself unnaturally still. "Can you feel your legs? I'm going to have to pull you up before the water breaches."

"Legs are fine. I can move them. It's the bloody ankle I'm worried about. Think I might have broken it. Hurts like buggery."

He restrained his snort of laughter and took hold of the other hand, his shoulders straining. "Mind your language, Duncan or I'll let go."

"That's the last time I give you any of my best scotch. For god's sake, man, be –" A stifled shout as he was hauled out of the water and onto the track, both of them shuddering and soaked. Duncan's hands and face were scraped and bleeding, the gash on his forehead needed stitches. It was no good taking him back to the gatehouse, he looked like death and Fiona would never forgive him if he left the elderly man without proper medical attention.

His throat tightened and he forced himself to relax. "Stay where you are. I'll bring the car."

"No need to rush. I'm not going anywhere."

He had to half-carry the man the couple of paces to the car, the slender frame heavier than he had expected. The damaged ankle was already swollen and he helped him onto the passenger seat, trying not to jar the damaged joint. "Strap up." He hoped Fiona would understand.

Duncan was still shivering but his face looked less ashen beneath its gruesome mask. "Take me home. I'll be fine."

"Like that? Bollocks." His hands were filthy and his parka only fit for the bin now, but he had a handkerchief in one pocket, somehow still folded and clean from the last laundering and he pulled it out and put it over the bloody slash. "You need to get that cut seen to for one thing."

"No time." He put one hand over the improvised dressing. "Blu's missing. I'm feared he may have gone up the road and when he sees the bridge, he might try to cross over. But I've no way to search for him, and…" He flinched and extended one leg. "No way I can, now."

"Blu? He hasn't returned? I saw him about three hours ago, on the foreshore. He was heading for the point."

Duncan grabbed the steering wheel. "You've got to turn back. I know where he's going."

"Where? Where's he gone?"

"Where his mother went last time she was here. The headland where the caves are." He slumped in his seat, exhausted. "I'd see her out there every low tide. She said she was beachcombing but there's nothing out there but the rocks and barnacles and the old caves and no one goes there now. Too dangerous with the waves racing in as they do. I can only hope he's had the good sense to make his way back."

The tide was coming in.

A short drive, though he took it slow, the smell of blood and muck and his own fear, a tiny hiss of pain from his passenger as the car jolted down the slope towards the Hall and over the surviving bridge.

Fiona must have seen him coming. She was waiting at the top of the steps, frowning in displeasure, hands on her hips as he stepped out and went to open the other door. For a moment his mind refused to think of what to say and then he took a breath, and another, willing himself to be calm and get the words out. It worked.

"Duncan. Came off the quad bike."

It was enough to have her hurry over, offering an arm to help her old friend clamber out, ungainly and hesitant. "You need to get to hospital, but the phone's dead. The line must be down." She shook her head at Peter. "Help me get him into my car. There's a surgery fifteen miles away. I'll drive him. Quicker than waiting for an ambulance."

He prayed his voice would not fail him again. "No. The stone bridge is down."

"Down? What do you mean? It can't be."

Duncan held up one hand. "He's telling the truth. A tree took it out. It'll have taken down the phone line as well. We're stuck until someone comes to get us or we walk out along the cliff path. No other way out of here. And I won't be walking anywhere soon." He took another lurching step and cursed under his breath. "Peter. Please. You've got to find him. Before…"

Something he had heard flashed into his mind. "Do my best. Stay here. F…five minutes. Getting someone to help you." He managed the last phrases, the briefest of sentences, her face staring at him in either distrust or loathing.

She said nothing. He made sure they were down the steps and Duncan seated on one of the sturdy kitchen chairs before he ran back to the car.

No time for pleasantries when he reached the cabin. A huge Christmas tree was propped against the outer wall, far too tall to be taken inside. His hammering on the sturdy door had Jon Wilson hurrying to open it and Peter pushed past him into the living room.

They were preparing to go out for the day: kitted out in waterproofs and sturdy walking shoes, hats and walking sticks, a map of the area spread out on the table, Jon's wife packing a rucksack with fruit and bars of chocolate.

"Mrs Wilson? You're a doctor?" His abrupt appearance in their cabin, blood-smutched and filthy with mud, was enough to startle the hardiest of men, and yet she showed no repugnance or fear. A small woman, dwarfed by cagoule and hat, her expression cheerful despite the weather.

"A doctor? I suppose so." She gave him a concerned look and put the rucksack down. "I mean, yes, but I haven't practised medicine for a good few years, not on a patient. Why? What's happened?"

Another deep breath, his throat loosening, the words coming easier this time. "Duncan. Came off his quad bike. Can you help? He's at the Hall."

She was already picking up a set of car keys from the coffee table. "Medical supplies? I don't have much myself, only the basics." A cool voice, controlled and with no sense of panic. Her calmness made it easier to speak.

"There's plenty there. I think he's going to need stitches and he's hurt his ankle, could be broken. I'd take you up there, but I need to look for Blu." He was already turning to go back to his car.

"Jon? You can drive me. I'll need you anyway."

They drove off at speed, leaving him behind in a spray of water, forgotten and unneeded. His sodden trainers were hopeless for walking on wet rocks and he grabbed his walking boots from the car and put them on, cursing the time wasted in tying laces. A fast run back to Duncan's, the door unlocked and no response when he shouted, and another run to the harbour steps. He could see the waves catching on the headland. There had been no sign of the boy since that brief sighting a good while ago.

He nearly came a cropper on the steps, cursing them as he skittered down, but once on the shore itself the footing was easier and in the daylight it was possible to avoid the worst of the mud. Even the rain had its uses, washing the dirt from his face and hands, and for once the bitter temperatures had eased enough for him to unfasten his parka and race on, the wet sand slowly reclaiming his footprints, his shouts drowned out by the rain.

CHAPTER 16

The hike out to the headland was treacherous with mud and sand and the need to cross the stream. Silt and debris darkened the bitterly cold water and he struggled to stay on his feet, let alone hurry. But there was no other way to get to the place where he had last seen Blu, so he soldiered on, ignoring the numbness creeping through his legs.

A difficult trek that had him ankle deep in thick silt at times, his jeans weighted down and his boots mired in mud. The waves were closer. Anyone out on the other side of the headland would already be trapped. He dug in the pocket of his parka for his phone, but there was no signal. There hadn't been one since he followed the damned dog down the road.

He hurried on, stopping every hundred yards to call out and catch his breath. The tide was already drowning the far rocks and encroaching further on the headland. In the end he stood there, bent double with hands on his knees, taking great lungsful of cold air and despairing of ever finding the lad.

The growl startled him, a deep rumble that might once have had young Peter Sinclair turning tail and running, but not now. He was too exhausted to do anything other than look up.

A wolfhound, coat black as sin, eyes blazing. The same dog that had haunted him since Friday night, the same one that had – only a short time ago – stood on the bridge and prevented him leaving. He straightened up, wiping water from his face and pushing back strands of wet hair. Over the last few days he had learned this was a place of secrets and mystery, of strange dogs appearing from nowhere and small children singing in the night.

"What do you want from me?" For one moment he was a child again, curled up in his cold bed in the dormitory listening to the older boys telling ghost stories with the sole intent of frightening the newcomers. Banshees and poltergeists, headless horsemen and drowned lovers, and ghostly black dogs luring travellers to their deaths in quicksand. A gruesome death. There was no one around to rescue him if the same thing happened to him. And Blu was out here. "Let me get the boy to safety. He's only young. I don't care what happens to me."

And he didn't. No job, no future, not much of a family really. If he could save Blu from drowning it would be enough.

He expected bared teeth and slavering jaws, anything but a wagging tail and a soft whine as the dog began trotting away, turning once to see if he was following.

He was either on his second wind or the footing was firmer, but the going became easier and he broke into a clumsy run, boots skidding in the sand and on the bare rock surface until they were running through the incoming water towards the bottom of the cliff below the headland, the dog leaping through the water in great bounds.

By the time he reached the cliff wall itself the tops of the crests were reaching the bottom of his parka, plucking at the hem of the heavy coat in their efforts to drag him down. His shouts to the boy were lost in the roar of waves breaking against stone. The dog had found refuge on a huge slab of fractured rock and was looking down at him. A single, urgent bark before it turned to face the cliff and disappeared.

The tide was racing now, the wind howling triumphantly, the rain battering against his back as if to push him forward. It took him three attempts to scrabble to the top of the rock. He slipped once, managed to find his footing again, water sucking at his feet and trying to pull him down, but he clung on, gripping the jagged edges until he found his footing again. By the time he reached the top of the rock, his hands were raw and he lay there for a minute, numb and sore and gasping for breath. Salt spray dashed into his face and he pushed himself onto hands and knees, groaning with the effort and wondering if the dog had abandoned him here to die.

Rain poured down on his head, running into his eyes and mouth and he spat, pushed himself up and wiped one arm across his mouth. It was tempting to take off the parka to give himself more freedom of movement, but without it he would freeze. He fastened it with numb fingers and then he saw the dog, waiting in a large gap in the cliff wall a few feet away.

Two choices. Jump or drown. A huge wave surged towards the rock and he jumped, sprawling himself flat over the pebbled floor of the cave. For cave it was, the thin grey sunlight behind him revealing a long passage sloping upwards and tall enough for him to walk along with care. The dog had gone.

A couple of paces took him out of the reach of the wind and rain, the roar of the waves softer once he was inside. He would go a few feet further in and hunker down until the tide waned, curl up to retain body heat and hope the water didn't reach him. The thought of making his way through the narrow passage ahead was enough to make him sweat, despite the cold. Shivers racked his body, his hands and face stinging where barnacles and sand had scraped his skin, water had trickled down his neck leaving his t-shirt stuck to his back, his sweatshirt unpleasantly damp.

"Is this what you wanted all along?" Bitterness made his voice gruff. He tried stuffing his hands inside his pockets but that made little difference. "Leave me here to die alone? What about the boy? I made you a promise."

The wind dropped, a lull in the roar of waves and he heard a faint cry from somewhere up ahead. Blu. He had to go further in. He could not see the dog and once he took more than a few strides along the passage he would be in darkness. With luck the flashlight on his phone would be powerful enough, but it drained the battery.

One step at a time, keeping his head down, the light brightening his way. Walls washed smooth by water and time, the floor sloping upwards. A spur of rock brushed the top of his head and he hunched lower, aware of the danger. "Blu? Can you hear me?"

"I'm here."

A faint and fragile voice echoing down the passage. The boy sounded terrified and no wonder. This was a nightmare place. Walls pressed in on him, the weight of countless tons of rock waiting to collapse, and instead of answering he found himself unable to do anything other than rest one hand against the rough rock wall and try not to vomit. Water rushed towards him, heralding a much larger flood and he pushed himself away from the wall and staggered on, the light bouncing off damp walls.

"Blu? Stay where you are and I'll find you." No sign of the dog, not even a footprint in the random patches of sand littering the pebble-strewn floor. The stench of rotting fish, of seaweed and filth. A tangled mass of orange rope and broken lobster pots and the corpses of seagulls lay to one side and he wondered if the boy had pushed it there earlier.

The slope increased until it was an effort to clamber up the incline and then he came across the first step. Not a freak of nature – a hand-hewn step carved from the rock itself and as narrow as the steps in the turret, the shoulders of his parka brushing the walls as he climbed. Each step was different: shallow risers, deep treads, sloping in every direction. Each step needed his whole concentration if he was not to fall and yet all he wanted was to run, to get to the top of the steps in the hope of finding a way out.

Sounds echoed around him: his own stifled gasps, the splash of waves below, the rumble of pebbles rolling as seawater flooded in. The flashlight dimmed and he checked the display. Not enough. He would be trapped here in the dark. The rough surface of the wall snagged at his coat as he slid down, hunkering on the narrow step and trying to push away the surge of panic threatening to overwhelm him.

He had no idea how long he remained there, shutting out Blu's voice and the pounding of the waves below until something nudged his cheek. A gentle whine, a warm tongue licking his fingers. The light was dimmer now but he could see the dog just inches away on the step above. It was time to put his trust in the beast. He stood, shaking his head at his lack of courage, and took another step, and another, the wolfhound always within reach and making no effort to leave him. They passed the highest water mark so far – a dry and withered tangle of long-dead seaweed and fragments of driftwood – and the steps became wider and more regular, the roof higher, his breathing easier. It was a matter of trusting the dog.

It was impossible to calculate how far he travelled – the passageway twisted and turned and all the time climbing upwards. And he recalled Fiona's words: 'Stories say there was once a secret passage from the caves up to the dungeon but nothing's ever been found from this end.'

If Blu had discovered the right passage they would come out somewhere inside the Hall itself. It was their only chance now. There would be no way back down until the water retreated in ten hours and he was already shivering. It would be worse for the boy.

Urgency spurred him on, Blu's cries ever louder, the dog leading him steadily upwards, his fear lurking below the surface.

The flashlight flickered and he lost sight of the dog, but a clatter of claws on stone and a reassuring 'woof' came from close by. "Blu? Where are you?"

"Here." A sob of relief, the voice high-pitched and wavering. "I didn't think anyone would find me."

"I'm nearly there. Hang on lad. Have you got a torch on you?" He managed to keep his voice calm.

"The battery died. I couldn't…"

"I've got one. We'll find our way out, no worries." His father would have thrashed him for the lie. The flashlight brightened and he could see a bend in the steep tunnel ahead. "A few steps more and I'll be…" He forced a smile on his face. "…here. Are you hurt?"

Even in the fading torchlight the streaks were visible on the boy's cheeks. As was his pallor. Lips blue with cold, skin ashen, hands tucked under his armpits. His only protection a thin anorak and ragged jeans. He was soaked to the bone.

Peter pulled off his own parka and then, without hesitation, his sweatshirt. "Strip off and put these on. Can you manage?"

A tiny nod of the head. "I think so." The sweatshirt dwarfed the boy, the arms long enough to cover his hands, but it was warm and relatively dry. The parka was even bigger but Peter helped roll the sleeves back and pulled the zip right up. It would do for now.

"Come on then." The boy weighed nothing. All skin and bone and suppressed fear. There was a story here, but that would have to wait. The priority now was to get them both out of this hellhole. "I'll lead, you stay behind me. Not too close, mind you. If I slip I don't want to knock you over."

"Are we going up?"

"Where else. There's no way out of here until the tide turns, and we don't have that much time." He rubbed his bare arms, the thin t-shirt no protection against the bitter chill turning his limbs numb and making his teeth chatter.

He listened for a moment. The faint echo of waves crashing below, the boy's harsh wheezes, his own juddering gasps. Nothing else. "Come on. Let's go."

"Wait."

He paused.

"Don't you want to know what I was doing here?"

"No. You can tell me later if you want to. Now hurry before this battery dies as well."

The threat was enough to get the boy moving. They made better speed than Peter had anticipated, the lad a couple of steps behind and the climb getting easier, but the cold was beginning to eat into his bones. He scraped his shoulder on the rock wall, slipped to his knees more than once, each time finding it harder to regain his footing. It would be so easy to sit down and rest, to wait it out here in the cold, but his father's words when he was sixteen echoed in his mind. The scorn and disgust when he refused to follow the family tradition and join the army.

"I always knew you'd turn out to be worthless." Cold and callous and without a shred of affection. The memory filled him with anger. They had to be close to the surface now. He would not give up.

He resorted to counting steps. Ten, thirteen, seventeen, and then the steps came to an end and they were in a small cavern, about ten feet long and not much wider than his outstretched arms. The space ended in a wall made of the same blocks as the original tower house. A dead end.

"There." Blu pushed him aside and pointed upwards. "Look. Up there."

He swung the fading beam of light up at the high roof. The rock had been chipped away, revealing a square-cut flagstone. Red stone. He'd seen something like it, but his mind was thick and dulled and refused to work. A small plastic box lay on the floor below the stone and he picked it up and held it, unable to make sense of what it was doing down here in the dark and cold.

"Mr Sinclair."

He looked down to see the boy's fingers digging into the flesh of his arm, but he could feel nothing. He tried to speak, but it was too much effort.

"It's up there. You have to lift the stone. I'm not tall enough to reach it. Please."

"Stone?" His tongue filled his mouth.

"You're tall enough. Try pushing the stone up and see if it slides across."

He put the box down. If he stood on tiptoe he could reach the square stone above. Hands flat on its smooth surface, a tiny push to see if it would give, and it wobbled for a second before falling back with a heavy thud. The second time he had a feel for how it was balanced and he held his breath, taking his time and getting the stone just... his arms burned with the strain and then one quick sideways shove and it slid across, leaving a pale square hole above them. The smell of dust and decay. A dim light.

He looked down. The boy was stuffing the plastic box into a pocket of the borrowed parka. Time to worry about that later. "Blu? If I lift you up, d'you think you can get out?"

"I'll try."

He bent down, hands round the slender thighs before lifting the lad up. "Mind your head." Hands pressed down on his shoulders, feet digging on his hips, and then a quick scrabble as knees pressed on his shoulders. He pushed upwards until the boy was half-in, half-out of the hole. One last upwards thrust of his hands to boost the lad further and then he was alone. His legs gave way and he slid to the floor as the flashlight dimmed to nothing.

CHAPTER 17

F iona brought another bowl of hot water across to the table. Dr Wilson had taken control of the situation the moment she arrived, getting Duncan out of his waterproofs and demanding clean towels and hot water. A practical woman, used to having her orders followed, though Fiona wondered how her patients had tolerated such a brusque attitude.

The worst gashes had been cleaned and steri-stripped with rapid efficiency. A difficult enough task given the man's inability to sit still. And then the ankle.

"Sprained. Not broken but bad enough. Pass me the ice pack."

She swallowed down her instinctive answer and handed the pack over, slightly in awe of this competent woman who had invaded her privacy and pushed her, metaphorically, to one side. Her husband was doing other things: boiling the kettle, washing up the mugs in the sink, making everyone a drink of tea. Keeping out of the way, though Fiona suspected he could be as useful as his wife, should it be necessary.

"You'll not be bandaging my foot, now." Duncan was trying to get out of the chair, face still streaked with dried blood and lips tight with pain. "I've a lad gone missing. I need to find him and I can't do that with my foot strapped up like some soft southerner."

"You'll do as I say, Mr Grant. Otherwise you might damage this ankle beyond repair. Now sit still and let me finish."

Fiona put a hand on his shoulder. "She's right, Duncan. There's no way you can walk on that. Please, sit still and let the doctor finish. Mr Wilson and I'll search for Blu once we know you're alright."

Jon Wilson dried his hands on a tea towel and hung it on the rail of the Aga. "Where did you see him last? Blu?"

"I didn't. It was Peter who saw him. Out on the foreshore heading for the point about three hours ago. I think the boy might be trapped inside one of the caves. There's a network of them out there. Only fools go out there now. Too easy to get caught when the tide comes in." He shivered and Fiona hurried through to her sitting room to fetch one of the thick woollen throws from the back of the sofa and wrap it round his shoulders.

Wilson pulled up a chair. "So what happens if Sinclair's found him? Is there any way they might be able to sit it out in the caves until the water retreats?"

A long silence. Fiona couldn't bear it. "To be honest?" She couldn't bear to look at Duncan. "It's unlikely. This is private land and not easily accessible and no one's ever done a proper survey of the system that I know of. We know the lower level caves all flood at high water. And another thing." She fiddled with the pair of surgical scissors Dr Wilson had been using. "In this weather, there's the real danger of hypothermia."

"So we'd better start looking for them." Jon Wilson pushed his chair back. I've got an Explorer map back at the cabin. We can plot a search pattern – you and me, Miss Cameron. I'll go and get it while Laura finishes with Duncan. The sooner we get organised the better."

"Wait." The old man held up one hand. "My desk, Fiona. You know where that is, don't you? In the top right-hand drawer there's an old map underneath my log book. 1895, twelve inches to the mile and it shows the main caves and the danger points. It's old but the coastline hasn't changed much since then. Bring it here and I can show you where he was most likely heading, and perhaps you should check Peter's cabin while you're about it? He may have left a note there?"

She grabbed her coat and car keys.

The gatehouse stood grey and forbidding in the heavy rain, the door unlocked as always and she went through to the living area and the old desk tucked away in one corner. No need to rummage through assorted papers or piles of miscellaneous junk mail – the gamekeeper kept his desk as tidy as his house. The map was exactly where he said it would be. She gave it one quick glance, shut the drawer and went back to the vehicle.

Cabin 3 was empty. A mere husk, all trace of his presence gone. A neat stack of boxes in the hallway, labelled and ready to be collected. No sound when she called his name. It even smelled empty. A quick glance into the bedroom – he had stripped the bed, wiping away any evidence of last night – and then into the living room and she was about to leave when something caught her eye. The razorbill skull stared at her from on top of an envelope on the table. Her name. 'Fiona'. It could only be Peter's handwriting. She hefted it – more than a single sheet of paper, much more. Rain clattered against the windows, a reminder of why she was here. She put the razorbill's skull to one side, tucked the envelope under her jacket alongside the map and hurried back to the Land Rover.

Laura Wilson was tweezing gravel from Duncan's palms when Fiona returned. Jon had cleared the table and she handed him the map and sat as he unfolded it and spread it out.

Duncan looked up at her. "You didn't see Peter did you? I was hoping…"

"No, and the tide's well on its way in now. I'm sorry."

"Not your doing, lass. The fault's all mine." He sat back, eyes bleak with despair as Laura plucked gravel and splinters from the pads of his work-hardened fingers.

Fiona traced the shoreline on the map. A faded and intricate line showing more detail that she had ever seen before. The harbour steps and the stone bridge, the slabs of flat rock and large boulders, the three small stacks standing on the other side of the point. "I've never seen this map before."

"The laird gave it to me a good while back. His grandfather got a few copies when they first came out and Richard found them while he was going through the records. Knew I'd appreciate it." Duncan pulled his hand away from the probing tweezers and pointed to a group of rocks close to the foreshore. "Maw Craig. Many a ship came aground there. And here – Laird's Seat. But what you're looking for is along here." A stab of the finger. "Caves. Most of them nothing more than a crack in the rock and no deeper than a few yards, but here, and here…" The finger stabbed again. "That's where the real caves are. The ones used by smugglers. One of those leads up into the Hall. Or at least it did, a long time ago. I can only pray that the boy found the right one and might find his way here, or at least be safe somewhere. There's no chance of searching the caves now, not until the tides gone down."

"You knew all along didn't you?" Fiona couldn't decide whether to be angry or delighted. "About the secret passage. Richard told you."

He had the grace to blush. "I was sworn to secrecy years ago. The laird had a copy of a much older map, hand drawn and showing the entry and exit points, but he kept that hidden and never showed me. Not that I wanted to know. It was a wicked time for everyone involved and best forgotten. Let sleeping dogs lie, he said. If he'd told anyone, we'd have had the newspapers up here and the treasure hunters and historians, all of them traipsing down the foreshore and no doubt getting themselves into trouble."

Laura Wilson took his hand back and picked at another piece of dirt, ignoring his attempts to stop her. "So, this secret passage. Where does it come out?"

"I have no idea. The dungeon perhaps? Or one of the outer storerooms? It could be anywhere. All I know is that he went down it once in his lifetime, but he said it was an evil place, not fit for man nor beast." He endured the removal of a chunk of gravel. "Perhaps I should put my trust in Bess. If anyone can save a child, she will."

Jon Wilson looked up from the map. "Bess? Have I met her?"

Fiona shared a glance with Duncan. "If you've seen a black wolfhound or heard a dog barking, that'll be Bess. She's not easy to see, but if you need her, she'll find you."

"Your dog? I didn't know you kept a wolfhound here?" Tweezers clattered into the bowl.

"I don't. She… she belongs to the Hall."

"A guard dog? Can't be too careful nowadays, though I don't expect you get many break-ins down here do you?" Laura wiped away a speck of blood and inspected Duncan's hand. "That looks fine. I'll put a dressing on this hand and then we're done, but you need to keep that foot raised for a while and no walking without a stick." She stripped off her latex gloves and threw them in a plastic bag. "You were lucky, Mr Grant. Most of my patients who've come off quad bikes don't have such a fortunate outcome. At least this time I didn't have to do any stitching."

"You're a surgeon, then?" Duncan held out his hands and examined them. "A grand job. The local nurse wouldn't have been as quick. Or as gentle."

"No, Mr Grant. Jon and I met when I was doing the autopsy on a murder victim and he was investigating the case. Until I retired early this year I was a senior forensic pathologist. My patients don't usually wriggle when I pick gravel from their hands. It was quite a challenge I can tell you." She reached for a sterile dressing and took hold of his hand again.

Fiona burst out laughing. A terrible thing, considering the seriousness of the situation, but Duncan's expression was priceless. "We're grateful, Dr Wilson. Without you,

Duncan would have had to manage with my first aid skills. I don't know what I'd've done if it'd been more serious."

"Oh, I think you'd have managed. You'd be surprised how well people cope in an emergency." Laura Wilson put the last dressing in place and sighed. "Done. Now you can make Duncan a cup of tea. He's looking a little pale. Have you got somewhere he can lie down for a while? Kitchen chairs are not that comfortable, and those painkillers I gave him will have him asleep fairly soon."

It took a while for Fiona to get the elderly man stretched out on her sofa, mug of tea and chocolate biscuits close at hand and the blankets from the back of the sofa warding off any aftereffects. Laura Wilson had threatened to undress him down to his underwear and put him to bed if he didn't do as she said, and the warning was enough to make Duncan biddable for once. He looked old and frail and tired, and Fiona was only too glad to have a doctor on hand to make him settle down. The fire was coming to life and the room warming up and she followed Laura out, closed the door and left him dozing.

Laura gave her a smile. "I wouldn't worry too much. He's as tough as old boots, but I do hope we find this boy of his. It doesn't sound good. Is there anyone else who might be able to help? The Coastguard perhaps?"

"It's not only the bridge that's down, there's no phone either. In an emergency someone could always have gone to the phone box a couple of miles away, but now we're stuck here." Fiona pushed a strand of hair away from her face. "If Blu doesn't turn up soon I'll try walking out along the cliff path but it's risky enough in the best of weather and there's no way I can do it once dusk sets in. That'd be suicide." The thought made her wonder, yet again, if Richard had done that all those years ago – gone up on the cliff tops like he had done before erosion brought the cliffs perilously close to the footpath. The only way to access the cliff path was from the other side of the Hall, a steep narrow track leading west.

"My advice is to wait for a while. You don't know what's happened to the boy or even where he is and going out alone would be foolish right now. If Peter is out there, then it's likely he'll turn up here before long and we'll have a better idea of what's going on."

"I'm worrying too much, but there was no sign of him when I went to the house. And there's not that many places he could be now."

"I'd be the same myself, but you have to be sensible. There's no point in risking your life without knowing all the facts."

She was right, but that didn't make the words any easier to hear. Peter was out there as well, and even if she never wanted to see him again, he'd saved Duncan.

Her jumper was stained with blood and dirt though she hadn't noticed until now, and she went into her bedroom and found a clean one, pulling the stained one off with a sense of revulsion and dropping it in the bin. She would never wear it again. She tugged the duvet into some semblance of neatness and closed the wardrobe door. Nothing worse than coming back to a messy bedroom last thing at night. It was strange locking the bathroom door after so many months of living alone. The boiler rumbled into life as she turned the tap. Hot water and soap to clean her hands, a flannel soaked and wrung out and pressed against her face, eyes closed against the heat and tears.

By the time she had composed herself and checked on Duncan – fast asleep, his face relaxed and looking years younger – Jon Wilson had brewed another pot of tea and was busy finishing off the rest of the biscuits while his wife tidied up the First Aid box, tutting over the contents and making a list of things needing to be replaced. Jon passed her a mug. She took it with a nod of thanks. No one spoke. The clock ticked away the seconds, the roar of rain from outside, the wind howling, the kettle hissing on the Aga.

The map was still spread out on the table, its edges torn and ragged, fold lines cracked and brown. The envelope was on the end of the table, forgotten in the urgency of seeing to Duncan and looking for the missing boy, and she picked it up and went to sit in her favourite chair over by the Aga.

A tumble of papers fell into her lap. The sketches she'd seen last night, or was it this morning? More than a dozen, each one individual, each one exquisite. She flicked through them, aching at their beauty and treachery. A modern design, all glass and steel and water, a round house in the style of the traditional Scottish houses, another one floating above the foreshore. She stared at a detailed sketch of the harbour, a handful of buildings spaced out along the edge. Richard would have loved these. But however beautiful they were she could not forgive him. He had come here under false pretences, tricking her into taking him round the Hall so that he could survey the state of the building. Richard would have been turning in his grave now, if he had one.

And that was the thing that hurt most. She had betrayed the Hall and its laird.

A plastic folder slipped onto the floor and Laura Wilson picked it up, glancing at it for a moment before handing it back. "This is excellent. Who drew it?"

She slid it out. A delicate pencil drawing, the invasive weeds and scruffy stonework and overgrown ivy erased, leaving the Hall looking elegant and proud. "It must be Peter. I didn't know he'd done this." Underneath the drawing were several sheets of paper covered with writing and she pulled them out, her eyes filling with tears as she read his letter.

The thud of feet on stone broke the silence. The muffled sound of someone calling for help. Jon Wilson pushed his chair back with such haste it clattered to the floor and then, before she even had time to wipe her eyes or register what was happening, Blu was pushing open the door and half-falling inside the kitchen, filthy and shaking and wearing a familiar thick parka.

Peter's coat.

"Blu? What on earth –?" She dropped the letter on the table. The boy looked like death, his face streaked with mud and tears, jeans and trainers wet through and filthy, the stink of harbour mud filling the kitchen.

"Mr Sinclair. He can't get out by himself. Quick. Help me." The boy was tearing at the zip of the bulky coat, his fingers made clumsy by the long sleeves and his own shivering.

Jon Wilson put a hand on the boy's shoulder. "Steady, lad. Laura? He's freezing. You'd better take a look."

Fiona pushed Jon aside. "Peter? Where is he? Where?"

Blu shrank away. "In the smugglers' tunnel. It comes out in a room down there."

The storerooms. It could only be one of those. "Show me. Now." Her fingers dug into the loose cloth of the parka, pulling him away from Laura Wilson and she pushed him ahead of her along the passage. His face was pinched and cold, skin pale as marble.

"There." He pointed. "In the corner. There's a sort of trapdoor."

"Fiona. Let me take him." Jon's voice broke through her desperation. "Start looking. I'll be back in a minute."

Fiona watched them go. The man with his arm round the child, a slight figure hunched over and staggering a little and looking even smaller in such a large coat. Peter's coat. He would be freezing without it. She hurried into the storeroom.

"Peter?" The packing case with Richards's decorations was still waiting to be taken through to the living room – she'd forgotten to ask Duncan for a tree – and she could see the empty space where it had stood, no doubt for years. It wasn't a shadow in the corner, it was a hole, wide enough for a man to go down. "Peter? Where are you?"

The faintest of answers. "Fiona?"

It was impossible to see much – a darker shape in the darkness below, but he was down there, she could hear him breathing. Shallow gasps as if every inhalation was an effort.

The ladder was dusty and showing its age. She couldn't remember when it had last seen service. Her father had his own set, lightweight aluminium ones stored in the roof space of the utility room and only brought out for serious tasks. The wooden struts scraped on the floor as she dragged them over to the gaping hole and stood there, not knowing what to do next.

"Leave that to me." Jon Wilson took hold of the ladder. "Get a blanket or a coat. Something warm."

Blu was sitting in the kitchen, hands wrapped round a mug of chocolate, his face sticking out from the blanket that covered him from head to foot. Laura Wilson was sitting beside him, watching like a hawk but the look she gave Fiona was enough to tell her that the boy would be fine. No time for anything else – she darted back to her own bedroom and ran back, arms full of her pink woollen blanket from the end of the bed. The warmest thing she could find.

Jon had the ladder in place and was climbing down.

"Don't come down yet. Wait until I tell you."

She took hold of the side rails, the ladder groaning with each downward tread. A creak of old wood and he paused, his upturned face white in the darkness for a second before he continued. She held her breath, not daring to distract him yet desperate to do something. The ladder stopped grumbling. He was down. It was an awkward spot – the opening right in one corner of the room, the stone flag which had concealed it now lying to one side.

"Drop that blanket down will you?" A flurry of pale wool tumbling down the rungs to land in Jon's outstretched arms. "Give me a minute."

He turned away and she could hear him talking to Peter in a quiet voice, no sense of panic or urgency. But that was a lie. She'd seen the concern on Jon Wilson's face as he clambered down, and although the atmosphere in the storeroom made her shiver, the space beneath the room was worse. A killing coldness, especially for someone already soaked to the skin.

"Fiona?" A different tone now.

She leaned over the hole. The light from Jon's phone pooled in the centre. She could see Peter curled up on the floor. He looked asleep.

"Tell Laura I need her. Hurry. And stay with the boy."

Need, not want. She ran.

CHAPTER 18

Blu was shivering and sullen. The mug of chocolate was empty and Fiona took it from his hands and put it aside. The door to the hallway was open and she could hear faint voices coming from the storeroom. Laura had given her brief instructions before hurrying down to the storeroom. 'Keep him warm and find him something sugary to eat. Chocolate, biscuits, anything sweet. Don't leave him.'

There was a secret stash of her favourite chocolate in the cupboard, bought for emergencies and still plenty left from her last shopping expedition, and she pulled a couple of bars out and plunked them on the worktop. Thick milk chocolate. Rich and warming and melting on the tongue. "How are you feeling? Any warmer?"

"A bit." He scowled at her. "She undressed me." His pale cheeks darkened.

"Oh." Embarrassing for a boy of his age. "I wouldn't worry. She's a doctor, she's used to doing that." She unwrapped the bar and snapped off a double row of glossy squares. "Eat this. Do you want another drink?"

He shook his head, engrossed in munching. His cheeks were still pale but she could see the colour returning to his lips, his shivering almost gone, his body relaxing. A good sign.

"You know Duncan's here?"

He gave her a look of utter panic. "Where? Was he looking for me?"

"No. He had an accident on the quad bike." She held up one hand. "He's alright, I promise, nothing serious other than cuts and scrapes and a sprained ankle, but he's asleep on the sofa in my sitting room if all the noise hasn't woken him already." It was unlikely. She'd seen the painkillers Laura had given the man – far stronger than she would dare hand out. "Finish that and I'll take you through and we can both stay there with him, out of the way if you want."

"He'll ask me what I was doing and I'll have to tell him."

The lad was close to tears. And not from any pain or the shock of his rescue. This was fear. "I'm sure he won't be cross. He was worried about you."

"You don't know what she's like. No one does." He rubbed his arms and drew his legs up.

'She'. Not 'he'. So it was a woman who frighten the boy, not Duncan. Fiona handed over the rest of the chocolate. There was more in the cupboard, and in the storeroom for that matter. "Whatever it is, you need to talk to your uncle. He's a good man for all his scowling. Yes, he might get angry and shout at you, but that's all he'll do. He'll be glad you're alive. Nothing else matters. Believe me."

She went over to the Aga, sliding the kettle over the hot plate to boil. Peter's coat was heaped on the floor along with what could only be the boy's jeans and t-shirt and an overly large sweatshirt. She picked up the coat and a box fell to the floor. A cheap plastic container bought to carry sandwiches, but there were no sandwiches in this one. It was too heavy for that. The lid was taped down, the tape yellowed and peeling away and she lifted the box higher to look at its contents.

"I didn't want to do it. She made me. Please don't tell him." Blu was sobbing now, curled up on the chair, his hands over his head. And she realised. The thought made her feel sick to her stomach.

"Blu. I give you my word. Whatever you think you've done, I won't let anyone hurt you." The blanket had slipped from one bony shoulder, revealing a fading bruise. The sort of bruise made by heavy fingers digging deep into vulnerable skin. She looked at him. "Duncan didn't do that. It was your mother, wasn't it?"

"She told me where to find the box. She said she'd be waiting at the top of the road tonight and if I wasn't there with it, then she'd leave me behind and tell Duncan and then he'd throw me out as well."

She handed him the box of tissues. The voices from the storeroom were louder now, but she couldn't leave the boy, not in this state. And he didn't need any more distress right now. "Come on. I'll find some more biscuits and we'll go and sit with your uncle where it's quiet. You can tell me the whole story. It's going to come out, sooner or later."

Duncan was still asleep, the soft light from the table lamp enough to illuminate the room. Blu bent over his uncle, reaching out with one hesitant hand to touch the man's cheek. "He's going to be alright? You promise?" A mere whisper.

She wanted to put her arms round him, wanted to hug him and hold him and take away the hurt and fear, but he was still too scared. Instead she knelt down beside the sofa and tucked the blanket closer round the sleeping man. "Dr Wilson looked after him. She said he'll be fine and I trust her."

"He looks so…"

"Old? Frail? He isn't." She put her hand on his shoulder, the lightest of touches, aware of him flinching even with that contact. "Trust me, he'll be up and about tomorrow. And needing your help I expect. A sprained ankle doesn't make life easy. Now, sit down and drink your milk or Dr Wilson'll be after me."

He snuggled down on the second sofa. "I like having a proper fire. Duncan says they're hard work with all the wood cutting he has to do, but I think he likes them as well. I'll have to see if I can get his fire lit. I've not done it before, but he'll need it tonight."

"I think your uncle might have to stay here, but we can talk about that later. Oh. I'd forgotten. Tomorrow's Christmas Eve." Her first Christmas alone. Last year, as he had done the year before, Matthew arrived on Christmas Eve loaded down with gifts and stockings and enough food to feed an army. They'd eaten smoked salmon for breakfast and drunk mimosas and opened presents in bed together. She'd cooked a meal – fillet steak – and they'd made love afterwards, and then curled up on the sofa and watched Christmas films until it was time to go back to bed. This year it would be a frozen ready-meal eaten in solitary silence in front of the fire. Not even a decent dvd.

Duncan stirred, a gentle slurring snore, eyelids flickering for a moment before he was quiet again.

She perched on the footstool. "He's flat out. So tell me. If you could have anything at all – anything – what would you like for Christmas?"

"Anything?" He rubbed his arms again. "I'd like a new name. What sort of mother calls their son, Blu? I hate it. Everyone laughs at me."

"What would you like to be called?"

He leaned forward, tugging the blanket higher. "Something ordinary. An everyday name like Peter. I bet he never got bullied at school over his name. Or maybe…" Firelight turned his cheeks pink.

"Go on."

"Ben. I like the name Ben. It's not too different and it's ordinary. I think I'd like to be Ben Grant more than Blu Capson. But she won't let me."

"Once you're sixteen no one can stop you, and until then there's no reason at all why you can't be called Ben if that's what you want." She tilted her head, trying to listen for any sounds from the storeroom. Nothing. She checked her watch. It seemed ridiculous, but it was only ten minutes since she'd sent Laura Wilson out of the kitchen. Too soon to start worrying. Her fingernail tore as she chewed at it, a tiny drop of blood seeping along the edge. "What else? Go on. Anything."

He was watching Duncan, the rise and fall of the old man's chest, the strong fingers hidden beneath white bandages and lint, the dressing on his forehead, bruises beginning to darken his cheeks and jaw. "I never thought

I'd like it here. I hardly remember coming when I was young. I remember a tall man being angry at my mum, and shouting at her, but I'd forgotten him tucking me up in bed and reading me a story when she didn't come home at night. And he made sure I always had enough to eat." He rubbed his eyes. "I don't want to go back with her. I want to stay here, but he won't have me, not now. Not when I'm a thief."

It was hard to know what to say, but she could hear the desperation in the words. "What did you steal? Something of his?" She waited.

"Steal from Duncan? I wouldn't do that." His look of horror was reassuring. "It was the box. She told me where it was. She'd been cleaning, she said, for the old man who lived here, and she'd found a watch hidden in the desk where he spent a lot of his time and she didn't think he'd notice. But she knew Duncan would find it if she took it back."

"So she hid it in the box for later? And then what?"

"She'd seen a map he had – Old Dick, she called him – and it showed her where the tunnel was so she went down to the storeroom and pulled up the flagstone and dropped the box down inside. No one else knew anything about it, see. She thought she'd have plenty of time to get it later, even if it meant going up the tunnel from the cliff. The map showed where the entrance was, so she knew where to go."

"But she never got the chance?"

He shrugged. "When she went back a couple of days later to see if there was any more stuff, all his papers were gone and the desk was empty. She didn't dare hang around to see if he'd called the police and she never got the chance to come back."

"So she dropped you off here and expected you to find it."

He nodded. "I didn't want to, honest, but we had no money left and nowhere to live and she owed people. She said if I didn't help she'd leave me and I'd never see her again." He buried his face in his hands. "I don't care now if I don't. I'd rather stay here even if it means I never see her again, but I don't think he'll want me now. If he ever did."

Her throat was parched. She would make another drink and see if she was needed. Blu would be safe for a few minutes. "Stay there. I'm going to see what's happening."

"With Mr Sinclair? I hope he's alright. I still don't know how he found me. My torch died and I'd was trapped in the dark and he gave me his jumper and his coat because mine were wet through. I've left them there. She'll be cross with me."

"Don't worry about clothes. Concentrate on resting and getting warm. Promise me you'll won't leave this room? I'll get your jeans washed and dried in a couple of hours, but until then you'll have to make do with the blanket, I'm afraid. Are you warm enough?" She put one hand on his cheek, warm and smooth and damp with tears. "It's going to be alright. I promise…Ben."

He gave her a thin smile. "I promise. Do you think he'll wake up soon? I'm going to tell him as soon as I can."

"Good lad. He'll be proud of you. Now. Get yourself comfortable. I'll be back as soon as I can."

∾

The Wilsons had got Peter up into the storeroom and wrapped him in the blanket. She had no idea how, or what it had cost both of them. They had undressed him as well – boots and socks, jeans and t-shirt – a sodden pile of clothing heaped by one of the boxes, and he was awake but looked like death. She stood in the doorway, not daring to come in.

Laura turned to her. "I told you to stay with Blu. Is he alright?"

"He's warm and alert, eaten some chocolate and biscuits. He's in the sitting room with Duncan. He wanted to be alone with him." It was like reporting to the police or her old headmistress at secondary school. "How can I help?" She stepped inside.

"I don't want to move him, but he needs to be somewhere warm so we'll have to risk it. A bed would be the best place as long as the room's not cold. No hot water bottles, nothing like that. It's not as bad as it could be – his temperature's above 32 – but it's not going to get any higher in here."

"My bed. The heating's on and it's quiet and warm." She moved closer, and knelt down, the floor cold under her knees. "Peter? Blu's fine. He's upstairs with Duncan." She wanted to say more, but Jon was there beside her.

"Okay. Peter? Time to get moving. I don't know about you, but this floor is too hard for my old bones."

Afterwards she remembered little about the struggle to get him out of the storeroom other than the weight of his arm round her shoulder and the frightening coldness of his skin where her hand wrapped round his waist. Laura Wilson's quiet encouragement, Jon on the other side taking most of the weight.

Step by step, Peter struggling to lift his legs and then they were outside her bedroom and she let Laura take her place and hurried to get her bed ready, grateful that she'd made some effort to tidy up earlier. A quick tug to pull back the duvet, a moment to fluff up the pillows, then she stood there, in the way and yet wanting to be involved. To tell him she had been wrong and she had read his letter and the picture was beautiful and Blu was going to be fine. But he was as pale as marble and she left them to it and made her way back to the kitchen where she collected the boy's clothes and took them out to the utility room. A cheap pair of socks worn thin at the toes and heels, a red t-shirt with a washed-out logo, a pair of supermarket jeans torn at the knees and with fraying hems.

She suspected there would be little else in the way of clothing back at the gatehouse. And Duncan, for all his good intentions, was not a man who would notice such things. It was too late to buy the lad anything new, but she could at least make sure that what he did have was clean and dry. Another trip to collect Peter's clothes and add them to the pile of washing. The parka was too dirty to go in the machine with the rest of the things and she tossed it into a corner to be dealt with later, once the clothes were clean and dry.

The box was where she had left it, on the table. Duncan would have to know about it sometime. The yellowed tape pulled away in a shower of dried glue and fragments, the lid coming loose as soon as she pried it off.

A watch. She'd seen it only once when she was a young teenager and a decidedly nosey one at that. It was hidden at the back of one of the drawers in his desk. Not that she'd been searching or anything. In fact she'd never noticed it before and so, ever the curious one, she'd slipped it over her hand to see what it looked like on her bony wrist. Gold-link strap, some fancy foreign name, dials and diamonds and the look of serious money. Richard had taken it from her wrist in silence, put it back in the drawer and never mentioned it again.

She turned it over, her thumb polishing the back to reveal an inscription and the family crest. 'W.E.M.F.' His father's watch. A valuable piece, and yet it had remained hidden and unworn for all those years.

Jon Wilson came into the kitchen, rubbing his hands and breathing out heavily. "He should be okay in a few hours. Laura wants to give him some warm milk if you have enough? Plenty of sugar and some chocolate as well if you have some."

She sagged against the Aga, relief making her legs tremble. "Chocolate's on the side there, and more in the cupboard above. Don't worry about milk, there's plenty more in the freezer. I'll get some out later." She hurried to get it ready, milk splashing on the hot plates with a loud hiss and sizzle. "What about you? Tea? Or something else?"

He looked at the clock. "Is it that time? We seem to have missed out on lunch somewhere along the way. I hadn't realised."

"Let me get this sorted and then I'll make something but I need to check on Duncan and Blu first."

"Go ahead. I'm quite capable of heating milk." He smiled at her. "We seem to have taken over your house I'm afraid. Laura can be like that at times, but she's the best person to have around in an emergency of this sort."

She was getting to know this man more – he seemed

content to let his wife lead the way, but she suspected he had his own unique strengths.

"Clean mugs in the dishwasher." She grabbed another packet of biscuits, put them on the table and headed back to the sitting room.

Blu was curled up asleep. Fiona added more wood to the fire and stood there, watching the boy.

"He's a brave lad." Pain roughened Duncan's voice. "I knew my niece had her problems, but no child should have to do that. I don't think I'll ever be able to forgive her."

Fiona knelt down beside him. "You heard him? I'm sorry, I didn't know you were awake."

"Aye. I did. Thought it best to keep quiet and let it all come out. He's done nothing to be ashamed of and I'll tell him that when he wakes. He's still a child and I don't hold anything against him. He'll always have a home with me, if he wants one." He pushed the blanket away, wincing as he tried to move his ankle. "What's happened to Peter? Is he alright?"

"He's fine. Laura Wilson has it all under control." She shook her head. "If they hadn't been here…" Her eyes stung and she pressed the heels of her hands against them. "You could have died."

"Me? It was a tumble, nothing more. Though if Peter hadn't come along, things might have been different. Seems like he saved both me and the boy. Ben. He suits it. My grandfather was called Ben." He put his hand on her shoulder. "Go and find me a walking stick will you, lass? I know there'll be one somewhere in this warren. Then I can get up and make myself useful."

"No. Stay there. When Blu wakes he'll want to talk to you. And I don't want him to wake up and be alone."

"Maybe you're right." He settled down again, grumbling, but she could see the relief in his face. "I'd better get used to calling him Ben, seeing as he's going to be living with me for a while."

"Oh, Duncan." She tucked the blankets around him again. "I'm going to miss you so much."

"I know, lassie. I've got used to having you living in the Hall again. It won't be the same without you. Nothing will."

CHAPTER 19

Peter had vague memories about getting up the ladder: a strong pair of arms helping him climb, someone above hauling him out of the hole as if he was a sack of rubbish, the helplessness as they undressed him, dragging wet denim off his legs despite his feeble protests.

And then the nightmare walk: the blanket slipping from his shoulders, Fiona close beside him, someone else holding him up on the other side. He'd wanted to talk to her but it was too much effort and then he was here in this quiet room and everything was coming back to him. The warmth in his body, the tingling sensation of blood returning to numb limbs and his mind clearing.

He turned his head to look at the wall, startled to feel a woollen hat covering his head. He was wrapped up like a mummy, the duvet tucked tight around him, swaddling him in goose-down. The thought made him want to laugh but his tongue was like a drunkard's, thick and clumsy.

"Awake. Good. I've got a drink here for you. Hang on a minute."

The voice was familiar. He blinked. "Doctor…?" His voice sounded pathetic. Weak and feeble and wavering. He tried again. "Dr Wilson?" Better. He coughed. "Blu?" He awarded himself first prize for effort if not clarity.

"He's fine. Nothing more than mild hypothermia. You can see him later on. And Duncan has a sprained ankle. Painful, but not serious. Now…" She slipped one hand behind his neck and raised him up. The mug clattered against his teeth but the drink was warm, wonderfully warm, slipping down his parched throat like a dram of Duncan's best single malt. He drained the contents and licked his lips.

"More?"

"Please." Less of a croak this time. The way things were going it would only take a few days before he sounded human again. He heard liquid pouring. It was hotter this time – not enough to be uncomfortable, but heat spread down his body with each mouthful.

"Good. Your temperature's coming back up nice and slowly and your pulse is strong so I'm going to send Jon through to sit with you while I check on Duncan and the boy. Don't try talking. Lie still and let your body recover. Understand?"

He nodded.

"Excellent. I like it when my patients are quiet and don't make a fuss. You and I will get on famously."

The room seemed empty when she'd gone. He'd been lucky. As had Duncan and the boy. The pillow beneath his head was soft and held a delicate perfume. A familiar scent, and although he could not recall from where, it was soothing. His feet were coming back to life, as were his hands. An unpleasant sensation but one for which he was grateful. His eyes closed.

Daylight was fading when he woke again and shadows filled the edges of the room. The hat itched. He wriggled one arm free and reached up to pull the horrid thing away but a hand caught his wrist.

"Leave that alone. You're supposed to be resting you know."

Laura's voice. He wondered how long he had been asleep. Hours of dreams and people talking to him, of wandering dark passages in search of someone lost. "Where am I?" In the Hall, that was obvious, but he couldn't remember seeing a bedroom.

"Miss Cameron's bedroom." The hat was tugged back into place.

Fiona's room. Her bed. "Does she mind?"

"Not in the least. It was her suggestion, although I think she was running out of places to put people. Duncan and Blu have taken up residence in the sitting room and I wanted you somewhere warm and quiet and out of the way so she offered her bed. I don't think there was anywhere else to be honest. The other bedrooms down here don't look as if they've been used for some time."

She wouldn't want him hanging around here now, not after last night. And yet there was no chance of driving back to Glasgow now. He was stuck here until after Christmas, if not longer. How long did it take to replace a bridge anyway, or perhaps the Coastguard would have to ferry everyone out. It wasn't something he'd ever considered. He could always ask Duncan if the attic room was available though the man had enough on his plate right now from the sounds of it.

He tolerated Laura's examination: temperature, pulse, reflexes. A more intimate examination than anticipated, warm fingers touching his skin, her hands helping him sit up, the hat removed. The urge to run his fingers through his hair to get rid of the itch. "When can I get up?"

"Now if you feel up to it. Fiona brought your car back to the courtyard and your suitcase is at the end of the bed so find yourself some clean clothes when you're ready to get dressed. You can have a shower or a bath, whichever you prefer."

A bath. The thought was tempting. Not as enticing as a long soak in the hot tub but, despite Laura's assurances, he was still cold. A shiver deep in his bones that would take a long time to ease. Even now, in the warm bed with no hint of a draught or any aftereffects, he could feel the chill air in the tunnel, the dread of being trapped there, alone in the dark.

She refused to leave until he was out of bed and able to stand unaided. He stood there, clad only in his boxer shorts, the blanket draped round his shoulders, his legs a little wobbly and aware of her watching him with interest.

"How are you feeling?"

"Fine."

"Any dizziness?"

"No. A headache, that's all."

"That'll go once you've eaten something. Don't have the water too hot and don't stay in too long. I'll leave you in peace. The bathroom's next door but leave the door unlocked or Jon'll break it down."

The bathroom was modern and well-equipped. A

decent bath with a separate shower on the other side, sink, toilet. White tiles on the walls, and pale grey ones on the floor. Towels stacked on shelves, bottles of shampoo and conditioner, shower gel, bath oil. He opened one. The fragrance reminded him of Fiona and he put the lid back on and placed it back on the shelf.

The hot water was plentiful and the bath deep. He locked the door only while he used the lavatory and then ran his hand through the bathwater. Deep and warm enough to melt the icy fear from earlier and he stripped off his boxers and stepped in, sinking down into its welcome heat and leaning back to submerge his shoulders, water lapping against his chin. Bliss. Showers were fine for everyday use; the one in Glasgow adequate at best and unsatisfying most of the time, but this? He could get used to this. Enough length to stretch his legs out, wide enough that his shoulders didn't feel squashed, the hot tap producing a gushing waterfall. All he needed now was something to take away the dreams and the fear of being lost forever.

The knock on the door had him hauling himself upright, water slopping over the edge to soak the bath mat. "Yes?"

"Can I come in? Laura wants me to check you're alright."

Fiona. He cleared his throat. "There's no need. I'm fine." The thought of another confrontation was more than he could bear. The door opened and she came in, closing it behind her. It was the hot tub all over again: the bath towel out of reach, her standing there watching him.

"You look a lot better. Your hands are a mess though."

Hands? He hadn't noticed the scrapes and bruises. He

held his hands out, stared at them, lowered them onto his lap. There were other scrapes as well: both knees, a long scratch on his right forearm, the sting of raw skin down his shoulder. He reached for a flannel.

She sat on the end of the bath, hands clasped in front of her. "I wanted to see you."

"There's no need. I'll be out of your way as soon as Laura allows it." Though he had no idea how he was going to leave now. Perhaps Duncan would put him up for a while, but it would be an imposition.

"Thank you. For the drawings, I mean. All of them."

He dipped the cloth in the water, pressed it against the stiffness on his shoulder. It stung. "I thought you knew I was an architect. I didn't… I mean… I was scribbling some ideas down. It's something I used to enjoy doing and when I saw the harbour and the cabins…" He straightened up and fixed his gaze on her. "They were doodles, nothing important. Not the Hall though. I did that one for you, I thought you might not have a recent picture of it." He soaked the cloth again, leaned forward to dab at both knees.

"I haven't. And it's beautiful. And…" She came and knelt down beside the bath, arms resting on the edge. "I read your letter. I'm so sorry. I got it all wrong. It's just that, when I saw the cabins and they looked as if you'd been working on them for months, I thought…"

"I was here working for Richard's heirs? I've no idea who they are and since Friday I'm out of work anyway. The firm I worked for didn't think I was good enough for promotion. Maybe it was stupid, but I couldn't face the thought of designing office blocks for the rest of my life." He laughed, but it was a hollow sound, like his future prospects, and he leaned forward, legs bent and hands wrapped round his knees. Water trickled down his chest. "God knows what my family are going to say. I'll probably end up like the prodigal son, returning home in shame. Only there won't be a fatted calf for me, or much of anything. I'll be lucky if my parents even notice."

"We make a good pair don't we? In a week or so I won't have a job either, or anywhere to live. It's going to be hard, leaving all this behind." A warm hand touched his cheek and he wanted to lean into the caress. "But I love the picture of the Hall. You've drawn it as it should be, as I want to remember it. And that means more to me than anything."

He edged away from her touch. "I'm glad. I'd have liked to spend longer on it, but it was the best I could do, given the time."

"It's perfect." Her hand trailed in the water. "And the lodges are stunning. I don't expect they'll put up anything quite so beautiful or fitting, but in a way I'm glad I won't be around to see. I can't imagine how Duncan's going to feel, living here while the estate gets torn apart."

The water was cooler and he reached out to add more, glad of the diversion. "How is he?"

"Duncan? As you'd expect. Complaining about being idle, wanting to be up and about. But he's had a long talk with Blu and they've sorted things out between them. Blu's going to stay with him for a while, only he'd prefer to be called Ben from now on."

"Ben?" He swished the hot water. "That's a good name. It suits him."

"He feels awful you risked your life for him." Her

fingers flicked water at his face and he wiped the droplets away with the back of his hand.

"He's a child. There's no way I could have left him in there. Anyone would've done the same. He was a lot braver than I'd have been in that situation." He soaked the flannel and ran it over the back of his neck. "You might think I'm imagining it, but I saw the same dog again. Bess. I swear she was waiting for me on the shore, and when I followed she led me to the cave. I had nothing to do with it really."

"Don't sell yourself short, Peter." She stood up and pulled a towel down from the shelves. "I was wrong about Bess as well. She's been guarding this place since she rescued the Fitzwilliam sisters from the smugglers all those years ago. If she wants you here, then there's a good reason for it. Look, get yourself dry and dressed and join us in the kitchen. Jon's cooking, and in case you're wondering, you're staying here tonight."

"I don't…"

"Please. You saved Blu. I felt awful when I realised you'd been doing those drawings for yourself, so letting you stay here is the least I can do to try to make it up to you. And anyway, where else could you go? I could make up the bed in the cabin again, but it seems a lot of work when there's a bed here. Unless…?" She bit her lip. "Unless you'd rather not."

"What about Duncan?"

"Laura says he'll be fine to go home after he's had a meal. He'll be happier in his own home. She's promised to keep an eye on him, but he should be able to manage the stairs. The swelling's coming down and I've found him a couple of walking sticks. What worries me is that if there is a problem there's nothing we can do, not with the road out and the phone line down."

"Has it happened before? I mean, being cut off like this?"

"More often than you'd think when it snows. Sometimes the road's blocked for several days, but the telephone's never failed before. Mobiles are a different matter. It's a miracle if you can get a signal down here. I don't know what we'd do in a real emergency now. No one comes as far as the bridge unless it's the postman, and most of the mail gets redirected to the solicitors, unless it's for me." She held the towel up. "Jon's doing spaghetti and tomato sauce for everyone and I found an apple crumble in the freezer."

A tempting thought. Apple crumble had been one of the few good things about school dinners. It was something of a surprise to realise how hungry he was. "Sounds good."

"Comfort food, my mother called it." She shook the towel. "Come on, before the water goes cold and you end up shivering."

A moment's hesitation. There was a world of difference between being naked in a hot tub and the situation he found himself in right now. Had it been Laura Wilson standing there he would not have given it another thought, but Fiona's earlier rejection – although forgiven – was not so easy to forget after a childhood of being unloved and ignored, the taunts and bruises and insults from his peers at school, Hamilton's cool contempt.

It had been too long since someone showed any interest in him as a man, let alone kissed him. The longing to be held and touched, to feel someone's skin against his own, to be wanted for who he was. But in the cold light of day, it had been wishful thinking on his part. No woman could possibly want someone like him – a man without any prospects, and with a distant family who cared nothing about him.

"Leave it there, will you? I'm not ready yet." He didn't look at her, but he could hear the hitch in her breath, the way she paused before placing the towel on the edge of the bath within easy reach. "Thanks. I'll be through in ten minutes." He picked up the flannel and made a show of washing his face, hearing her footsteps across the tiles, the door opening, closing, and leaving him alone.

CHAPTER 20

The aroma of tomato sauce and garlic and herbs filled the kitchen. The hiss of boiling water, the clatter of plates, the click of the oven door shutting. Peter edged his way down to the far end of the table to join Duncan and the boy.

The table had been laid for six; cutlery, napkins, wine glasses, two bottles of something red at the other end, and he sat himself next to Duncan and opposite the boy who was wearing a pale green sweatshirt too big for him. Fiona's. He gave the lad a smile. "Ben. It's a good name. Much better than Blu, if you don't mind me saying."

The boy blushed and ran his fingers through shaggy hair. "Duncan likes it as well. It seems strange, but I'll get used to it."

"You will. I understand you're going to be staying here for a while, with your..." Great Uncle sounded far too formal. "With Duncan."

"He is." The old man's voice was strong and clear and proud. "We've come to an agreement, Ben and me. He's

209

offered to call me Granddad if I call him Ben. It'll take a while, but I think I can learn to like it." His grey eyes flashed with humour and he nudged the boy. "Nay lad, I'm proud that you might think of me as that. I've always wanted a grandson to take fishing and walking on the hills, but the truth of the matter is I never found a woman I loved enough to want to marry."

Fiona was grating cheese, her back to them, ignoring the conversation. Jon stirred sauce and dipped a teaspoon in before tasting it. "Perfect. Plates ready, Laura?"

A bustle of movement and noise, sights and smells: hot plates clinking down on the table, the gurgle of pasta draining, laughter as a strand slithered free and fell to the floor, the tang of tomatoes and the bright splash of the sauce against pale spaghetti. Plates handed out, Ben staring at the stands of spaghetti before looking at Peter, pleading and scared.

A murmur. "Like this." A twirl of the fork, a few fat strands coated with thick sauce. "Easy enough. Try it? I think you'll enjoy it."

Duncan was already digging in to his food, his appetite undiminished and the boy took a mouthful and then another, his hesitancy so far unnoticed.

Peter took another mouthful. "I haven't tasted sauce as good as this for a long time Jon. What do you put in it?"

Laura shook her head. "It's his signature dish, the only thing he makes without me having to nag. I keep telling him he needs to expand his menu, but he says he prefers my cooking." She added a spoonful of grated parmesan to her serving. "Want some, Ben?"

Fiona, sat between Ben and Laura, was quiet, concentrating on her plate, dabbing at her lips with the napkin, not looking at anyone. Peter took the bowl of parmesan and sprinkled a helping over his plate then put the bowl down in front of the boy. "It's strong, so don't add too much until you've tried it." The spoon shook. He raised his voice. "So come on, Jon. What's your secret? I can taste red wine and garlic. I'm betting there's basil and a dash of vinegar, but there's something else."

"Have a guess." Jon put his fork down and picked up one of the bottles. "Grape juice anyone? I thought, seeing as Ben is too young and Duncan can't drink with those painkillers, we'd all stick to the healthy stuff this evening." He unscrewed the cap and poured his wife a generous amount. "I've a bottle of Shiraz for later if we need it. Peter?"

He took the bottle and poured glassfuls for the lad and Duncan. "Fiona? What about you?" She shook her head and he saw the brightness in her eyes. He ached for her, but it was all for the best. She would forget him soon enough, when he had left this place and she'd moved on and found a good job and a place to live. She would be free to find someone who could give her a better life than any he could provide.

He raised his glass. "So, Jon. You can't leave us in suspense like this. Secret ingredient. Dried seaweed? Crushed mussel shells?" He heard Laura laugh, but Fiona was still staring at her plate. She had not eaten much, whereas Ben had cleared his plate and was scraping up the last dregs of sauce.

"You were on the right track with vinegar –"

"Hah!" Ben raised his hand and high-fived Peter's.

"– but it's not your everyday vinegar. I use balsamic, aged and infused with blackberries and rosemary, and then…" He paused for effect. "Then I add a good table-spoon of dark brown sugar."

"Sugar?" Ben frowned. "In this?" He poked at the sauce with his fork.

"You enjoyed it didn't you?"

"Well, yes. I've never had pasta like this. It was mostly Pot Noodles before. Mum didn't…." His cheeks reddened again.

Peter reached across for the pepper mill. "I think your grandfather will be more than happy to teach you how to cook, won't you, Duncan? That soup we had on Friday night was better than any I've ever tasted, which reminds me, what are you doing for Christmas Dinner? Turkey and all the trimmings?"

There was an uncomfortable silence. Duncan frowned. "I had plans to do something with a haunch of venison I've been saving, but I think it'll have to stay in the freezer. I won't be able to do much in the kitchen for good few days. Not with this ankle. I'm sorry, lad. I'll make it up to you at Hogmanay though."

He focused on eating. The grape juice was too sweet for his tastes, but he downed the glass and put it aside, his stomach churning. He should have gone back to the cabin and stayed there, even if it was all packed up. It wouldn't have taken long to make up the bed and light the fire and try to forget her.

Fiona's voice broke the silence. "It's obvious isn't it? You and Ben can come here for Christmas. I've got the space and Ben and I can do the cooking while you super-vise. I've never done a proper Christmas dinner before so it should be fun. And Peter's going to stay here, aren't you?"

Everyone else had finished, plates scraped clean, Ben running one finger round the rim to collect the last scraps of sauce before licking it off.

He put his fork down, no longer hungry, even though the sauce was delicious. "It's more work for you and the cabin's fine. There's all the food still in the fridge and freezer, so if it's alright I'll stay there, out of your way?" He picked up his plate, reached for Duncan's and stacked them together and made his way round the table, collecting the other plates as he went. No one spoke. Somewhere close by an unseen dog growled, a menacing sound that filled him with terror, and he let the plates clatter onto the worktop and stood, hands splayed flat as he struggled to stay on his feet.

"Peter?" Her voice came from miles away. A distant call, a hand on his arm and then he was sitting at the table again with a wet cloth on the back of his neck and an arm round his shoulders. "I thought you were going to faint. You've gone white."

He shook his head. Cold water soaked his neck, trickled round his throat to pool in his collarbone. "I heard a dog. It was her again. And it was like…." He shivered at the recollection of the children's faces in the window, of the sense of dread and loss and sheer anguish. The horror of being left alone. "I have to go."

A chair scraped on the floor, cold fingers took hold of his wrist. "You're not going anywhere tonight, Peter. Not until I'm sure you're well enough to be left alone." Laura Wilson touched his face. "You didn't eat much, really."

It was easier to say nothing, to let everyone think it was the aftermath of the day's drama. Ben sitting opposite, a tiny smudge of tomato sauce at the corner of his lips, Duncan at the head, fiddling with his wine glass and clearly worried. The smell of hot apples and cinnamon and sugar. Jon's quiet voice over by the door. It had to be Fiona behind him, removing the wet cloth and drying his neck. He wanted to lean into the contact, to feel her breath on his skin, ask her to forgive him. But the moment passed and he put his head down on his arms and tried to calm his racing heart.

It was Laura who rescued him, who took him through to the sitting room and got him comfortable on the larger of the two sofas, Laura who brought him a bowl of apple crumble with a generous helping of custard and who sat with him while he forced down a few small mouthfuls.

She said nothing, but her fingers took hold of his wrist more than once, and he could see the faraway look in her eyes as she counted out heartbeats while he willed himself to take the next breath and the next, each one deeper, each swallow less of an effort until he could eat once more.

He finished as much as he could bear and put the bowl down on the coffee table. "What now."

"What do you want? I could make you go to bed, but somehow I don't think you'd sleep, and the kitchen's too noisy right now. Do you want something to read?"

Fiona had left a stack of paperbacks on the floor. Better than sitting there worrying how he was going to get out of this mess. He picked up the first one – historical romance – and put it back again. "I'll sit here, if that's okay. I feel better now. Probably over-tired." His stammer had not made an appearance. No doubt it was lurking in the background ready to cripple him later on. It would be a fitting end to a nightmare of a day, and all he deserved.

The fire was dying down when Duncan came to join him, a halting and painful trek across the room aided by two walking sticks.

"Stay there, lad, there's no need to get up. I can manage well enough. How are you feeling?"

He shuffled to one end of the sofa to give the older man room and took the sticks, leaning them against the worn leather. "Better."

"What happened in the kitchen? Do you want to talk about it?"

"Not really." He folded his arms and leaned back, leather creaking beneath his head as he stared up at the ceiling.

"Tell me to mind my own business if you must, but I thought the two of you –"

He jerked his head forward. "There's no 'two of us'. I have nothing to offer a woman like Fiona, and as soon as I can, I'll be leaving. She won't miss me."

"She will, if I know Fiona Cameron. That lass has been waiting her whole life for you, only she doesn't realise it. Bess knows as well."

He gave a snort of derision. "A bloody dog. And not a real one at that." But it was his distress talking. He'd seen the dog more than once, been comforted by her touch in the long cold tunnel, heard her joyous barks and savage anger and witnessed her determination to keep him here at all costs. For what? If he had not followed the animal on Friday evening, he would never have found this place, or been trapped here.

"She has her reasons. We might not understand what she does, but it will all come right in the end. Trust me, Peter. And trust her as well. I do." He dug in his pocket and brought out a pack of playing cards. "Fiona found these for me. How about a game of rummy, while we wait for the others to finish washing up? One advantage of a sore ankle." He gave Peter a quick wink and then he became serious. "I wanted to talk about what Ben was doing in the tunnel. I know he won't mind me telling you. Fiona knows, but she won't say a word."

"Neither will I. You have my word on it." He waited as the cards were shuffled and dealt, and then the old man started talking. It was hard enough to listen, it would have been even harder telling the story.

It was, in many respects, worse than his own childhood. At least he had been fed and properly clothed and he had a home, of sorts. But Ben's short life had been in utter turmoil and he could feel his anger raging that anyone could treat any child in such a way. "You're going to take care of him from now on?"

"As long as I'm able. He's the only family I have now, other than his mother, but I doubt I'll ever hear from her again and she's welcome to his Child Benefit if it keeps her away from here. I'd thought about applying for legal kinship of the boy, but I think it's better if I just take him into my home. I don't want money; it's enough that he's here and safe. Now. Shall we play?"

They were in the midst of their fifth game by the time the others came to join them, Laura carrying a tray with mugs and a plate of chocolate biscuits. "Coffee for anyone who wants it. And in case you're wondering, it's de-caff."

"Rescued at last. I was beginning to wonder if you were going to leave me with anything at all." Peter dropped his cards on the sofa. "How much do I owe you?"

"Five million or thereabouts and I expect full payment

by the end of the year." Duncan scooped up the rest of the cards and gave a wry smile. "Pity it's not real winnings. Think what I could do with that much money."

"That's easy. Buy a boat and a new quad bike for starters." Ben was perched on the footstool beside the fire, his hands wrapped round a mug. "And a bigger run for Sock and Mitt. They'd enjoy that."

"The ferrets? I didn't think you liked them?" Peter took his own mug and stretched out his legs.

Ben leaned forward, hands clasped together. "I always wanted a pet, but mum wouldn't let me have any. Not even a hamster. She said they were too much work and there wasn't the money anyway." Bright flames cast a red glow on his cheeks. "So whenever I stayed where they had some pets, I didn't have much to do with them, because I didn't want to..." He shrugged and looked up at Peter. "You know."

He did. "Get too fond of them? Because when you left you'd have to leave them behind and it would hurt too much. And even if you desperately wanted to keep them, there was no way you could look after them properly." Everyone was staring at him and he leaned forward and put his mug down on the table. "I know the feeling."

"Oh Ben." Fiona's voice was thick with tears, but she was staring at Peter. "I'm so sorry. I didn't understand."

Duncan coughed. "Well, lad, perhaps you'd change your mind about them when you've had to clean their cage out a few times. And as you're thinking of staying a while, I might look at getting another dog in spring when the weather's a bit warmer. There's a farmer I know who breeds good working dogs. Not cheap, but you only get what you pay for. Mind you, I'd expect you to do most of the training and so on. But, you didn't say what you'd buy for yourself?"

"Me?" The boy's hands clasped tighter on his knees. "I'd like some walking boots and a camera. Not one on a phone, one I can use to take proper photographs. And…" He paused and glanced up at everyone as if expecting them to laugh. "If I had enough money, I'd like to go to university."

He hadn't expected that answer and from Duncan's face, neither had the old man.

Jon straightened up and nodded with approval. "Any particular subject?"

"Wildlife conservation, or something like that, maybe with photography as well. I've missed a lot of school but I'm not stupid, I've just never been given much of a chance." This was not the timid boy speaking, the child abandoned by his mother, this was a young man with hopes and ambitions and the whole world ahead of him. Peter held his breath. All it would take was one comment from anyone else to ruin this child's dreams.

Jon Wilson was the first to speak. "A lot depends on whether you want to specialise in one aspect of the science. I mean, endangered species, arctic, mammals, that sort of thing? There's always going to be good careers available in conservation and with a good degree, you'd have more than enough options."

Ben shrugged. "It's not going to happen. It takes money to go to university. A lot of money."

His father had said as much, followed by the refusal to give him any financial support at all. But he'd done it anyway. Student loans and part-time jobs. Pulling pints in a bar, stacking shelves in a warehouse, picking fruit and potatoes, anything which earned him enough money to pay his rent and tuition fees. He'd lived off cheap food but he'd graduated with a First.

Duncan spoke up, his voice full of passion and defiance and anger. "No one in my family is going to miss out on his dreams for lack of money. If it's what you want, then the money will be there. Mind you, lad, it's not easy. You'll have to work hard to catch up I expect, but I can help with that as well. I may be getting on, but I've been catching up on my 'A' levels for the past few years." He ticked them off on his fingers. "History, Mathematics, English Literature. The last one was Law."

"Duncan! You kept that secret. What else have you been hiding?" Fiona was sitting, mouth open in surprise.

"Nothing, lass. Well, nothing that concerns you at any rate. Now, Laura, tell me what you'd do with your winnings? Not a sports car, please."

It was going to be alright. Peter sat back, aware of Duncan deftly taking the attention away from both him and Ben and happy to let the conversation flow around him. It had been a long time since he'd been part of a group like this – an unusual experience, no one making snide comments or subtle hints, no 'shop talk' or gossip, only friends chatting. He was listening to Laura describe one of her more interesting cases when he caught Ben trying to hide his yawns behind one hand. Duncan looked even more exhausted, scrapes and bruises darkening his face, but neither of them wanting to spoil it for the other. It made him aware of his own weakness, his head aching and his eyes gritty.

It was not difficult to fake a yawn. "I hate to spoil

things, but I'm ready for bed, wherever that is, and I'm sure I'm not the only one."

Fiona glanced up at the clock. "Oh heavens. I hadn't realised it was that time. And I wanted to talk to everyone about Christmas and what you want to do. How about coming for breakfast everyone? There's plenty of food here. Nine o'clock too early?"

Laura yawned and stretched her arms out, before wrapping one around her husband's shoulders and pulling him closer on the sofa for a hug. "That would be lovely, wouldn't it dear, and we can pick Duncan and Ben up on the way. It'll give me the chance to change those dressings. Fiona? We'll see these two back to the gate-house tonight. I want to check Duncan's ankle before he goes to bed, and I'd like to meet these ferrets as well."

The four of them headed out in a chorus of 'thank you' and 'goodnight' and 'sleep well' leaving Peter alone on the sofa and Fiona, sitting cross-legged on the other one, watching him. She pushed herself off and stretched.

"I need a decent drink after that. Ben wanting to go to university and Duncan doing A levels? I'd never have guessed. Whisky? There's some in the kitchen."

He nodded. His back ached from the sofa, and Duncan had left the playing cards behind. An untidy stack, slipping down the crack between seat and armrest. They had the thick feel of well-used cards, a little battered around the edges, rather like Duncan himself. He could imagine the man sitting at his kitchen table playing cards in the evenings, a glass of malt within reach, maybe a ferret scampering underfoot instead of studying law or writing essays about Shakespeare. There again, Ben's ambitions had startled all of them, himself included.

Fiona arrived, carrying a bottle and two tumblers. Not the elegant cut glass ones favoured by Duncan. These were cheap and chunky, similar to his own purchased in a discount store after Georgia had taken his expensive ones. A generous half-inch of whisky, a mere splash of water. She handed one over and took her seat again. "It's nothing special, but you look as if you need it. It's been an unusual sort of day, hasn't it?"

"And you've got a Christmas lunch to think about now." The whisky was better than he expected and he took another sip. "It's too late to get a tree."

"I'll make do. I can always hang some tinsel up, and there's a holly bush not too far up the road, on this side of the bridge. It'll be better than nothing."

Stilted conversation. Another sip, the liquid lying on his tongue before he swallowed. "I'll give you a hand in the morning. If you want."

"Thank you. I'd like that. I was wondering…" She put her glass down on the floor.

"Yes?"

"I was thinking about asking the Wilsons for dinner on Christmas Day as well."

"Laura and Jon? That's a good idea. They can always say 'no' but I don't think they will. They're a nice couple."

"If they come I'd like to have dinner in the Great Room." She tilted her head. "Or am I being silly?"

Silly? He'd eat every single meal in there if he had the choice. No one could possibly get tired of sitting at that table, in that room. "I can't think of anywhere better. Hard work but worth it."

"I'd have to light a fire, it'd be far too cold otherwise, but it's the only chance to have one last meal in there.

Duncan would love it. And I think Ben should get a chance to see it as it once was. We can even use the best dinner service."

He could see her hesitation.

"But what about you? Would you come?"

The whisky was gone. "If you want." He could see the pain in her eyes. "I'm sorry. That was all wrong. Everything's wrong." The bottle had a screw top. Duncan and his father would have been appalled, but he didn't care. A slosh of alcohol, splashing up the sides of the glass to spill over the edge. He screwed the lid back on and sat back, sucking the surplus from his fingers. "I never wanted to hurt you. It's just that... dammit, Fiona." He could see the bright sparkle filling her eyes. "You deserve better than me. Blu had it right. I mean, Ben. He refused to get attached to any animals because he didn't think he could give them a decent life. I'm the same."

"You understood what he was talking about." She was running her finger round the top of her glass.

"I do. Look at me. I have no job. I live in a cheap flat which I share with a man who brings home a different woman every weekend. I'm not proud of my life and, although I have a feeling you and I have something special between us and it could easily become serious – very serious – I have nothing to offer you. If I had a decent home, or a job or something – anything at all – I'd ask you to come with me. But I don't." His glass was empty again, but he was too tired and distraught to refill it. "Please, go to bed. I'll sleep here on the sofa."

"You're wrong about having nothing to offer me. I think there's some reason you're here, and I don't think Bess will let you leave until you've sorted it out, whatever it is. But I'll let you have it your way for now. I'll fetch you some pillows and a couple more blankets for tonight, but don't think I'll give up that easily. In a couple of weeks, I won't have a job or a home either. And I'd rather be poor and with you than have all Duncan's pretend millions and be alone."

The door closed softly behind her and he made his way to her bedroom to retrieve his bags and then headed for the bathroom. By the time he was finished she had put pillows and blankets out for him and stoked up the fire. The whisky had done its work and he undressed down to t-shirt, boxers and socks, crawled under the blankets and was asleep within moments.

CHAPTER 21

Fiona turned over, wide awake and restless. It was far too soon to get up. An uneasy night's sleep, the shape of his body still pressed into the mattress when she'd pulled back the duvet, a smaller dent in the middle of the pillow. She'd hoped to find some remnant of his scent, the intimate masculine warmth that clung to his skin, but there was nothing of him left and so she'd curled up where he had been, put her head in the hollow and closed her eyes, knowing she would not sleep much. A night filled with restless, uneasy dreams, the pillow hot and lumpy, the wind howling outside. It was picking up speed and the sea would be wild later on.

Perhaps he was right. Without jobs or homes what chance did they have of building any sort of relationship? And yet something inside her refused to accept it was hopeless, or that this was any more than two lost people leaning on each other. It was more than that, much more.

She lay there, listening to the language of the Hall: the click of radiators, the creak of cooling wood, the sea roaring in the bay. No children singing now or a dog welcoming them home. It looked like Bess had abandoned them.

And today was Christmas Eve.

When she was a child this day would have been spent helping her mother make herb butter and mince pies, roll bacon strips and chop chestnuts, but now she huddled under the duvet trying to summon the courage to brave the cool air and make her way to the bathroom. The heating had kicked in during the night, but it was not enough to make the rooms comfortable. In the end she gave up trying to sleep, flung the duvet aside and found her thick dressing gown. A quick shuffle of feet into slippers and she opened the door, dashing to the kitchen to turn the heating as high as it would go.

A long luxurious shower, washing her hair and turning the temperature higher until her skin tingled with heat. A mug of tea, two slices of toast eaten while sitting close to the Aga. Peter's designs were on the sideboard and she picked them up and leafed through them before putting them aside to show Duncan later. The drawing of the Hall was too precious to leave out and she put it back in its cover and took it through to the sitting room, out of the way of greasy fingers and splashes from the kitchen sink.

He was asleep, stretched full length on the sofa, one arm behind his head, one foot sticking out from under the blankets. His sock had a hole in the toe. Her mother used to darn socks, not from lack of money, but from the pleasure in the task, but nowadays it was cheaper to buy new. She tugged the blanket under his foot, tucking it close to keep the chill out. He stirred, mumbling something, a flicker of eyelids, a frown lining his forehead and then he was still again and she bent down and kissed his forehead then poked the fire back to life and put more wood on. Flames curled up the sides, crackling as the fire took hold again and, satisfied, she curled up in the other sofa to watch him sleep.

Today she would start getting the Great Room ready for tomorrow, something she had not ever intended. Even if it was only her and Duncan and Ben for dinner, it would be worth doing. The thought filled her with both dread and anticipation: the silver to polish, the dinner service to wash and dry by hand, glasses and candles and linen napkins to sort. And the food to get ready – there was a turkey crown somewhere in the main freezer, not a huge one but large enough to feed six.

She'd not bought any crackers this year. You couldn't pull a cracker on your own and paper hats were tacky and the jokes even worse. Matthew preferred expensive crackers, with 'proper' gifts as he liked to call them – no cheap plastic fish or tape measure and no silly giggles over the dreadful jokes. They'd have to manage without this year. And presents. She had nothing to give anyone. Unless….

Sod the new owners. What the eyes didn't see, the heart wouldn't grieve over. She uncurled herself from the depths of the sofa and headed out, grabbing her coat and scarf, her rucksack and the key to the Hall. There was a roll of Christmas wrapping paper among the decorations and some unused cards. This might be a makeshift Christmas, put together in a rush, but it would be a good one if it was the last thing she did.

The rooms welcomed her, each one wanting her to

linger, to wipe away the dust and cobwebs, to sweep the carpets and rehang the rotting wallpaper. It was as if the whole house held its breath, waiting for someone to come to its rescue. She picked up the billiard cue in the games room. A beautiful piece, balanced and – even after all these years – still looking as clean as the day it was put down on the table. No. That was not right. She put it back, knocking a red with its tip so that the ball rolled a few inches to clack against another, the sound echoing in the dimness of the games room. A ghostly echo of the past and she shivered. Nothing in here.

By the time she'd appropriated suitable gifts for Duncan and the Wilsons, and put them safe in the rucksack, she was feeling the cold. Two more items. The turret staircase was draughty, the wind finding its way through every crack in the mortar and it was with sheer relief that she found herself on the top floor.

Richard's room was the same as ever, a fact that disquieted her. For some unknown reason she expected to see the fire burning brightly and Richard turning from his desk with a welcoming smile.

"Where are you?" she whispered. "All I want is to give you a proper burial. The one you deserve."

There was no answer and she put the rucksack down on the floor, hoping he would not object to her taking his things. It was unlikely – the heirs would have no qualms about selling everything to the highest bidder and this way at least a few of the laird's personal belongings would go to people who would cherish and use them.

The camera was unused from the looks of it – its battery long dead – but the cable was there as was the instruction booklet. Not a cheap camera either. Ben would love it.

Peter. She knew exactly what to take for him. A last look round the room and then she said her goodbyes and left. She would not go in there again.

The next hour was spent recharging the camera, wrapping and labelling and all the while seeing Richard's face, hearing his quiet voice. He would have liked Peter and Ben and the Wilsons. And he'd always liked Christmas as well, especially when her mother was alive.

After her death some of his energy and spirit deserted him and he aged, so that when she came back from university he was stooped and tired and diminished. The weight of years, her father called it, but it was more than that. He'd lost the spark of joy in his eyes and the smile she had come to expect whenever he saw her.

There was her present to get as well, the one left when her dad and Abby headed off on their holiday. She'd already sent her presents to Gainsville, but she could put her impromptu presents under the tree –

The tree. It was too late now to get one.

She was heading for the storeroom to get another loaf when she saw the sitting room door open and Peter standing there, half-asleep and drowsy, hair sticking up and looking as if he'd dragged his clothes on. She let him be. He would come through when breakfast was ready.

The sausages were browning in the cast-iron frying pan when her guests arrived in a flurry of wind. The door slammed shut. Duncan looked tired and she guided him to the large chair at the head of the kitchen table and found a footstool. Ben was blowing on his hands and stamping his worn trainers.

"Ben, what size shoe do you wear?"

He stuck a foot out and looked at it. "Seven. I think."

"In the hallway there's a cupboard on your left. There's a pair of walking boots inside, left by one of the guests and they didn't want them back. They're brown leather, more or less brand new, and too big for me. Try them on after we've eaten, and if they fit you're welcome to keep them." She turned back to the sausages, a quick check of the bacon crisping up in the oven, the eggs ready to fry, the toaster loaded. Black pudding and fried bread on the hot plate, butter and tomato sauce on the table.

"Plates are in the warmer, knives and forks in the drawer over there. I'll put everything on the table and help yourselves, okay?"

He still hadn't appeared. She cast a quick look at the door. Laura was laying the table, quick efficient movements that made Fiona think of a surgeon setting out scalpels and forceps. Napkins and the sauce bottle. Had she cleaned the lid? There was nothing worse than congealed sauce crusted round the spout. Still no sign of Peter.

She slid sausages onto a serving plate, added crisp bacon slices and black pudding, put it on the table with a thud. Six eggs cracked into the pan with a deft hand, scooping up the hot fat to baste them, the scrape of serving spoons on plates as Laura dished out, and then she was sliding the eggs onto a server and adding it to the table. A discordant 'ding' as the toaster threw out four hot slices and she grabbed those as well.

A quick check: everyone seated, everyone with a plate full, butter being spread on toast, knives cutting sausage links. And then the door opened and he came in, dishevelled and unshaven.

"Sorry." Eyes dark from lack of sleep, his hands twitching, face grey with more than tiredness.

"You timed that well. Grab a seat." It was kinder not to ask if he slept well. She grabbed a plate and served him – not much, but enough to whet his appetite. Personal experience had taught her how overwhelming a full plate of food could be at times like this, and she put it front of him without a word and took her own seat, close by.

Everyone was busy eating and she joined them, relishing the forbidden delights of fried bread. He cut up a sausage then put his fork down again, his head down to avoid catching anyone's eyes. She wanted to reach out and comfort him, but the last thing he needed was to be embarrassed in front of everyone and she concentrated on her own plate, surprised by her appetite. The serving plates emptied as people relaxed and helped themselves to seconds. He had eaten virtually nothing.

"Duncan?" She chased an errant piece of bacon around the plate with her fork. "How's your ankle?"

"A bit tender, but nothing to worry about. Ben's been looking after me." A quick nod at the boy in appreciation. "This is good. Makes a change to eat a meal I haven't made."

"I agree." Laura waved a fork loaded with fried bread and bacon. "I'm usually the one doing a fry up so this is a real treat. Thank you for inviting us. How did you all sleep?"

Ben looked up from dipping sausage in runny yolk. "Okay, I suppose." For a moment Fiona thought he was going to add something, but he looked over at Peter and bit his lip.

"You were up first thing to make me a mug of tea. And a good brew it was." Duncan put his knife and fork together. "Grand breakfast, Fiona. Maybe you can come to ours before…" He shrugged. "Before you leave us."

She reached out. Gnarled fingers and strong knuckles under her own slender fingers, the softness of bandages against rough callouses. Work-worn hands. "Let's not think about that today. Tomorrow's Christmas Day and I'd like to have a proper celebration here. As Richard used to do."

"The Great Room?" A rare smile lit his face. "Lass, I can think of nowhere better. I took the venison out of the freezer last night and it'll be ready in plenty of time if you want? It's a fair size as well, boned and rolled and I did a good job of butchering it if I say so myself."

Roast venison. Her mouth watered at the thought. "Laura and Jon? Would you like to join us? If Duncan's supervising I can promise it'll be worth it. And it'll be the last time we eat at the table in in the Great Room."

Laura looked at her husband and waited.

"Here? Are you sure? You have enough to do as it is."

She nodded. "It'll be a bit of a botched job, and there's a lot to do, but yes. I'm going to do it. We'd love you to join us."

The quickest of glances at his wife before he turned back to her. "And we'd be honoured to accept. How can we help?"

She hadn't thought much about the practicalities, let alone planning the meal. "I have to get the room ready first. And I should take you through so you know what you're letting yourselves in for. There's the silver to polish and the dinner service to wash. The chimney needs checking..." A crushing amount of work. She'd been a fool to even consider it.

Duncan raised his hand. "Leave the chimney to Ben and me. We'll sort it out. And I can sit and polish silver with the best of them. Peter? What about you? Any good at laying a fire?"

He looked up, frowning. "Me? I'm sorry, I wasn't..."

"Did you sleep at all last night?" Laura cut in.

"A bit, but I had..."

"Nightmares?"

He shuddered. "You could say that. I'll be fine. I just need some fresh air."

Fiona smiled. "You could go and cut that holly for me, remember? I'll find you some secateurs. But make sure you wrap up."

"No." Laura shook her head. "Not by yourself. Fiona? I'll see to things in the kitchen, you go with him. And don't be too long. It's bitterly cold out there."

Fiona bit back the 'yes, ma'am'. Laura was the professional here, and although the Hall was Fiona's domain, she knew little about medical matters. She pushed back her chair and went to get her coat.

The secateurs were in the utility room, along with a ball of string and she stuffed them in her pocket and led the way out of the courtyard. "Why didn't you sleep?"

"No reason."

He trudged on, long strides taking him ahead of her and she grabbed his arm. "Don't do this. Please."

"What? I'm doing what I was told."

He looked utterly miserable. She tightened her grip.

"Tell me what happened last night. I came in around six and you were fast asleep."

"Nothing happened. I didn't sleep well."

"Don't you dare lie to me. You look like death warmed up and if you don't tell me I'm taking you straight back inside."

Ten strides, eleven, her hand still on his arm, his shoulders hunched. "I heard… God this sounds so stupid." He took a deep breath. "I kept hearing… voices. All night. Someone whispering in my head, children crying in the background and that bloody dog howling. Every time I tried to wake up they pulled me back. And the dreams." He stopped and she felt him shake with the memory. "Rooms and rooms and rooms. It was like I was trapped in a maze. So many rooms I couldn't find my way out. And I was alone and dying and the worst thing was knowing I'd abandoned you, that there were things I wanted to tell you and I'd never had the courage, even though…"

"Peter? Even though?" They were outside the court-yard now, the harbour ahead, the wooden bridge waiting for them to cross. The stream was still in flood, the churning water filthy, the sea wild, white waves throwing spray against the point of the headland.

"Even though I loved you more than life itself. And I had been so stupid, so bloody, bloody stupid." He looked around. "I can't explain. I don't know what happened, other than it was me in that dream, and yet it wasn't. I saw myself in a mirror and it wasn't my face. I was someone else."

She wanted to hug him, but he was too distant, too

absorbed in recalling his nightmare. "That must have been terrifying. Do you know who you were seeing?"

"I didn't recognise the face but I know who was inside my head. I know what he wants. But I don't know how I can do it. He told me his name." He turned to her and put his hands on her shoulders. "Richard Edward George Fitzwilliam, laird of Black Dog Hall. And he wants me to find him before it's too late."

CHAPTER 22

Any thought of collecting holly to decorate the Hall was forgotten. He let her take his arm again, and they walked back to the bridge and he leaned on the rails, looking down into the water.

"You should come back inside. Try to rest."

He shook his head. "I can't. You don't know what it's like, the hopelessness and desperation. And I couldn't do anything. A stubborn pig-headed old man – that's what he calls himself – and he'll be in my dreams as soon as I try to sleep. I know how strong he is." The water mesmerised him, rippling and swirling, eddies and whirlpools, the dips and hollows where undercurrents pulled at it. He could have watched it for hours, the power and strength and contempt for man's feeble attempt to tame it. If the floodwaters rose any higher, even this sturdy bridge might crumble.

The Hall waited for him a short distance away. There was no escape from here, no way to avoid the insistent voice echoing in his head. "You must think I'm mad, that what happened yesterday made me lose my mind. That I'm making it all up."

"I never told you Richard's full name, or that the house is known as Black Dog Hall by the locals. It's something we don't mention to visitors. And 'stubborn pig-headed old man' was his favourite reply whenever he wanted to do something risky, like walk along the cliff path to his beloved bench where he used to sit and watch the dolphins. That's what we think happened to him – he went out and slipped over the edge. It's the only thing that makes any sense."

"He didn't. I can tell you that much. He never expected…" He grimaced with the memory. "He thought he'd have more time to get things properly sorted."

"And he died? Where?"

He turned his back on the stream, leaned against the strong rails and looked across to the Hall. "I have no idea. I wish to god I did, but if he'd died at home, they'd have found his body, surely."

"They searched everywhere. And I mean everywhere. I was at university and I came home as soon as I could. It was awful." She gave him a brief, painful smile. "Police and search parties, the coastguard, everyone. And they didn't find a thing. Dad was devastated."

"And you?" The wind was picking up again, biting into bone. He wanted to wrap his arms round her. "It must have upset you as well."

"I nearly dropped out – it was my last year but I didn't care. It was like losing my mother all over again. I don't think anyone realised how close we were, but Dad and Abby persuaded me to stick at it and I went back for the new term determined to make Richard proud of me and get a First. He'd had been so thrilled when I got accepted and if I'd come home it wouldn't have made any difference. He'd gone. It took me a long time to accept that he was dead, even if it was never made official."

"Until now. And you're about to lose everything. From what the impression I got I don't think he meant that to happen, but I'm only guessing. But he's full of grief and regret and anger at himself and nothing's going to help until someone finds him." A gust of wind took his breath away, and he gulped for air. "I'm sorry. We've forgotten to get the holly. Do you want to go back for it?" He hoped not. Even this short walk had exhausted him. He was like an old man, weak and feeble, legs trembling.

"It's not important, we can do without."

But she was lying. She wanted the Great Room looking perfect for tomorrow. "Maybe later on?"

"What did you mean? When you said you loved me more than life itself? I mean…" She broke off, her face red with more than the raw wind. "I know that wasn't you talking, was it. That was Richard."

It would have been easier to lie to her, but he couldn't. Not to this woman. "You know he thought the world of you? He was so proud when you went to university, the first one in the family –" Where had that thought come from? "Your family, I mean. He was planning a party to celebrate your graduation, the Great Room and all that."

She was looking pale now, the sharp wind making her eyes water, her shoulders hunched. "Let's get back. I'll ask Jon and Ben to get the holly later if we need it."

"Fiona? It wasn't Richard. I mean… He wasn't the only one thinking… Oh damn it." He leaned down. A fleeting and shy brush of lips, the fear that she might turn away from him, or worse.

And then she caught his face in both hands and took him, her kiss fierce and wild and it was not the wind that took his breath away this time. "Once all this is over, we need to talk. Boxing Day. You and me and the hot tub. Properly this time."

He was too flustered to answer. Her next kiss was gentle but no less fervent and it was his turn to pull her close, tongues and lips and breath mingling as if they were one.

The sound of a car coming out of the courtyard pulled them apart and they stood there, flushed and embarrassed like schoolchildren and trying to look as if nothing had happened. Jon Wilson pulled up alongside and opened his window. "Laura's sent me to fetch the tree from our cabin. We asked Duncan to get a decent sized one, and he took us at our word." He shook his head in amusement. "I was expecting one about six foot. Darned things a good eight-footer at least, if not more. Can't really fit it in the cabin but Duncan says it would look wonderful in the Great Room. I could do with a hand if you're up to it?"

A Christmas tree. He managed a quick smile. "We'd love to."

It was bliss to be out of the wind even on such a short drive. Manhandling the tree however was less enjoyable – a fraught few minutes hauling it up onto the roof rack without breaking any branches and then roping it down. He sat in the back of the car, hands clasped together to stop them shaking, but it was no use. As soon as he was back inside the kitchen, Laura pounced.

"You're not doing anything else Peter, until you've had

a rest. You're my responsibility at the moment, and if you don't at least go and put your feet up for a couple of hours, then Jon and I will not be coming tomorrow. Understood? And before you start to argue, think about Fiona, about what she wants."

Her tone was enough. Ben was at the sink, washing up and pretending not to listen, Duncan drying plates, Jon dragging the tree down the steps in a rustle of pine and it was Fiona who came to his rescue.

"I'll get the fire going in the sitting room and make sure he's comfortable. Ben?" She put the heavy key to the Hall on the table. "I'll leave this with you. Don't lose it. If you want to look around the Great Room, that's okay, but please don't go anywhere else." She hesitated. "I'm sorry, I didn't mean…"

Duncan slid the key over to Ben. "What she means, lad, is this is still the laird's home and we need to treat it with due respect. Don't fret, lass. We'll have a look and see what needs doing and you get Peter out of here before he falls asleep standing up."

The thought of closing his eyes and dreaming made him shiver. He would get her to leave him alone and then he would find something to read. Anything to keep him awake. Tonight was another thing altogether but he would deal with that when the time came and without a word he followed her down the corridor into the quiet seclusion of her sitting room.

He put his hand on her arm. "I can see to the fire, and anyway, you've enough to do without babysitting me."

"Not a chance. You seem to have forgotten that we're cut off from the outside world. No phone, no internet, no road, and no way to get help if something happens to any of us, not without a miracle anyway. And right now you're the one who needs looking after. So, you can take your pick. Laura or me?"

She was right, but it didn't make it any less embarrassing. He sank into the soft leather of the sofa and picked up the book from the pile. It looked even less appealing than yesterday, but it might keep him awake. "I'll sit here and read."

She pulled the paperback from his hand and tossed it to the floor. "No. You're not here to read. Lie down and close your eyes. And no talking."

"Mr Archer used to say that before lights out in the dormitory." A bitter memory. The silence, the door closing, footsteps fading and then the rustle of bedclothes as the other boys climbed out of their beds in search of entertainment.

"Shh. Look, I'm staying here, so don't try to get out of it."

"I'd rather talk for a while, if you don't mind." Richard was still there, a ghostly presence lurking deep in his mind, together with other even more unpleasant nightmares. Boarding school had left him with a fear of enclosed spaces and the dark and Georgia's betrayal had only increased his sense of failure.

"As long as you don't expect me to leave you by yourself." She moved to sit next to him, curled up in the corner with her legs tucked beneath her.

"I won't." Leather creaked as he relaxed, one arm outstretched along the back, legs crossed, ankle resting on his knee. "My ex-wife liked modern furniture. No antiques, no real artwork, everything stylish and uncomfortable. She would have hated this."

"And you don't."

He waved an arm. "What is there to hate? There's real history in here: the fireplace, the furniture, even the walls. The sort of place that could tell a story if you only knew how to listen or what to ask." He breathed in, a long slow intake. "Old buildings are soaked in the memories of people who lived and worked and died in them. You have to give them time to show you."

"You'd have loved Richard. He felt the same way. I used to find him in the library, just standing there as if he was waiting for something. I asked him once what he was doing, and he said the house was talking to him. Once, he told me he knew it was in pain and he was waiting for it to tell him where."

He didn't laugh. He'd done something similar on occasions with a design – laid it out on his desk and sat there, waiting for the drawing to show him where he had made a mistake. "And did it?"

"Turned out one of the roof tiles had slipped. When the leak showed up a few days later I asked him if that was what he had been looking for. He smiled at me and told me I should try listening as well." She stretched her legs out to the fire, kicking off her shoes. "He was part of this house, his family lived here for generations, a long line of Fitzwilliams tracing their family tree back to well before this Hall was built. He was bound to have some sense of what was happening in the building, though I don't really think it talked to him. He was most likely listening for unusual noises. A bit like Duncan does, when he goes shooting. You should go out with him one day. I think you'd find it fascinating."

Shooting animals wasn't his idea of a good time.

"Maybe." The fire was blazing now. He yawned. "I never liked guns. My father used to shoot grouse in the season. He took me with him once." He toed off his own shoes and leaned back again.

"How old were you?"

"Twelve I think. Or maybe older. He didn't take me again. Told all his friends how pathetic I was. I didn't care. I'd stopped caring what he thought by then."

"And then you refused to follow the family tradition. Shame on you." But she was smiling.

"I'd have made a rubbish soldier. Once I learned about architecture, I had something to work towards. I suppose I could have done art or maths, but I love the challenge of designing something different. My parents, of course, see it as a betrayal of the family ethos."

"Which is?"

"Better than the rest? Promotion at any cost? Something like that anyway. A Sinclair isn't allowed to be 'ordinary'. We're expected to rise above everyone else, usually by trampling them underfoot."

"And they think you're ordinary? What a bunch of idiots. I mean, look what you did for Ben, and Duncan."

A log cracked in the fireplace, his back ached and he rolled his neck and shoulders to ease the discomfort. "My brothers would be the first to disagree with you." He blew out a long breath. "You've no idea how good it feels knowing I don't have to spend Christmas with them."

"Won't they be worried when you don't turn up? My parents know how bad the wi-fi is so they won't be too concerned when they can't get through. And we swapped gifts before they left. I suppose I could put my present from them under the tree when Jon gets it up and we've decorated it. I love doing that."

"I never got to decorate a proper tree. My ex insisted on a fake one, already trimmed. And when I was a boy my parents had theirs done before I arrived home from school. They get a professional in to do it now, I think. Perfect symmetry, matching ornaments, complementary colours, that sort of thing. As for presents under the tree, we opened them on Christmas Eve. It kind of spoiled the magic when I was younger and it made Christmas Day a bit of a damp squib." He hid a yawn and sank a little lower in his seat.

"I bet it did. We did the whole Christmas thing right up until I stopped coming home for the holidays about three years ago. Mince pies and a glass of whisky for Santa Claus, stockings opened as soon as I was awake. Main presents round the tree before we ate. It was tremendous fun. Richard insisted on having dinner in the Great Room and then he held a party for Hogmanay a week later. Everyone came for that – pipers and roaring fires and a ceilidh until well after midnight. None of this modern fireworks and conga dancing. My dad first-footed for a few years until he started to turn grey and I remember Duncan doing it as well, but there'll be no point this year."

A child's memory of a man standing in the doorway, tall and dark and silent and holding a lump of coal in his hand. He'd been terrified and his brothers had teased him. It was hard keeping his eyes open. He stifled a yawn and shifted his position to turn away from the fire aware of Fiona standing to lift his legs up onto the sofa. And then he was lying down, his head cradled on a warm surface. Fingers brushed over his forehead.

"Trust me, it'll be alright. Close your eyes. I'll be here."

He could fight the darkness no longer and, reluctantly he let go, wondering what nightmares Richard Fitzwilliam would visit on him while he slept.

CHAPTER 23

Peter was sleeping dreamlessly from the look of him, his face slack and eyes motionless, no hint of distress or fear. Fiona shuffled back on the sofa to get more comfortable, wishing she'd thought to get a book or even a drink first, not that she regretted it. It was a new experience, having a man fall asleep like this. Oh, Matthew had dozed on the sofa plenty of times, but never with his head on her lap, like a child. It was surprisingly heavy. There was not even a cushion at hand.

The calm was broken by noises in the corridor outside: the rattle of boxes and creak of wood, a muffled curse as someone – Jon, no doubt – dragged the Christmas tree over the stone flags in a stiff rustle of branches, soft voices warning him to be quiet. For a moment she thought about wriggling out and going to supervise, but Laura and Jon were more than capable, and they would make sure Duncan didn't do much.

All went quiet again. The grandfather clock marked off the seconds. A ponderous tick, deep and resonant. She hardly noticed it most of the time, but now it filled the room like a heartbeat, slow and steady and reliable. It had been her mother's responsibility to wind the clock up each week, a task that thrilled Fiona when she was younger.

And then her mother had died and the clock left unwound, the weights at the bottom of their chains and the clock left in silent mourning until Richard stepped in, cleaning the dust off the mahogany case and lifting the key from the top where it had been left by her mother. Fiona had watched as the weights rose again and Richard's strong finger tapped the pendulum into motion. She'd never forget his face as he closed the glass door, or his gentle words to her. "This was your mother's clock. Keep it going. Please."

Her father had taken over the job when she left for university and over the years she'd forgotten Richard's face and the look of utter loss when he took down the brass key. But despite his words, the clock was listed as part of the Hall inventory. She would not wind it up again but, until it fell silent, it was a soothing reminder of her mother and all that she had loved here.

The door opened, a sliver of light brightening the dusky room. Ben. Quiet and slow and careful, coming up to her and handing her a mug of tea in silence. "You angel," she whispered. "How are things?"

He gave her a childish grin. "Tree's up and Duncan says the chimney looks fine. We're going to have a test fire first though. We're waiting for you before we start decorating anything." He handed her one of the cushions and helped her slip it under Peter's head and then pulled the blankets from last night over the sleeping man. "Laura says stay here. Do you want anything?"

"My iPad. It's in the kitchen." Hopefully recharged and even though it would be offline, she had enough eBooks on it to keep her busy for months.

He was back in two minutes: iPad, a couple of chocolate biscuits, plate with a thick slice of ginger cake. "Laura brought it." Then he was gone, creeping out as quietly as he had entered. He would make a good gamekeeper. She turned on her iPad and found something to read.

"What time is it?"

She lifted her hand from his shoulder as he spoke, his voice thick and blurry from sleep.

"Ten past one. You've been asleep for nearly three hours. Feel better?"

"I didn't dream." He pushed himself up off her lap. "I fell asleep on you? I'm sorry."

"I didn't mind in the slightest. I thought, maybe, if you weren't alone, if someone was with you, then perhaps you'd sleep better?"

He rubbed his face, the rasp of bristles, the crack of joints stirring, a long slow yawn. "It seems to have worked."

"I'll leave you to get up. Come through to the kitchen when you're ready. I'll have a brew waiting." She shuffled off the sofa, aware of his closeness, the warm, tempting smell of a man newly-woken from sleep.

"Have you been here all the time?"

"I said I wasn't going to leave you." She leaned forward

and kissed his cheek. "Hurry up now. You've missed all the fun of getting the tree in, and I suspect Ben is desperate to start decorating it."

By the time he re-appeared in the kitchen, the others had come back, filthy with dust and soot and cobwebs. Mugs of tea, toasted sandwiches, slabs of Laura's home-made ginger cake, a raid on the storeroom for more biscuits and bread. Ben's excitement infected everyone and she found herself caught up in the accounts of cleaning the chimney and dusting the table, of sweeping the walls and floor and flicking dead spiders from long-ignored webs.

"So you got the tree up?"

Ben laughed. "You should have seen us. We made Duncan sit down but he kept trying to help us and in the end Jon…" He flushed. "I'm sorry. Mr Wilson –"

The man held one hand up. "Don't apologise, Ben. We're all friends here and Jon is fine. 'Mr Wilson' makes me feel like a school teacher."

A slight hesitation. "Well… Jon told Duncan to stop pratting about –"

Fiona joined in the laughter. "Pratting about?"

Jon shrugged. "It made him sit down didn't it? I was worried about that ankle more than anything. But we managed it in the end, thanks to Duncan telling us where to find an old bucket and some bricks. Just needs trimming now, but I know my place."

Laura sighed. "Fiona doesn't want her tree decorated by a man who has no sense of design or style. If you do it, we both know it'll be a disaster. Remember last year's? On second thought, don't." She shook her head in mock horror. "I had to take everything down and start again.

You have no idea. Jon might have been a great detective, but he'd make a rubbish interior designer."

"We should let Peter do it. He's good at design." Fiona bit into her sandwich and waited.

"Oh no. Not that sort of design. I'd be hopeless. And anyway, I've never…" He fumbled with the crust of his sandwich. "I mean…"

"I'm only teasing. But I think you'd do a good job and Ben would love to help you. Am I right?"

She was. Ben swallowed the last of his sandwich in three enormous bites and pushed his chair back.

"Hold on, lad." Duncan put down his mug. "Don't you think you need to see what Peter says first? For all you know he may hate Christmas trees."

"Peter?" The look of eagerness on the boy's face was almost painful to see. Fiona held her breath.

He smiled at her first then turned to the boy. "Let me finish my brew first. Have you taken the boxes through? There's another large one in… in…" She could see him struggle with the word, and no wonder after yesterday. He gave her a desperate look.

"The storeroom, Ben, where the tunnel came out." She answered for him. "Jon can help carry it through. Be careful though, most of them are fragile so make sure you don't –"

"Drop them? I'll be really careful, I promise." His face lost some of its sparkle.

"No." She looked at him, his anxiety so close under the surface, waiting for a cutting remark or a reproof. She softened her voice. "No, I was going to say make sure you don't cut yourself. If they break, they break. It happens. But glass like that cuts deep, and I don't want you hurting yourself. Sod the decorations. You're far more important. Remember that."

Had his mother ever told him not to worry if something got broken, or he did something wrong? Had she cared for this child, this budding young man who was so eager to help and still so caught up in the magic of Christmas. And she wished she had more to give him than a second-hand camera. She wished she could offer him the safety of the Hall and permission to wander the estate and watch the oyster-catchers and the otters. He could have been the brother she'd always wanted.

Ben took Peter through and she busied herself tidying up, getting the veg out for tomorrow, the tin of chestnuts, dried herbs. Better to let them get on with it unencumbered by her watching them, though her fingers itched to help. She set about peeling sprouts and making herb butter and chestnut stuffing, then bacon rolls and cranberry sauce.

It was actually happening. A proper Christmas in the Hall. And not a half-hearted one at that. They would be friends and family together, for Duncan was the closest thing to family right now. And Peter would be here, though there was still some distance between them. He was like her father and Richard in some respects. Old-fashioned and courteous, gentle and thoughtful and unwilling to put anyone else in jeopardy, but there were times when you simply had to take a risk if you wanted something badly enough, the way she wanted Peter.

She'd never believed in love at first sight. Lust, maybe. In fact, definitely lust, but not the feelings she had for this man. It had been fun, at first: sharing the hot tub, the look of embarrassment on his face, his nervousness. And then it all changed. Now she could imagine herself living with him, loving him, the two of them growing old together. The thought thrilled and terrified her at the same time, but now was not the time to think about making a future together – she had Christmas Day to organise. And the first thing was to see how the tree was coming along.

"A little higher… yes, that one. And the star on the very top…. Careful!"

Peter was standing on a chair, stretching his arms up to the top branches of the tree, fingers full of shimmering glass, Ben directing him from below. She put her hand over her mouth. The tree was stunning – glittering and gorgeous – and she stood there and watched as Peter put the last decorations in place before jumping down. He was flushed with delight, his hands brushing needles from his sleeves and his eyes fixed on the tree. "I hope Fiona likes it. What do you think?"

"She thinks it's perfect." She stepped into the room as they turned to face her. Ben's smile even wider now. "You've done a wonderful job. Thank you, both of you."

"All the credit goes to Ben. He did most of the work. I just helped out with the higher branches." But she could see the pleasure in his face, the thrill of getting his wish granted.

"And we didn't break any, either." Ben stood tall amid the jumble of tissue paper on the floor. He looked across at Peter. "Can we go and get the holly now? If you want to, that is."

"Let's tidy up first and then we'll go. Is that alright

with you, Fiona, or have you something else that needs doing?"

The table shone, the sofas wiped clean of dust, the floor tidier than it had been since she moved back, the cobwebs cleared away. A small heap of logs blazed in the fireplace, waiting for more to be added once Duncan was satisfied. "There's only the candelabra to polish, but I'll ask Duncan to do those, or we can use them as they are. I don't mind."

She had, earlier. She'd wanted tomorrow to be perfect, everything the way it used to be, but seeing the tree and Ben's face lit up with the joy of Christmas, had changed things. It didn't matter if the candle holders were tarnished, or they used the everyday dinner service which was more practical anyway. Christmas was for sharing and loving, not worrying herself over silly things like polishing silver.

"Go. I'll tidy up here. You two go and get some fresh air. Ben? Find some gloves and those boots I told you about. The wind's fierce at the moment and I don't want you getting cold." She bent to pick up the tissue scraps as Ben ran back to the kitchen.

"Thank you. For..." Peter scooped up a piece of paper and spread it out on the table before folding it.

"Letting you help Ben? He was desperate to do it and I knew Duncan wouldn't be able to help. And Laura and Jon weren't the right people if you know what I mean?"

He nodded and took another piece of tissue – once red but now only the palest hint of the original colour remained – stroking it flat, folding it in precise lines to add to the tidy pile. "They're good people. But Ben? He'd have stood back and watched when all he wanted was to do it himself, even if he made a mess of it. But he didn't. He has an eye for lines and the way things fit together. I'd like to see if how good he is at photography."

"That was kind of you, to let him do most of it. I know…"

"How much I wanted to do it all myself?" He shook his head. "Maybe you'd have been right a few weeks ago, but I got far more pleasure out of watching him. Anyway, I got to do the most important part – I put the star on the top." A quick grin reassured her.

"Has anyone ever told you what a wonderful man you are, Mr Sinclair?" The scrap of tissue fluttered to the floor unnoticed, as she stood on tiptoe to kiss him. The scent of pine, the prickle of needles under her fingers, the urgency of his mouth and body inviting more from her, but then Ben was hurrying back, great clumping footsteps in his heavy boots and chattering about Duncan and venison and marinades, and she pulled away and bent down to gather up the rest of the paper.

It was dusk before the Hall was ready. Duncan had let them build a bigger fire and the heat had spread outwards, chasing away the years' long chill and bringing the room to life once more. Jon and Duncan set about polishing the silver, ending up with black hands and smudged faces, but the candelabra shone in the centre of the table. Holly branches lay on the stone window ledges, fat church candles white between glossy leaves and red berries. Ben and Peter had come back red-faced and gleeful, the boy hiding a small sprig of mistletoe behind his back, much to Duncan's astonishment.

"Where did you find that? I haven't seen mistletoe round here for years."

Ben stifled a laugh. "It was growing right in front of us in a hawthorn tree. Couldn't miss it. We only took a small piece, honestly." The boy held it up. "I'll have to find somewhere to hang it."

"Not in my house, you won't." Duncan found his coat and scarf and gave a fake scowl. "Come along lad, it's time you and I were heading back. The ferrets need feeding and so do we." He turned to Fiona with a slight bow. "Thank you for your hospitality today. We'll see you in the morning if you've not changed your mind? I'll have the venison ready to go straight in the oven if you could pick it up first thing tomorrow?"

"Of course. Hang on though, Laura said she'd drive you both back when you're ready. It's too far to walk with that ankle. And the wind won't help."

The house was strangely empty and quiet once everyone had gone. She went through to the sitting room, tidied up the cushions, neatened the blankets, pulled the curtains shut to keep out the dark. Simple tasks to avoid talking to him.

"Mince pies. Have you got any?"

"What? Sorry, I was miles away." The stack of books were in the way and she picked them up and stood there, arms full and aware that the pile was about to topple over. He caught them, scooping them all into his arms and dropping them on the sofa.

"Mince pies." He blushed. "I'd like to leave one out for Father Christmas." His eyes defied her not to laugh.

"A couple of dozen actually. Laura made them while you were sleeping. Far too many I expect, but they'll keep for a few days if they don't get eaten tomorrow. And we'll need a glass of whisky and a carrot."

"You don't think it's silly?"

"I'll let you in on a secret, as long as you promise not to say I told you. Duncan asked for a mince pie as well." The quiet request, the furtive wrapping in tin foil, hiding it in one of his large pockets. It wasn't silly.

Peter was frowning. "He won't have bought a present, will he? For Ben, I mean."

"I doubt it. No one imagined he was going to stay. Why?"

He smiled. A transformation from worried adult to the childish delight of a little boy. "Wait here."

He was breathless when he got back, hair mussed by the wind, cheeks wind-reddened, the cold clinging to him like a cloak, but he was carrying two large boxes and a couple of carrier bags. He put the bags in one corner and handed her the larger of the boxes, already wrapped in expensive Christmas paper. "It's a Lego set. I bought two for my nephew, but I think I'd rather let Duncan have that one for Ben and I can give him the other. What do you think?"

She wanted to kiss away his uncertainty. "It's perfect. And very generous. Look, why don't we walk down later on when he's asleep? You can give it to Duncan yourself. What do you want to do with the other one?"

"Put it under the tree for tomorrow. I just need to write new labels."

"I'll get you some later. I've got some things to put out as well so I hope I can trust you not to go peeking before tomorrow?" She put the parcel down and took his hand. "We've forgotten the mince pie. Come on."

A quick dash up to the hall with plate and glass. There was no need for lights – moonlight flooded the room and the tree was a tall cascade of glittering glass and silver. She forgotten how lovely this room was in the moonlight, and now, decked out for Christmas it had a rare, ethereal beauty.

"It's…"

"Beautiful?" She handed him the plate. "Go on. You do it."

He made his way to the hearth and put them down. She could see his hesitation, but he turned round and made his way back, feet silent on the floor.

"Wait." He pointed with one hand at the door jamb and the sprig of mistletoe stuffed there. "Ben?"

It was hard not to laugh. "Seems a shame not to make use of it."

His lips firm and welcoming, her breathing a little ragged, the warmth of his mouth against hers before she released him with a pang of regret, but this was not the place for anything more.

"What now?" he whispered.

She took his arm. "Now? We eat. I'm starving. Time enough for proper kisses later."

Pizza in the sitting room. A far cry from last year's Christmas Eve, but Matthew would never have eaten a meal like this, slumming it on the floor with bare feet warmed by the fire and a blanket wrapped round their shoulders.

"What will you do when you go home?"

He laughed, but it was hollow. "Home? I've got two

months' rent paid and then I'll find somewhere else. I'll have to look for another job, but it's not that easy. Although..."

She waited.

"I know someone who's emigrating. He said he'd put a word in for me, but it would've meant relocating and I was still hoping for promotion. I'll give him a call when I get back."

She nudged him with her elbow. "You've forgotten something. We can't leave here. Not until someone realises the bridge has gone. And that's not likely to happen out for a few days."

"What if there's an emergency, something really serious? There must be a way to get help."

She wriggled closer, relishing the warmth of his body, his arm round her shoulders, his bare feet playing with hers. "Dad told me once, when we were cut off in a snowstorm. Have you ever heard a maroon go off? It's a tremendous noise, carries for miles I believe. Anyway, there's a box of them, and several flares as well, in one of the top floor rooms. If we have to, we'd light a couple on the roof and then send up a flare. That should be enough to alert the coastguard that we need help, but it's never been tried before. I don't even know if the flares work, they've been there for so long."

"So unless there's a serious crisis, we're stuck here. No one in, no one out. I rather like that thought. We can take advantage of the hot tub."

"Tonight?" After getting so warm here, going out into the bitter night air and stripping off, even if it was to immerse herself in the deep heat of the tub, was not the way she wanted this evening to end.

"It's a bit too cold for that I think. If the wind drops, we could have a bonfire outside, toast marshmallows –" He looked worried, but it was a sham, the corners of his lips turning up in amusement. "You have got marshmallows haven't you?"

She snuggled even closer. "Toasted marshmallows are one of those things that sound good, but in reality they don't live up to the promise. Like candy floss. It looks lovely, but when you bite into it you're left with a sticky face and a mouthful of nothing. Like some people I knew."

"Plus fours and no breakfast."

She burst out laughing. "Exactly. All show and no substance. Matthew was like that, full of promises and grand ideas but nothing came of them."

"Is he still with his new woman?"

She shrugged. A few months ago that question would have cut her to the bone, but she was whole and restored and alive. "The last I heard. She's welcome to him."

"I have no idea what my ex is doing now. Once the divorce went through and she'd got what she was after, she sold the house and rented somewhere in London. The money won't last long."

"Does it still hurt?" She let her hand rest on his thigh.

"To be honest? No. She was only ever after money. And when she realised I didn't have as much as she thought and little hope of any handouts from my parents, the marriage simply fell apart. I don't even resent what she did, not now." His hand stroked her hair and dusted over her cheek.

The steady pulse of his heart against her cheek was reassurance enough. "What would you do, given Duncan's millions? You never said."

"That's easy. I'd buy this Hall."

"And then?"

"Then it becomes more difficult. It needs a huge amount spending on it, maybe as much as another half a million to get it fit for the next few hundred years. Some of the stonework needs replacing and probably all the windows and then there's the plumbing and electricals and heating. Not to mention the timbers. I daren't think what the roof is like. It all adds up, you know."

She sat up, heedless of the blanket slithering down from her shoulders. "But if you could, you'd do it? You wouldn't let it fall into ruin."

"Hell, no." He sat up as well, arms wrapped round his knees as he stared into the fire. "A place like this? Okay, it's not one of the great houses and it's too far off the beaten track to have any hope of attracting sufficient tourists, but that's no reason why it should be abandoned. Right now it's still saveable, but in a couple more years the damage might be irreversible."

"What would you do with it? Given the money."

He leaned back again, arms folded this time. She could see him thinking. "New lodges for starters. Only four of them and modern ones, exclusive and with all the things people expect nowadays. Decent internet connections, high spec fittings, smart tvs, that sort of thing. Appeal to people who want quality and privacy. Keep the log fires but have underfloor heating. Go down the environmental route with solar panels and ground source heating. Have welcome packages: local produce, cheese, chocolates, that sort of thing. And I'd build them right on the edge with the track running behind. That way you'd have the view as the selling point and they'd bring in a decent income once the initial costs were paid. And a year or so down the line you'd be getting about a hundred and fifty thousand or more gross profit once the word got out."

"And the Hall?"

"Ah. That's the hardest part. To be honest, I can see why the heirs don't want to keep it. No." He turned to her. "I don't like what they want to do, but they're businessmen looking to make a profit like anyone else. You can't make a building like this –" He spread his hands wide. "– into a conference centre. It's not got the right structure, or the size. There aren't enough rooms for starters. And I can think of nothing more obscene than turning the Great Room into a meeting area with display screens and rows of plastic chairs or even make it into a lecture theatre. Given the chance I'd make the whole house available for location work – you know, hire it out to TV companies, maybe even film studios. As it is right now I think it would be even more desirable and of course you've got the smuggler's passage. That's an added bonus."

"You've thought about this haven't you?"

"A little. It's hard not to, when I think about this being lost forever. So what would you do with it?"

What would she do? All her ideas required money, and even if the house was saved, it needed an income beyond that of any holiday lodges. "I don't know. I hoped…" Her shoulders ached and she was tired, and tomorrow would be busy. She took hold of his hand. "Come on, grab your parcel and we'll take it to Duncan before it gets too late. I'll drive."

~

The gatehouse door opened. "You're out late, Miss Cameron."

She held one finger up to her lips. "Shh. Is Ben awake?"

"In his bed these last two hours, and that's where I was about to go, unless you need me. Is there a problem?"

"Peter has something for you."

"I hope this is alright." He shuffled his feet on the doorstep. "I bought this for my nephew for Christmas, but I thought you might like it, to give to Ben in the morning. I've got a smaller one to give him." He shook the box. "Lego kits, both of them. It's pure luck I brought them with me and I'm not going to use them now."

Duncan was silent.

"If you don't…"

"For Ben? You're giving it to Ben? That's a generous gift."

"No. I'm giving it to you to give to him. Fiona said you might not have a present for him and I have a spare. It's yours if you think he might like it." He glanced at Fiona, his eyes lined with worry.

"I see." Duncan rubbed one hand over his face. "And there I was worrying myself sick over what to give the lad. I'm in your debt, Peter." He took the box and hefted it. "I'll be sure to tell him where it came from. Now, d'you want to come in for a dram?"

She reached up and gave him a kiss, his cheek whiskery and warm, the scent of earth and whisky and peat on his clothes. "You're giving Ben a home and a family. That's the best Christmas present he could ever have. Don't ever forget that. Now, we'll take the venison with us if its ready, and then we'd better be getting back. It's going to be busy tomorrow."

The kitchen was dark. She dropped the car keys on the table, slid the large joint into the fridge and took his hand.

"Come on, let's go to bed."

"I…"

"No, Peter. You're not sleeping on the sofa. It's been a long day for both of us and if you insist on staying in here I'll lie awake all night worrying and neither of us will get any rest."

He followed her in silence. The room was cold and she pulled back the duvet and shook her pillows out. A nighttime habit after an encounter with a spider when she was thirteen. He sat on the bed, tugging his sweatshirt over his head leaving his hair ruffled. The ends were beginning to curl. By the time he had folded that, and taken off his t-shirt, she was under the duvet, shivering at the touch of cold cotton.

"Hurry up, my feet are freezing." She turned on her side, watching the slow deliberate movements of a man unsure of himself.

He stood to unfasten his jeans, his back towards her as he unfastened his zip, the sluff of denim sliding down his legs to pool on the floor. Picking them up, folding them, draping them over the back of the small chair. And still he hesitated.

"Stop messing around. Anyone would think I'm going to chain you to the bed and do naughty things to you."

"Sorry. It's just that…"

"Don't tell me. You've never slept with a woman before? It's a bit late to tell me now, don't you think?"

He laughed, broad shoulders shaking with the release of tension and then he lay down, tugging the duvet up and turning to face her. "Good lord, woman, you're freezing. Turn over so I can warm you up."

His arm over her body, one hand slipping under the top of her pyjamas, the heat of his chest against her spine, his thigh pressed against hers, feet intertwining for warmth. The roughness of bristles on the back of her neck. She snuggled closer, wanting every last contact, even the soft coolness of his belly in the small of her back. "This is nice. Cuddling together, I mean."

"Better than a hot tub?"

"Much better."

His hand moved a little.

"Peter?"

"Yes ma'am?" His leg slid upwards along her thigh and she rolled over to face him, flushed with desire, her body trembling with urgency. Cold skin under his hands as held her, his fingers clumsy and nervous, his body responding to her nearness.

"Please?"

He fumbled with her top, edging it upwards over the rounded softness of her breasts and she raised her arms and let him slide it over her head. And then his hands were trailing over her body until she was writhing with each touch, each kiss and suck and nibble and nip. He took his time, letting her guide him with soft cries and clenched fists. One finger dipped into her moistness, her moan of anticipation, her hips pushing upwards, frantic, panting. A longer kiss this time, deep and urgent, tongues encountering each other, kissing and nipping, until she slipped her hands under the cool cotton, dipping down to encounter his hardness. Only then did he pull away, sitting on the edge of the bed to rip off his boxers his erection springing free, hot and tight and eager. He cursed his stupidity. "I can't. I don't have…"

"Yes you can. I'm on the pill, and I trust you."

"I promise, there's been no one else since –"

"Shh. Enough." She pressed her fingers against his lips. "I want you. Tonight." Her hands welcoming, mouth and tongue reassuring him and he sank into her embrace, and then her body was beneath him, soft and shaking, her nails digging into his shoulders and scraping down his spine, her tongue on his neck and then teeth in his skin as he pushed into her, burying himself deep in her tightness. He was aware of her deep moan of pleasure, of her hips beginning to move under him until he could feel her urgency, her trembling turning to a shudder and he hastened his own rhythm, bringing her to climax moments before his own release left him shaking and sweaty and raw.

And they lay there, together, clammy and hot and wonderfully, gloriously satiated. Muttered words from mouths pressed against soft flesh, cold air shivering exposed skin, until he rolled away from her, sticky and limp and wanting more. She was drowsy and sweaty, her eyes half-closed and he pulled the duvet up to keep them both warm and rolled onto his side watching her amid tangled limbs and the fading scent of sex.

It was a shock to realise how wrong she had been about sex and her own needs. Fiona stretched cat-like, relishing each memory: his tongue lapping at her throat, her nipples hardening under his fingers. It was more than sex. Much more.

It was the way he watched her body and learned her secrets: that she liked her earlobes nibbled and the hollow in her collarbone kissed, her longing to feel his tongue lick her – there, and like that. And how wonderful it was to indulge herself with his body as well. To have his leave to explore every part of him and take control, to kiss her way down his spine and feel his back arch beneath her fingers, to watch his face as he came gasping and trembling in her fingers. He was deeply asleep now, limp and boneless in the aftermath of their last slow coupling, a silky sheen covering his body. He was beautiful. Wide shouldered and narrow-hipped, skilful fingers and slender feet.

It was close to midnight, the sheet crumpled beneath their bodies, the duvet somewhere on the floor. Pillows scattered everywhere. He lay face down on the bed, one arm above his head, the other relaxed by his side and she ran her fingernail down his spine and back up again, watching him shiver. And again, this time up into the hair at the base of his skull.

"Stop it." A grunted murmur, a stifled snort. His hand reached out to grab her thigh and she pulled away with a shriek of laughter and scrabbled off the bed to find the duvet.

"I'm freezing and you promised to get me warm."

A loud, jaw-cracking yawn. A sly grin. "Come here and let me warm you up again."

"Stop it. Right now." She stifled a giggle and slid under the cover alongside him. "Seriously, you need to go to sleep or Father Christmas won't leave anything under the tree for you."

"It doesn't matter. Whatever happens tomorrow, this has been the best Christmas I can remember." His lips touched her neck in a delicate and tender kiss. "Thank you. For everything."

～

"Peter? Wake up."

Someone was shaking him, strong hands pulling him away from the tree, baubles tumbling to the floor and shattering in the cold moonlight, shards of razor thin glass slicing through Fiona's skin.

Blood. Blood on her face and her hands, blood soaking the floor, life pouring from her as he screamed his throat raw. He was Richard and he had failed her.

"Wake up. Come on, open your eyes. Peter? Are you listening?" A sharp pain on his cheek made him gasp, and he woke, sweating and shaking, the taste of blood in his mouth. His throat ached.

"Fiona?"

"You were dreaming again, and not nice dreams from the sound of it. Richard?"

He sat up, head on his knees. Deep shuddering breaths. His mouth dry. "Yes. And you were there." Her hand on his back, long soothing strokes easing the pain and the horror. "He doesn't have long. Only a few days."

"Do you want a drink? Cocoa might help you sleep."

It was unlikely, but he'd try anything. "Please."

"Stay here. I'll be as quick as I can." She slid out of bed, leaving him bereft and cold. The door creaking shut, her feet pattering along the hallway, the soft whine of a dog close by.

"Bess?" Stupid talking to a dog that had died hundreds of years ago. And yet her presence calmed him. "I don't know why you need me here. I don't know what I can do to find Richard. Seems to me everything's already been done." He didn't even know if the wolfhound could hear him, even cared what he was saying. Anything was worth trying. "And I'm not going to ruin Fiona's last Christmas meal. But if you want me to look, I promise I'll try."

Silence. But the horror of his nightmare – or was it Richard's greater terror of being abandoned – eased and he lay back on the pillows and lay there, until Fiona returned with mugs of cocoa laced with whisky and he drank like a man dying of thirst and she made him curl up alongside her and put his head on her breast and he slept.

CHAPTER 24

Peter lifted himself up on one elbow, gazing down at her face and the tangle of auburn hair on the pillow. It was not yet dawn, but after his nightmare his sleep had been dreamless and restoring and he was wide awake.

Today was Christmas Day. No parcels at the end of the bed, but he had never expected anything. To wake with her next to him was enough and he ran one finger along the curve of her collar bone, watching the slight pulse in her throat, the tiniest movements of her lips, the flutter of eyelashes. Was she dreaming of Richard? He hoped not.

He had nothing to do other than lie back and wait for her to wake. No doubt in a couple of days someone would alert the coastguards and they'd be picked up by lifeboat and this would all come to an end. A return to normality. He would have to face his mother's cool displeasure and his father's total disregard of any explanation for not attending the family Christmas. And there was his career to think about. He'd have to phone Waterman and update his cv, work on his portfolio and include the lodges, and his life would go

271

back to the way it was before Fiona and the Hall, before Duncan and Ben and a black dog who had brought him here.

Fiona would let him stay here until New Year, though there was no certainty of rescue even before then. It didn't matter – there was enough food and supplies, and the Wilsons didn't seem worried about getting back home. There would be time for him to relax and work out what he was going to do once this was all over, though in all honesty, he already knew. She was stirring, sleepy yawns and warm body pressing against his and he leaned over and gave her a kiss. "Stay there, I'll make you a brew."

The chill air made him shiver as he slipped out of bed fumbling for socks to protect his bare feet, boxers and sweatshirt in place of a dressing gown. The Aga was rumbling away in the kitchen and all he had to do was slide the kettle over the hot plate and get the teabags out and cut slices from yesterday's loaf. Thick slices, and a little uneven but all the better for that. The toaster was big enough to take all four pieces and he found honey and butter, milk and sugar, plate and tray.

Fiona was stirring when he pushed open the bedroom door and put the tray down on the dressing table. "Happy Christmas. Early breakfast?"

She pushed herself up on the pillows, yawning. "Happy Christmas as well. I wasn't expecting this."

"Careful, it's hot." He put the plate in the middle of the bed. "I hope you like honey."

"Love it." She took a piece, crunched into the crust. "I can't remember the last time anyone brought me break-fast in bed."

He tugged off the sweatshirt and slid next to her under

the still-warm duvet. "I was thinking." Honey dripped onto his chin and he rubbed it away, his stubble itchy and irritating.

"About?"

"Afterwards. After Christmas, I mean. You and me."

"And?" She'd put her mug down on the bedside table and was watching him.

He edged himself further up the bed, the plate tilting on the duvet until he lifted it up and put it between them. "I've enough money saved to rent a flat. Glasgow, if we have to, or anywhere up here where we can both find work. Nothing fancy, just a roof over our heads to start with." Honey had dribbled onto the plate and he handed her another slice of toast. "What do you think?"

"Moving in with you?" She took a bite.

"We both need somewhere to live." He licked his fingers. The toast was warm and rich with butter and sweetness and he wanted to kiss her, wanted to promise her the world but she deserved better than lies. "Flatmates, if that's what you'd prefer at first? It's all I can offer you right now. But I'll make it up to you, I promise, once I've got a job."

She finished her last slice, stretched out her hand to stroke the side of his face. "Not flatmates. Not after last night." The rasp of fingertips over stubble, the look of understanding in her eyes, honey glistening on her lips. He sat, hardly daring to breathe. Fingers trailing along his jaw, sliding over his lips, down his throat, resting there for a moment as he swallowed, her hand trembling against the soft skin of his throat before tracing its way down his breastbone. "What time is it?"

He stretched one hand out for his watch, her fingers brushing the sparse hairs on his chest. "Eight-fifteen."

"Damn." She flung the covers back, cold air halting any thoughts of more than a cuddle. "I need to get up. There's loads to do."

He watched her leave, heard the bathroom door slamming, the shower running and he lay back, hands behind his head. A perfect Christmas.

A later breakfast in the kitchen – scrambled eggs and bacon – before they set to work peeling vegetables. The smell of red wine and apples and venison, and he folded napkins and polished glasses and immersed himself in the unfamiliar rituals of Christmas Day at Fitzwilliam Hall, or as he was starting to call it in his own mind, Black Dog.

Red wine uncorked to let it breathe, a bottle of crusted port decanted with consummate care, cranberry sauce ladled into small silver sauce boats. The carving knife sharpened and laid out on a silver knife rest. There was little conversation, the only music her collection of Christmas songs and even those were muted. They moved around each other in an elegant and perfect ballet. Stolen kisses, fingers brushing against fingers, sharing a spoon to taste sauces. Reaching behind her for the dishcloth to wipe up a spill, passing him a spoon to be washed, handing her a drop of the wine to approve, clearing a place on the worktop when he lifted the joint out to baste it.

And then it was noon and Jon's car drove up, disgorging everyone in a flurry of parcels and bottles and shouts of welcome.

"Happy Christmas!" Ben jumped the last few steps, landing in the doorway with a look of sheer delight. "Laura's helping Duncan and Jon's forgotten the cake so he's going back for it. Can you help bring everything down?"

It took several trips. Bottles of wine and non-alcoholic drinks, a stack of presents – hastily purloined from their personal supplies he suspected – and a large box of expensive chocolates.

Fiona looked bewildered. "This is far too much, honestly. I mean…"

Laura handed her a bottle of brandy. "We were expecting to have a quiet Christmas in the cabin – which would have been lovely – but this? This is beyond any of our dreams." She lowered her voice, became serious. "Thank you, Fiona. Jon and I always wanted to have a Christmas somewhere like this. You've made this one rather special."

"It's a pleasure, really. I don't know what we'd have done if you hadn't been here, either of you."

Peter held the door open to let Ben come through, laden with parcels and wearing a wide smile. "Do you want to take those through and put them under the tree? Duncan? Go and take the weight off that ankle before Laura shouts at you."

Jon's return was the signal for everyone to head up the steps to the Hall. Duncan was already ensconced in one of the chesterfields, a glass of wine in one hand and Ben sitting nearby, eyes fixed on the glittering tree and the packages hidden beneath its branches.

"Okay. How should we do this? One mad scrabble or everyone give out their own?"

Duncan put his glass down. "We'll start. Ben? You can do the honours."

A package for Laura, another for Jon, then Fiona,

before Ben was holding one out to him. Peter frowned. "For me?"

"Your name on it. It's from Duncan."

He watched as the others opened theirs with cries of delight: Ben's sailing boat made from a piece of driftwood, Laura's candle holder and Jon's book stand also in driftwood, Fiona's wind chime in wood and sea glass. A thing of beauty. And then it was his turn and he undid the wrapping and pulled the paper away.

He'd thought Fiona's wind chime was lovely. His present was exquisite. A single piece of driftwood bleached white by salt and sun, pockmarked with tiny holes and as light as a feather in his hand, but Duncan had stained the upper part of the wood and transformed it into a stylised bird with a deep bill. A razorbill. The wood was warm and smooth and he held it in his hand and looked over at the older man. No need to say anything.

Laura handed everyone a small parcel. "Nothing much, but I hope they'll be a reminder of this week." She looked embarrassed. "Just something I started doing a few years ago to relax after work."

Jon shook his head. "Don't let her fool you, she's won prizes for her work. I'm trying to persuade her to sell them online."

The weight was heavy in the palm of his hand and when he loosened the string, the folds of paper fell open to reveal a pebble the size of a child's fist. He turned it over, hearing Fiona's gasp as she did the same. A silhouette of the Hall in the moonlight, hand painted with tiny brushstrokes.

Laura shrugged off their praise. "I'm afraid they're all a bit rushed. I didn't have time to do anything else."

"It's beautiful. I've never seen anything so delicate." Fiona put hers on the table and Peter put his alongside – the Hall but seen from the courtyard with the turret and the moon behind the tall chimney stack. Duncan was turning his over and over, and Ben was passing his round the group. Things of beauty. Personal gifts they would treasure.

Best get it over and done with. "I didn't have –" he shook his head. "I can't come up with anything as good as Duncan's or Laura's, but I thought you might like these."

The scarf for Laura, the poems for Jon, space rocket kit for Ben. A look of glee on the boy's face as he shook the parcel. The whisky and hip flask for Duncan and finally the russet coloured shawl with a murmured 'with my love' as he handed it to her.

She tore off the paper and held up the shawl with a cry of delight. "This is gorgeous! How did you know?" The shawl was a perfect match for her colouring, as if he had planned the whole thing from the start and she hugged him with unfeigned delight and he leaned back with a sigh of relief. Ben had his box open and was skimming through the instructions with a look of trepidation mixed with eagerness.

Duncan held the bottle in his hands as if it was the last in existence. "This is too much Peter. Far too much. I can't take this."

"Yes you can. Please. There's no one else I'd rather give it to."

Jon was leafing through the book, eyes focused on the illustrations, his face solemn and yet enthralled, Laura wrapping the scarf round her neck with obvious pleasure. He breathed out.

"My turn now." Fiona was still wearing the shawl. "These are… Well, I chose them, but they're really gifts from Richard. I think he'd want you all to have them."

Silence as she handed them out. A small parcel, no longer than his hand and no heavier than the pebble. He turned it over, not wanting to open it and yet eager to see what was inside and he watched as one by one they were opened. Beautiful gifts, each one thoughtful and personal: Duncan's Tantalus, Jon's ornate silver corkscrew, a silver and glass inkwell in Laura's hands. Ben's shout of delight at opening his own parcel to reveal the camera. Richard's camera. And impossible as it was he could sense the man inside his head. The curiosity and the satisfaction and the sense of joy. They were waiting for him to open his gift and he ripped the paper away and sat there, speechless.

Richard's fountain pen and pencil in their original case, the laird's initials engraved on the gold plate. He lifted the pen out. It fitted his fingers as if it had been made for him, as perfectly balanced as his own much cheaper version.

"I can't take this."

"Yes you can. He'd like you to have it. Here." She passed him a notepad. "Try it out. I cleaned and refilled it. I think he'd be pleased to see it being used."

The notepad shook in his hand. He risked a tiny line, the nib releasing its contents without any need for pressure, sliding like silk over the coarse paper and leaving a perfect trail. His fingers moved automatically, writing the letters, drawing a quick line beneath and then he was done and slipping the cap back on. Only then did he look at the paper.

R.E.G. Fitzwilliam. Written in his own distinctive script. Everyone looking at him.

It was Fiona who broke the silence. "Come on. Back down to the kitchen. We'll be eating in about thirty minutes if I've got the timing right, so Ben, can you tidy up here? And then help carry everything back up?"

The kitchen was busy enough to not need his presence and he went into the bathroom, running his hands under hot water and then washing his face. It was his own face staring back at him from the mirror, but Richard was not far away. "Help me. If you want me to find you, then help me. Before it's too late."

And then Fiona called him and he was carrying the roast on its platter up the turret steps and hurrying down again for a stack of scorching hot plates, everyone able to carry something following behind with serving dishes and gravy boats and flushed faces.

A flurry of activity and chatter, Jon carving the joint and Fiona passing dishes round. He poured out drinks and a watered-down wine for Ben. Then everyone was seated, glass in hand and waiting.

He glanced at Fiona aware of the distress in her face, her indecision at what to say. There would be no other feast to honour the passing of the laird and yet saying those words would destroy her and he pushed back his chair and rose to face the empty chair at the head of the table.

"Peter. Wait." Duncan was standing now. The man knew. "It needs to be whisky. And a good one at that. More than good – the best, the one you gave me. Let me pour it."

The squeak of a cork as it was twisted out, the scent of

aged whisky, dark and peaty. The tiniest amount in each glass. Chairs scraping on the floor.

He turned back to face her. "Fiona. Would you rather...?"

"No. Do it. Please." She was crying now, but not tears of despair or overwhelming sadness. They were tears for a man long gone and never laid to rest. Ben had moved closer to Duncan and holding his hand, Jon and Laura solemn and still. Everyone with a glass in their hand.

He took a breath, preparing to send his voice to every corner of this huge room, and beyond. Those years of speech therapy. Of learning to project his voice, of having the confidence to speak aloud. And he was among friends here. He turned back again to face the chair.

"To the memory of Richard Edward George Fitzwilliam, beloved laird of this House. May he rest in peace and may his blessings fall on all those gathered here today, old friends and new." He raised his glass. "To Richard."

"Richard." A quieter response maybe than in previous times, but it was a toast among friends and those who loved him. And what more could a man want than to be mourned by the people he left behind.

The whisky was rich and potent, tasting of fire and strength and he savoured the small sip as it slid down his throat. Even Ben had drunk his tiny ration and was standing as solemn as the others. A mournful howl echoed through the still air and Duncan smiled. "You did well, Peter. A fitting toast and one of which the laird would have approved. Now. Shall we get started? Our feast awaits."

The roast was mouth-wateringly tender, the potatoes

crisped to perfection, vegetables piping hot and delicately flavoured with herbs. He ate well, aware of every bite, of loading his fork with venison, of helping himself to more when the platter was passed down, but for all that he found himself distanced from the conversation. An onlooker rather than a participant. As if he was half-asleep and yet he was not tired. Far from it – he was wide awake, his muscles coiled like springs. Something was going to happen and he had to be ready.

They had warm mince pies – the one left last night had mysteriously disappeared, as had the carrot and alcohol – and Christmas pudding complete with flames and brandy sauce. And then it was all over and he helped clear the table and carry everything back down. Ben was restless, wanting to start constructing his kit, but now was not the right time.

"Why don't you go outside and try out your camera?"

"Can I?"

Fiona waved her fingers at him. "Shoo, before I have you scrubbing pans."

Ben ran back upstairs, returning more slowly, camera in hand. "Peter? Want to come with me?"

Why not? Some fresh air might clear the fog in his head. He grabbed a spare coat from the kitchen and followed the boy out into the courtyard, walking round the perimeter and thinking about the gifts he'd received. All of them.

Dusk was approaching and the sky was clear. Another bitterly cold night ahead of them. The Hall looked dark, the windows black against the stone or blazing with light. The lights inside the Great Room were dimmed, and he could see the candles on the windowsills – small flickering pinpoints. He'd stood right here in this very spot on Saturday when he'd seen….

"Oh god. I've been such a bloody fool."

He left Ben taking photographs and he hurried back inside to the sitting room to pick up the drawing of the House he had done for Fiona. The others had finished tidying up and were drinking coffee and brandy in the Great Room and he took the drawing up and laid it on the long dining table.

"Peter? Are you alright?"

He held up one hand. Something about the drawing had irked him from the start, even though he knew it was accurate. It was in the picture. It was all there, if only he could see it.

"Peter?" Her hand touched his arm and he shook her off, not unkindly, but any distraction was unwelcome.

"Peter?" Laura's voice, more concerned.

"Give me a minute. Please. This is important." It was there. It had to be. What had Fiona said about Richard and listening to the House? He did the same now, letting himself relax, opening his mind to any sound, any smell, anything that might help. Eyes closed, he imagined himself walking along the top corridor and into Richard's room, looking out of the windows….

A child cried out, high and faint and pleading, the dog whined, and he put both hands on the table and stared at the paper until the answer leapt out at him, as clear and bright as the baubles on the tree.

'Fiona. What did you want for Christmas? Really, really want I mean.'

She was close to him, not touching, but he could feel the heat of her body. "Really? I wanted to find Richard."

He turned to face her. "I think I know where he is."

～

It took a long time. Duncan insisted on joining them, and Ben as well, though Duncan told the boy both of them had to stay at the back and do exactly as they were told.

Laura took Peter to one side. "Seven years. You know what to expect if you do find him? It might not be pretty."

"I know. It's important I go in first. I can't explain right now, but you have to trust me."

She put her hand on his cheek. "I do, but you need to take Jon with you, even if he's right behind you. You understand why?"

He did. "I don't think his death was suspicious, just unexpected. He told me he was planning the future of the Hall, wanting to make it secure."

"He told you?"

Heat surged through his face. "I've been dreaming about him the last couple of nights. More than dreams really." He waited for her scorn but there was only sympathy. "He's been trying to tell me where he was, only I wasn't thinking straight. I just hope I've got it right, for Fiona's sake."

They climbed the steps to the top level in a slow procession hampered by Duncan's ankle. Out onto the top corridor and along to Richard's private room. A glimpse of Bess in the distance before the dog disappeared. He let Fiona go in first.

"Where? Where is he?"

"Wait a minute." The panelling was a work of art, the intricate hand-carved folds designed to hide any joins in the wood and he began running his hands down the folds on one side of the fireplace, pressing his hands against the polished oak, tapping his fingers over the panels his head tilted.

"You told me all his notes had gone and then Ben told me about… well, about his mother stealing the watch from his desk. I think those two things were connected. Richard hated the thought of someone going through his personal things so he decided to… Ah. There." A click, a dark line revealed. He stepped back. "Most of these old houses were built with secrets. Hidden passages, spyholes, staircases inside walls. I'm pretty sure there's a secret chamber of some kind on the other side of this wall. If you look at the hallway outside and the length of this room there's a discrepancy. About three metres I'd guess. It's hard to say exactly without measuring. And with all the smaller rooms up here and the thickness of some of the walls, it would've been easy enough to create a hidden space without anyone suspecting." He slid his fingers inside the gap, feeling for a catch.

"How did you know?" Fiona was close to tears, Ben huddled next to Duncan who was perched on one arm of the sofa.

"The drawing. There was something wrong with it and I couldn't work out what or why, even though I knew it was accurate. Then I remembered something you said about Richard listening to the House and I tried doing the same." He frowned and leaned forward, eyes closed as he concentrated. "I should have realised on Saturday when I saw the children looking down into the courtyard. They weren't staring out of any of these windows. If I'm right, we'll find Richard's secret study on the other side of this door." A loud click, a tall section of panelling opening wide enough to reveal a dusty staircase. "Jon? I'd like to go first if that's alright?"

"Just remember – don't touch anything."

No one stopped him. Tears poured down Fiona's cheeks, Ben sitting mute and distressed with Duncan's arm round him, Laura calm and composed. Jon's footsteps followed him as he climbed. Only five steps but enough to keep the others from seeing much inside the small chamber.

It was smaller than he expected. A single bookshelf, a decent sized desk stacked with papers and books, a high wing-backed chair facing the window looking out over the courtyard. A barrel-shaped cut-glass tumbler on a small wine table within reach of the man sitting in the chair, but any whisky left in the glass had long since evaporated. The man in the chair could have been asleep, had it not been for the utter stillness and silence. There was no smell, no hint of the gruesome corpse he had expected, only a faded remnant of Richard Fitzwilliam, long fingers resting on the arms, feet in shabby slippers tucked under the seat, the proud face staring out to sea though his eyes were closed. A handsome man, even in death.

"Richard." He felt no horror or shock, not even sadness. Instead, the surge of overwhelming relief was enough to have him clinging to the door frame before his legs gave way.

Jon's hand grasped his arm. "You've found him. I think you should go and tell the others."

Jon was right although it was a wrench to make his way down the stairs to where Fiona waited. He nodded at her. "He's there, quite peaceful. It's as if he just fell asleep."

She clung to him, tears soaking into his sweatshirt. "Can I... can I see him?"

He glanced at Laura.

"As long as neither of you touch anything. We have to treat his death as suspicious until we have all the facts. Once you're finished, Jon needs to take photographs and I'll do an examination." She put her hand on Fiona's shoulder. "I'll come with you if you want? What about you, Duncan?"

"Let the lass go in with Peter. He'll look after her. As for me? I said my farewells a long time ago." A stern reply, but Duncan had the right of it, and had he asked to go into the room, then Ben would have felt honour bound to do the same. Richard's body, though nothing like the skeletal remains he had expected, would be distressing enough, particularly for a young lad who had doubtless never seen death close up.

"Is he...?"

"Frightening? No. Nothing to be scared about. Just an old, old man asleep in his chair. His eyes are closed and he's at peace. Whatever happened, I don't think he suffered."

She clung to his hand, her body pressing close as he led her into the chamber, her face turned away from the view, until he put his hand on her cheek.

"Take a look. Just the edge of his chair to start with, nothing more." He stood close, ready to take hold of her.

One hesitant step, and another, until... "Oh god. He looks..." She clung to his arm.

"Asleep. And peaceful. Keep that thought in your mind." He pulled her closer. "Now, we need to let Jon take over."

He allowed himself one last look before the retired policeman was guiding both of them away. "It's time to say goodbye. Laura and I'll take good care of him, trust me." Jon was pulling a pair of latex gloves out of his pocket, ones from the First Aid box. "Go on now. You don't need to be here. He wouldn't want you getting upset."

So they left, stumbling down the steps into the room where Duncan waited. "Come on, lass. You've done all you can. Let's go downstairs and get warm."

They drank brandy by the fire, even Ben, who was pale and shivering. Peter swirled the liquid round in its snifter. "I'm sorry I ruined the day for you all. And it was a wonderful meal as well."

"What happens now?" Fiona was hunched up in one corner of the sofa. "I mean… we can't exactly do anything can we?"

Duncan broke the silence. "Well, I'll be taking Ben home once Jon's finished and we know more. That's all I can do now. And as for ruining the day?" He laid a hand on Peter's knee. "It was the best gift you could have given us, and Richard for that matter, so don't fret about it. It's been a grand day, hasn't it?"

Ben took another sip of alcohol and put the glass down. "It's been the best Christmas I can remember. I'm sorry about Richard, but I think he'd be happy you've found his body." He put a hand on his stomach. "Is there anything to eat? I'm starving."

Peter let his laugh escape. "I agree. It's what… three hours since dinner? Time for cake and chocolates. I'll go and put the kettle on. Ben? Why don't you start on that model – there's room on the table and you won't be in anyone's way there."

"I can give you a hand if you like?" Duncan sounded surprisingly keen and Peter shared a smile with Fiona. Ben would lose himself in the task and the sadness would fade. He gave her a quick nod and she followed him down to the kitchen.

He perched himself on one corner of the kitchen table, arms folded, his shoulders hunched. "I'm sorry. I shouldn't have said anything, not today. I should have left it until tomorrow."

"Don't be. I'd have been devastated if I thought you'd kept it from me, even for a couple of hours. He's home where he belongs." She put mugs on a tray, added cake and plates and a box of biscuits. "I wish you'd come here years ago. No one ever considered looking for a secret room – we just assumed Richard would have told us about any. It was stupid. We wasted all those years. And what if you hadn't come? What if we'd left and no one ever found him?" The tray shook in her hands and he took it from her and put it down on the table.

"But we did. We found him, all of us." He kissed her forehead. "Think about it. If it hadn't been for Duncan looking after me when I arrived, and you showing me the courtyard and letting me stay in the cabin, or Ben getting trapped in the tunnel, then this might not have happened. And it was Bess and the children at the heart of it all. Bess brought me here and the children have been there, all the time, showing us the way. Fiona?" He pulled her close, let her head rest on his shoulder. "You'll be able to give him a proper funeral now. I know he'll like that."

Ben was starting on his second slice of Christmas cake

– peeling off the marzipan and icing to eat last – when Jon arrived with his wife close behind and looking tired. Duncan poured them a drink in silence. Ben finished his mouthful and put his plate on the coffee table. Peter edged, closer to Fiona to make room. Everyone waited.

Laura stretched out her hands. He hadn't noticed how strong her fingers were.

"It's good news. From a cursory examination, I'd say he died in his sleep, or at least so suddenly there was no time to react. There's no indication that he was in any pain, far from it, judging from the way his hands are resting on the chair. A post mortem should show the cause of death but I'd rule out a heart attack. I'd be looking at something like sudden cardiac arrest or an embolism, maybe even a stroke. Whatever it was, he didn't suffer."

Jon Wilson had seated himself on the arm of the sofa, beside her. "I've examined the room and taken photographs. There's no sign of anything unusual, no blood or unusual injury. Nothing to suggest it was anything other than natural causes. There's not much else anyone can do now. It's an unexpected death and in normal circumstances we should call the police now death's been confirmed, but that's not going to happen today. Our main concern is the condition of the body." He grimaced, "I'm sorry. I tend to go into police mode at times like this. What I mean to say is –"

Laura took over. "The body is remarkably well-preserved. Unusually so. In fact I can't ever recall seeing so little decomposition before, certainly not in someone who died seven years ago." She held up her hand. "And yes, indications show he's been dead for a considerable length of time. The room is undisturbed, and there's a newspaper on his desk dated December 14th 2011. And yet…"

"He was waiting." Everyone looked at him and Peter realised he had spoken the words aloud. "What did he call himself? A pig-headed stubborn old man? He's been here, waiting all this time to be found. Clinging to this world by sheer bloody-mindedness, and in a house protected by the ghosts of a dog and two children from hundreds of years ago. Is it any wonder his body is as he left it? There's a reason he needed to be found and I don't think he'll rest until we know why." He poured himself another brandy and drained the glass, not caring if they thought he was mad. Jon was watching him.

"I think the best thing to do is to leave things as they are for now. One last thing, Fiona." The policeman held out a large envelope. "I found this on his desk. It's addressed to you."

CHAPTER 25

It was her name on the front, the penmanship recognisable as Richard's writing, but even so she hesitated. A last message from the man she'd thought of as 'grandfather', the man who taught her to play billiards, who'd helped her set up a bowling alley in the Long Room one miserable summer when it never seemed to stop raining.

She turned the envelope over in her fingers, hoping to find some clue as to its contents. It was fatter than she expected, crinkling in her hand. Everyone was waiting. "Am I allowed to open it?" She half-hoped Jon would say no.

"I can't see any reason why not. It was in among a pile of papers he'd written about local history, so I doubt it has anything to do with his death. You can open it, or maybe you'd rather wait until later."

"I don't know." The words burst out. "What if it's…?"

"Don't. Don't think that." Peter's hand was gentle on her wrist. "He loved you. That's all you need to know."

The seal had come loose, not surprising after so many years. She slid one finger under the flap and eased it open, careful not to tear anything. Sheets of cream parchment-like paper stapled together.

"Last will and testament of Richard Edward George Fitzwilliam." The pages crinkled in her fingers, she didn't dare look up. "I, Richard Edward George Fitzwilliam of Fitzwilliam Hall, also known as Black Dog Hall, revoke all my former wills and codicils and declare this to be my last will."

"Is it dated?" Laura's voice. Calm and sensible.

She flipped back to the cover page. "November 2011."

Duncan grunted. "Not long before he died, then. Read on, lassie."

She wanted to cry. But she wouldn't do, not yet. Maybe later when she was alone. "I appoint my grand-daughter…" The pages fell from her hand. "Oh god. No."

"Fiona?" Peter. Bending down to pick up the pages, frowning as he read.

"His granddaughter. He calls me his granddaughter. He can't do that, can he?"

"He can." Peter handed her the pages, his voice grim. "You need to read the next page."

It was all there, words and phrases crossed out or smudged with ancient tears, the handwriting wavering in places, and blurred by her own tears, her voice faltering as she read it aloud.

'My dearest Fiona,

I was twenty-two and a foolish young man when I met Jean and fell in love. She was my life, my love, my future, my first and only love. To us it didn't matter that she was the daughter of one of our tenant farmers, or that she was a Catholic and I was not. We were in love and as soon as she turned eighteen I was going to make her my wife. And then she came to tell me she was pregnant with my child.

I went to her father asking for his permission to marry her, only to be thrown out of the house and told never to see her again. When my father discovered what had happened, I was sent to my uncle's house on Mull for the next six months. I wrote to Jean every day but there was never any reply and all I could do was hope that both she and our unborn child were well and she would get a message to me.

It was June when I returned home to find all my letters to Jean returned, unopened. The farm tended by her family for years had a new tenant and no one would, or could, tell me where the previous family had gone. In August that year I received a brief and anonymous letter from someone who had been with her for the last months of her life.

Jean had been sent to a convent for unmarried mothers, had given birth to a daughter, and died shortly afterwards. She was buried in an unmarked grave in the convent grounds.

I did the only thing I could. I found my daughter and arranged for her to be adopted into a family I knew well. A hard-working father, a loving mother. A couple who had not been blessed with children and who took my daughter to their hearts and gave her everything she ever needed. I could only watch from a distance, helping out when I was able, but never being part of her family.

When my daughter became engaged, and employment was hard to find, I offered the two of them the Housekeeper's Apartment and permanent jobs as Steward and Housekeeper of the Hall. And after too many years I was content. And then my daughter had her own child. My tiny, perfect granddaughter called Fiona. And though I do not have any pictures of Jean and *my memory is fading, every time I look at you I see her face staring back at me and I am happy.*

Please forgive me for not having the courage to tell you the truth. Just know this. I loved your grandmother and your mother, and I love you as well, more than life itself.

Richard.'

Moira. Richard's child and her mother. No wonder Richard had treated her like royalty. By the time she finished reading, she was sobbing, Peter's arm round her shoulders, a damp handkerchief doing little to mop up the flow of tears.

And the worst thing was that he had never spoken of it. For a moment she wanted to hate him, wanted to go back up to that room and scream at him, slap him for doing that to her mother. All these years and he had never said anything. Not to her or to her parents.

"Why didn't he tell me?"

"It would have destroyed your father." Duncan leaned forward, hands clasped together. "He hated the thought of being beholden to anyone. He's a proud man, and a good one and your mother loved him. Simple as that. If he'd found out that his wife was Richard's daughter, he'd have seen his job as little more than charity. And yes we both know it wasn't, but some men are like that. And I suppose, once the lie was told, there was no taking it back, not without hurting everyone."

"He'll have to know now." And Duncan was right. It would hurt her father to know Richard had lied. But not as much as losing his wife had hurt. And it hadn't been charity. They'd both worked hard.

"What else does it say?" Ben was sitting cross-legged

on the floor, cake and construction kit forgotten. "The will?"

Peter looked at her wordlessly. She scanned the pages, leafing back and forth, the words making no sense or too much sense. "That can't be right. He left me... everything?" Duncan had studied law and she handed him the pages.

Lips moving as paper rustled. A log cracked in the fireplace sending a shower of sparks up the chimney, Ben shuffled on the rug, Laura leaned back on the sofa, watching.

"It is. He left you the Hall and the estate and everything else other than a few personal bequests to friends. The nephews don't get a mention, not that they deserve anything." He pulled her to her feet and hugged her. A long hug, tight and heavy and trembling and full of relief. "You'll be staying now, I take it?"

"I'll need to go to court, won't I? They'll have to overturn the decision. Can they do that?"

Duncan nodded. "You have the will. And it looks legal enough, though you'll need a proper lawyer to look at it."

"Hold on a minute." Peter was hunched over, head down as if he was in pain. "Was it witnessed? And if it was, why didn't they come forward earlier? If it's not been witnessed, it's worthless."

"Here." Duncan turned to the back pages. "A couple from America. They were staying in the cabins. Addresses and everything. It's valid. I'm pretty sure of it. My guess is Richard wanted to change his will secretly. No solicitors or witnesses who might have gossiped about Fiona or her mother." He handed the document back. "You're a wealthy woman now. And wealth like that brings its own problems. What are you going to do with it?"

She had no idea. In the last few hours she had been granted her greatest wish, and her world had changed irrevocably. There would be no desperate search for somewhere to live or a new job. She would have to tell her father the truth about Richard and her mother, but that could wait. The immediate future concerned her more.

She reached for Peter's hand, wanting his strength, but despite the warmth of the room his fingers were cold and held little comfort.

"I don't want to stay here tonight. Not with…" She was abandoning the house, but there was no way she could sleep in her bed knowing Richard was in that small room. And she needed time to think, to get all her thoughts in order.

"The cabin? Everything's there."

She turned to him. "It'll be freezing."

He pulled his hand away. "I'll go and turn the heating on, but it'll take a while to warm up."

Duncan shook his head. "I'd come with you, but I think I'd be more trouble than it's worth. Take Fiona. She knows the system better than anyone." The elderly man yawned and rolled his shoulders. "I'm inviting you all to my home for the evening. There's room for everyone and it's not fair on Ben having to sit around with adults talking when he's got a couple of space stations or whatever waiting to be built, and ferrets who need letting out. What d'you think?"

An evening at Duncan's. She smiled. "I'd love to."

"What about everyone else?"

Laura gave her husband a quick glance and nodded.

"We'd be delighted. I'll tidy up here while Fiona and Peter get themselves sorted. What do you need Duncan? There's plenty of venison left and mince pies and so on."

Duncan rubbed his hands together. "Bring whatever you want. I've got cheese and bread and plenty of good whisky. Ben? You need to start putting your things together, lad."

The Great Room felt cold as she followed Peter out, the fire burning down and the dark shadows of night creeping in from the corners. It was a frightening thought – this would be her responsibility in a month or so, or whenever things were made legal, and there would be inheritance tax and repairs to deal with and decisions to make about the cabins.

And there was Peter, a proud man like her father and not someone who would take the easy route despite his childhood. A man who had fought for his independence even at the cost of alienating his family and giving up his job. No wonder he had been withdrawn. If she ended up as wealthy as Duncan intimated – Richard's properties in London had to be worth a fortune at least – it might shatter any chance of a future together. And who could blame him. A failed marriage to a wife who married him for money and a family who ignored him. A man who, in his own words, had nothing to offer her.

He would leave. Not because he wanted to, but because he would believe it was the right thing to do. And she cursed Richard for doing this to her.

CHAPTER 26

Wind howled round the courtyard, rattling the windows, lifting a slate from the roof of one of the outhouses and send it clattering to the ground in a volley of loud cracks. Peter had to turn his back on the wind in order to breathe but they managed it, the car doors slamming shut to lessen the noise though not the sensation of being buffeted from one side to another.

"Sure you want to come?" He turned on the ignition, a rattle and stutter before the engine caught and he could ease his foot off the clutch. It would be a miracle if he managed to get the car back to Glasgow once all this was over.

"I'm here now. And Duncan's right – it'll be easier with two of us."

She was quiet. He kept the car in low gear, fighting the gusts coming inland. A wild night and if the storm didn't ease, the morning tide would be crashing against the harbour wall. It would be impressive at the very least though it would no doubt leave his car covered in salt and sand and whatever the sea flung at it. They were in for a restless night, not that he expected Richard to make another appearance in his dreams. The man was at peace – he'd felt it the moment he'd stepped into the room. The rush of gratitude and joy tinged with such sadness. But for all his faults Richard had done his best, and that was enough.

He glanced at Fiona sitting in the shabby passenger seat, her hands clasped tightly together. "It's been quite a day."

"Not what I expected. Not what anyone expected really." She sounded numb, and who could blame her. A Christmas Day complete with corpse and then the discovery that she was the real heir. Whatever happened, the Hall would be safe now.

The cabins were in darkness. He flicked the headlights to high, the rough track and the buildings and low cliffs eerie in the harsh beams.

"I'm sorry didn't get to thank you properly for the pen. It's something I'll always treasure."

"I don't know anyone else who's left-handed and I knew you'd appreciate it. Richard used it all the time. I tested the reservoir before I filled it – it would have been awful to give it to you and find it leaking everywhere, but you might want to have it checked properly." She hadn't looked at him. He could feel her stiffness, the way she held herself rigid and contained.

He gripped the steering wheel even tighter, the vehicle jouncing from pothole to pothole, the wind trying to find a weak spot. It was a relief when they reached the cabin and he could park close enough to get some protection from the storm.

A bleak and bitter interior – no trace of the warmth and comfort he had found here just two nights ago. Strange how some buildings returned to nothing but a soulless shell within days of being abandoned, retaining no memory of the humans who had lived and loved inside their walls. And yet the Hall had kept Richard's memory alive for years.

Fiona flicked on the lights, the brightness casting dark shadows that added to the bleakness of the interior. "Close the curtains will you? This might take me a few minutes."

He stood at the window. Tomorrow they would have to get someone down here, even if it meant finding a way back up to the top road or along the cliff path, though from the sounds of it that was perilous at the best of times. Maybe they could make some sort of rough bridge strong enough for one man to cross over the stream. If it hadn't been in flood he would have risked fording it – but then the bridge wouldn't have collapsed in the first place. There was no easy answer. He heard the click of the boiler coming to life, a steady thrum as it began work. The log burner was clean and empty, and he began laying a new fire.

"Can you give me a hand?" She called him from the hallway, standing amid the pile of boxes and bin liners. "I can't find the bedding."

"This one." He tore open the black bin liner and tipped the bedding out. The radiator was warming up and he hung the sheet over it while he found pillows and duvet, giving each one a fierce shake in an effort to dispel the lingering cold.

Something crashed against the outside wall – a heavy thud that reminded him of the tree crashing into the bridge and he grabbed Fiona. "Stay here. Away from the window." She was pale and shivering and he hurried to the front door and tugged it open, the wind strong enough to have him doubled over in an effort to keep his footing outside.

A gust had caught one of the wooden patio chairs and tossed it aside. It lay broken and defeated on the patio, but that was the only damage he could see. The hot tub was secure, its lid fastened tight and too cumbersome for the wind to lift, and he dragged the remains of the chair into one corner where it would be protected by the heavy bulk of the tub. The wind was a living thing, long fingers searching for any weaknesses and he hurried back inside, forcing the door shut and locking it against the intruder while they finished setting the cabin to rights. It was going to be a wild night, but at least the rain had held off.

A quick dash into the Hall to help Fiona collect her things, the precious papers from Richard sealed in a plastic bag, the shawl bundled up under her arm. He left his gifts on the coffee table, cautious of the weather and then they were heading out again, locking the oak door behind them and driving up to Duncan's where the others waited.

"Fiona?"

She looked at him.

"We need to talk."

Her shoulders drooped. "Later. When we're alone. For

Ben's sake let's not spoil tonight, let's just enjoy what we have right now. Please."

Right then he wanted nothing more than to kiss her, but that would only drag out the pain of separation. Better to make a clean break while she was too busy to miss him. He closed his eyes, for some inexplicable reason wishing he was back in the Hall. "Later then."

Duncan was at the door as they pushed the gate open and hurried up the path, fighting the gusts of wind with every step. "Welcome." He ushered them into the living room. "Now. What's it to be? A dram of my best, or a glass of port?"

It set the tone for a long Christmas evening: drinks by the fireside, ferrets scampering between legs and over the backs of chairs, sneaking food from plates until Ben grabbed them both and put them safe out of reach of forbidden delicacies. The change in the boy was astonishing. Peter could see his confidence coming to the fore, a poise and composure that had been lacking throughout his own childhood, and he envied the young man. It would be a fine thing, growing up here on the estate with Duncan watching over him. A good place to raise a child.

"Peter? Were you listening?"

He blinked. Fiona was looking at him. "Sorry, no. I was... daydreaming."

"It's well into Boxing Day and high time we were leaving. You look half-asleep as it is."

A round of goodnights and friendly hugs and handshakes, a quick kiss of Laura's cheek, her words quiet in his ear. "Take care of her. She looks fragile." And all he could do was nod.

The tide was out, but he could hear the breakers

crashing over the headland and down the edge where he had followed Bess into the tunnel. He took Fiona's arm and saw her safe into the car, his headlights pointing out to where the sea was white with spray and crashing waves. Laura and Jon followed behind, waving as they drove past to their own cabin and he saw Fiona inside and went out onto the patio for a last look.

"It looks angry – the sea, I mean." She had come up behind him to lean on the wooden balustrade. "I can't remember the last time we had a storm like this. They can get very dramatic at times. I used to like watching the waves, but now all I feel is sadness."

"I could stand here and watch for hours. My family didn't do seaside holidays. By the time I was two my brothers were all in the army and I spent most of the school holidays at home." He leaned on the rail, feeling it move slightly under his weight. "Don't get me wrong. I had acres of land to roam in, trees to climb, streams to paddle in, everything a boy might want. I just like watching the sea, that's all."

"There'll be plenty of time to stand and watch, together."

He turned to face her. "Will there? You're the new laird – or is it 'lady' – here, the inheritor of a huge domain and enough money from the sounds of it to renovate the entire estate. You'll have wealth beyond most people's dreams whereas I'm an out-of-work architect who can't even afford a decent car, let alone a house. Can you imagine what people will say?"

"Does it matter? Really? We talked about me working from the Hall – why can't you do that as well? Set up your own business and run it from here? You can help build the lodges as well."

He snorted. "Matter? Of course it matters. They'll take you for an idiot, tricked by someone only after your money. I care too much to let that happen to you. And…" He paused, folding his arms and staring at the stained flags of the patio. "I don't want anyone's charity."

"You're the idiot, Peter Sinclair. Who cares if people think you're after my money. You weren't last night when I had none. And what if Richard's will is declared invalid? What happens then? Tell me that, will you, because right now my whole world has been turned upside down and I'm not sure how I can cope with it, and all I want is someone to give me a hug and tell me everything's going to be alright. Even if they're lying. Can you at least do that? Please?"

Heat surged through his face and he wrapped his arms round her, pulling her close and holding her tight. "I'm sorry. Forgive me." Salt spray stung his cheek. She was shaking, her hair damp and smelling of the sea. "Let's go inside and get warm."

"I don't want to leave it like this."

"I'm tired, Fiona, and so are you. It's been a hell of a day what with one thing and another and we both need some sleep. We'll talk in the morning. Go inside and I'll make sure everything's secure."

The wind scoured his cheeks, numbed his fingers and fought him for every breath. He could hear it howling, or perhaps that was the dog, and in the end he left the waves and the wind alone and went inside, locking the door behind him and treacherously hoping she would be asleep when he joined her. It took him a few minutes to tidy up their few belongings: spare cake and sandwiches from Duncan stored in the fridge, his phone on charge though with no signal there seemed little point, Richard's will – still sealed in the bag – on the small dining table along with the razorbill skull. Somewhere out there, in the wild weather, a single razorbill waited for a partner who would never return. His coat was damp and he hung it in the hallway near the radiator and opened the bedroom door.

She was curled under the duvet and facing his side of the bed, the cashmere shawl a patchwork of gold and russet on top. He undressed and slipped under the cover, careful to avoid waking her. Salt drying on his lips and crusted on his eyelashes, the thunder of the waves outside, the delicate scent of her perfume and he turned his back to her, tugged the covers round his shoulders and closed his eyes.

"Don't leave me."

A cold hand touched his shoulder and he flinched. "I thought you were asleep."

"There's no way I can sleep now."

The pillow was twisted and he sat up and thumped it a couple of times before lying down again. It hadn't helped. "What can I do?"

"Tell me. What if you'd been the person named in the will? What if Richard had left it all to you? Do you think I'd have gone off in a sulk, because everyone would think I was only after your money?"

The idea horrified him. "Of course not. You're not that sort of person. And an inheritance like that would horrify me. Throughout my childhood I had it drummed into me how the family estate goes to the oldest son: the land, the house, the responsibilities and so on. I'll be lucky to get anything at all, and that's fine by me. I can think of nothing more stressful that having to run the family estate, especially by..." He swallowed, sat up and rubbed his face. "Christ, I've been behaving like a spoilt schoolboy, haven't I?"

She leaned against him, her face hot and wet. "Yes. You have. But I understand why. I think I'm going to be rather wealthy and it terrifies me to be honest. I have no idea where to start."

"Richard's funeral. That's the first thing you have to think about. Then rebuilding the bridge." He smoothed away her tears. "And then? Well, I think the Hall will tell you what needs doing next. Or Bess will."

"You know she won't let you leave even if you wanted to. You're part of the Hall now."

He pulled her closer and lay down, her head on his shoulder, both drained by the events of the past twelve hours. She was asleep within minutes, her hand limp on his breast, her breathing light and easy, her body boneless in slumber while he thought about the bridge. They would use the old stones as much as possible but make the roadway wide enough to take a good size lorry, and high enough above the water so that no flood could destroy it. And then the Hall. With sufficient funds, they could start replacing the crumbling stonework...

At half-past-seven he was wide awake, his mind still racing with ideas and plans. Fiona was fast asleep, but the wind howling round the cabin made him restless and uneasy. In the end he got out of bed, grabbed his clothes from where he had left them and went through to the kitchen for a brew and one of the thick venison sand-wiches left over from last night. It was still dark.

One glance at the weather had him shivering and he wrapped his fingers round his mug and thought of how he was going to explain his absence to his family. Water splattered against the windows, the waves roared. And a louder sound as someone banged on the door. A violent hammering, Ben's voice shouting, and he dropped the mug and ran to open it, the boy staggering into the hallway drenched and shaking and looking terrified.

"What's wrong? Is it Duncan? Is he alright?" He was aware of Fiona, now awake and out of bed, struggling into her jeans. Too late to protect her from whatever horror the lad was about to unleash.

"You've got to leave the cabin right now. Duncan says there's a storm coming. No." The lad shook his head, water dripping from hair and face and sweatshirt. "A storm surge, that's what he called it. The cabins are in danger and he says everyone's to go to the Hall."

He turned to Fiona. "Storm surge? What does he mean?" Even in the dim light of the hallway he could see the fear in her eyes.

"Low pressure, a windstorm and high tide all at the same time. It pushes the water levels much higher. There hasn't been one here for over seventy years but if Duncan's right we need to warn Laura and Jon and get to safety."

He handed the boy a towel. Fiona was pulling on her shoes. "How did you get here?"

"Ran."

The boy was still gasping for breath. He grabbed his car keys, tossing them to her. "Fiona? Go right now. You take Ben in my car and pick up Duncan, I'll get the Wilsons. Quicker that way. We'll meet you at the Hall."

She reached for her jacket and shawl and he ran into the bedroom to get his boots. When he came out, the tail lights of his car were a distant glitter in the darkness, the waves now throwing themselves against the harbour wall in their efforts to invade the land. And high tide was not due for another two hours. They would be overwhelmed by then.

He raced to the end cabin, sea spray soaking him to the skin in seconds. Was it only Sunday that he'd done just the same thing – bursting in on the couple in his desperate plea for help? It took longer this time to rouse them but once he explained Duncan's fears, they were quick to get dressed.

"Phone and coat, that's all you need, Laura. Nothing else is important." Jon was urging her out and waiting to close the cabin door. "The presents are still in the boot if that's what worries you. Come on!"

A nightmare drive, even in the Wilson's more powerful vehicle, the waves now clawing at the bottom of the harbour wall. By high tide the track would be submerged and all the cabins flooded. He wondered what would become of the four buildings once the sea had wreaked havoc on the small stretch of coast. Would the narrow strip of land remain once the sea retreated?

The Hall was high enough to weather any storm surge, but even Duncan's house could be in danger. He'd seen a video of high tides on the news a few years back, but nothing had prepared him for the power and ferocity of this wild sea.

Waves chased them, lapping at car tyres, spray leaping

over the harbour wall to pound at the windows until he thought they would shatter, and then he heard the thrumming of rubber on wooden slats and they were over the bridge and into the courtyard where the sea could not reach them.

"Good. You're here." Duncan was holding a wicker basket, Sock and Mitt peering between the open weave of canes. "It's going to get worse, but the Hall isn't in danger, thank goodness. We can hold out here until the worst's over, but I fear for the cabins and I should have expected this, with the weather as bad as it's been."

"Not your fault, and you've warned us in time. As for the cabins, those can be rebuilt." Laura made her way down the steps to the kitchen. "People can't." She took hold of her husband and kissed him. "Not quite the Christmas we expected, but certainly one neither of us will forget. I'm glad our presents were in the car. I'd hate to lose any of them."

Richard's pen and pencil. They were in the Great Room along with all his other things – the painted pebble and Duncan's carving. His laptop was also somewhere in the Hall, along with his suitcase. All he needed.

It took a while to get sorted: the ferrets allowed to run free in one of the inside storerooms where there was little to damage and plenty of mice to chase, hot drinks for everyone, toast and marmalade handed out. Fiona was distracted, flinching every time they heard the rattle of glass or the lights flickered, and Ben went to check on the ferrets and came back with an armful of candles from the pantry.

"Thought these might be useful." They rolled across the table: fat cream cylinders smelling of vanilla and reminding Peter of long hours spent kneeling in church. Fiona sat at one end of the table drinking instant coffee and looking grim, Laura opened yet another packet of biscuits and handed them out. Everyone waiting.

Fiona broke the silence. "I need to check a couple of things upstairs. Won't be long." She grabbed a bunch of keys from the hook behind the door. "Peter? Can you get some firewood for the sitting room, just in case we're stuck here for a while?"

"Sure." An easy enough task. Ben joined him and they filled two baskets with logs and hauled them through, stacking them in tidy piles on the hearth.

Fiona was nowhere to be seen when they'd finished and, concerned, he hurried back to the kitchen. "Duncan? Where's Fiona?"

"She went up to the Great Room I think. If she came down again, I must have missed her."

Elbows scraped on the narrow turret walls. He slipped once, cracking his shin on the edge of the step. "Fiona? Where the hell are you?"

The room was in darkness and he turned on the lights, scanning the space for some sign that she had been there. His pen and the other gifts were on the coffee table, along with her wind chime and painted pebble and her shawl draped over one of the sofas, but there was no sign of… and he cursed his stupidity.

Richard's will. He could see it as clear as if he was looking right at it – the plastic bag lying on the dining table in the cabin.

"Duncan? I think Fiona may have gone back to the cabin. I'm going to look for her."

"What in god's name made her do that in this storm? Is the girl mad?"

"We left Richard's will there."

"Christ, man, be careful. I'll do what I can here. It'll be dawn in half an hour. If you find her, get somewhere safe and I'll try and alert the coast guards."

The Land Rover had gone and he fought the gusts of wind until he was inside his own car, praying it would hold out until he found her. The engine started first time and he tightened his grip on the wheel and drove out of the courtyard into the full ferocity of the worst storm surge to hit the small harbour in living memory.

The sea was up against the harbour wall, waves flinging themselves towards the cabins and splattering the cliff walls behind. Engine juddering in second gear, he pushed through the flood, terrified of being overwhelmed by the water and in the dim and wavering light of his headlights he watched, horrified, as yet another wave broke against the stone defences and a wall of water, reaching higher than the cabins, flung itself upwards. It hung there for a long moment, shimmering in the faint beam of his lights, before it dropped.

The noise was deafening and, despite its weight, the car lost contact with the ground and slithered sideways across the rough gravel on a rush of water and sand and god-only-knew what else. There was no time to open the door and make a run for it, and even if he had, there was nowhere safe, not with waves crashing and spray blinding him. All he could do was cling to the steering wheel as the surge lifted the vehicle and tossed it towards the cliff. The crunch of metal, glass shattering on one side, water soaking him within seconds. The engine died and he clambered across the passenger seat, glass tumbling from his clothes. Seawater poured across the footwells and he fought to push open the door, panic making him clumsy.

"Fiona!" Spray blinded him, stinging his eyes, the roaring waves drowning all hope of hearing any reply. Ahead of him he could make out the dark bulk of the Land Rover, skewed across the track and lifeless.

CHAPTER 27

"**B**en!" Duncan limped to the turret door, ignoring Laura's protests. "Get down here, quickly boy."

The thud of feet coming down the steps, the boy reappearing with Jon close behind. "I can't find Fiona."

"We think she's gone back to the cabin. Peter's looking for her and I need you and Jon to help me up to the top floor if you're up for a rescue. Mind you, it'll not be comfortable so I won't think the worse of you if you say no. Laura, you stay here."

"But, you can't leave them out –"

"Enough, Ben, hear me? D'you think I want to leave them out there? What happens when the next man who goes out gets caught by the sea, and the next and then the next until we're all out there and drowning and no one left to save any of us? Tell me that?" He closed his eyes for a moment. "I've seen it before, too many times. The one thing we can do to help them is to get me to the storerooms on the top floor and then we'll see." He reached out to touch the boy's shoulder. "Trust me, lad. This is the only way we can help them."

He hurried as much as he could, his ankle screaming with each step, his legs faltering under the strain but he had Ben and Jon behind him ready to catch him should he fall, and then they were on the top floor and limping past Richard's room. No time to stop and consider what was in the small antechamber – time was short enough as it was. The storeroom door yielded to his desperate shove and he leaned against the jamb, panting. "That red box. Bring it here."

The hinges were stiff, but the contents looked clean and he picked out one of the two yellow tubes and handed it to Jon. "Maroon. Whatever you do, don't drop it." A pause, and then he handed the second one to Ben. "And the same goes for you." Two more cylinders, shorter and fatter, snug in one of his deep pockets, before he led the way back to the turret and up to the top of the steps where a heavy oak door opened onto the roof. "Put them on the top step and go back down. I can manage from here."

"Like hell you can. You're going out there?" Jon pointed a finger at the narrow parapet walk. "Not by yourself and with that foot. Tell me what to do and I'll go."

"It'll take too long." He gripped the stone frame of the door. "I have to do it, even if it means crawling there."

"Then I'll crawl behind you." The man was adamant, his hand now holding Duncan's wrist in a death grip. "We're wasting time." He let go and jerked his head at the narrow path. "Go on, man."

One last look at the boy. "Ben? Hand your maroon to

Jon and then stay inside. Don't come out whatever happens. Promise me?"

He could see the longing on the young face, but now was not the time for a youngster to be risking his life.

"I promise. But..." The swift hard hug surprised Duncan. "Be careful. Please."

He tousled the boy's hair. "I will. Wait inside for us."

Once out on the parapet they were at the mercy of the weather, the wind stealing every breath and leaving him gasping and struggling to walk. His hand found the iron railing along the low wall and he clung to it and limped along the path, Jon right behind him, fingers gripping the belt of his trousers, ready to tug him backwards. He hadn't even asked Jon if he was afraid of heights.

Despite the cold night air, he was sweating when the two of them reached the corner of the roof where a steel launching tripod faced out to sea.

"Jon?" He held out his hand.

"You've done this before?" The policeman handed over the first maroon.

"A couple of times. Not up here though. These were only put in the year before Richard... died. I just hope they work." A deft twist of his fingers removed the caps before he slid the cylinder down into the first of the steel tubes. "And the other." The second one readied and put in place. "Get ready. You might want to cover your ears." He squeezed the trigger. The maroons shot upwards, hundreds of feet into the sky before –

"Bloody hell!" Jon's hands pressed against his ears, but it was too late. Two thunderous booms deafened both of them, less than a second between the explosions. A brief flash of light accompanied each firework, but that would not be sufficient. Duncan leaned on the railing, listening. "Right. That should have got their attention but we'll give them a minute, just in case." The howl of the wind, the roar of waves ripping at the rocks. He waited, counting off the seconds, trying to calculate how long it might take. The rescue helicopter had to be scouring the coastline right now, but Fitzwilliam Hall was low on the list of priorities – they would be busy checking the larger communities first.

The flares in his pocket were the last hope. A quick glance over to the door. Ben was sheltering inside and watching. He twisted off the cap of the first, pulled out the cord and pointed the cylinder upwards. One hard tug and it was gone, arching into the night sky to hang like a brilliant star beneath its parachute before it was caught by the wind and tossed towards the cliffs behind the small group of cabins. The second fared better, lasting a good twenty seconds. He had done his best. Now it was up to the coastguards and whatever gods were looking after those caught out in the surge.

The walk back to the turret drained him of the last of his energy. Out of the wind it was easier to catch his breath. He let the boy lead the way and, although he was not a religious man, he found himself praying for the sound of helicopters.

CHAPTER 28

Peter's shouts were futile. The wind stole the words before they left his lips, the sea pulled his feet from under him more than once to leave him rolling under the water and fighting for air. A brief lull in the onslaught gave him a reprieve, and he bent over, gasping for breath. The sky was brightening or his night vision improving, for he could see the buildings, monochrome blocks in a dull grey landscape. Even the water was grey and sullen as it stormed the defences and crashed against the cabins.

He ran on, head down to avoid the worst of the falling spray, hands protecting his face from the stinging assault, bumping hips and knees and shoulders each time he fell, his hands bloody and his throat raw and the sky growing ever lighter.

"Fiona!" Water smashed into the wall and even above the roar, he heard the grind of stone blocks moving as the harbour wall collapsed inwards – a row of granite dominoes pushed by a giant finger. The sea leapt towards the cabin, smashing into the patio, turning balustrades to matchsticks and throwing itself at the door.

A figure appeared at the window and he dragged himself up the steps, water sucking at his legs while he clung to the splintered remains of the rails. The deafening roar of water pulling back in preparation for another assault and then Fiona was there, dragging him up and hauling him inside and slamming the door closed. "You idiot! What the hell did you think you were doing?"

He was too exhausted to answer. The interior of the cabin was a wreck, water swilling across the floor in great swirls, the stink of foulness, the fridge door swinging open.

"What do you think? I came to get you."

"Where's your car?"

He shook his head. "Useless. Same as yours. We can stay here or try making our way back, but that's not going to be easy. You've got the will?"

She held it up. "Watertight."

"Good. Hang onto it." He ventured a look outside, the window rattling, water leaking between wall and frame. "I think it's too dangerous to go back out. The cars are being thrown about like driftwood. If we're out there and they…" He shook his head. "I think we should stay here and hope the building holds up." There was nowhere else to go other than the cliff face behind and that would be a last resort.

"Why did you come?" Even out of the wind she was shivering.

"You were here, alone. What other reason do I need?" Water began trickling down from the ceiling. "Duncan's trying to get the coastguard, but I don't know how long that might take."

"It was stupid of me, but when I realised I'd left the will here I had to get it. At least I had to try. It was Richard's last wish and I'd have never forgiven myself if I hadn't done something. But now..." She was pale with fear and biting her lip.

The razorbill skull was still on the table and he picked it up and handed it across. "Keep this safe for me, will you? When we get back to the Hall I'm going to put it with the one Duncan gave me."

"A pair of razorbills, together. As they should be." She unsealed the plastic bag and slipped the skull inside, with Richard's will, before sealing it up and putting it deep into one of her pockets.

It was getting harder to talk, the wind screaming through cracks in the walls, the sea clamouring louder than thunder and all he could do was to hold her hand and pull her close as the door smashed open and the water surged in, deep and icy and killing. He shouted as loud as he could. "We have to get out. This place won't last much longer." Already he could hear the creak of timbers, the crack as tiles snapped. The cabin was on a propane gas supply. If the pipe broke.... "Ready?"

She nodded, eyes wide with terror and he hauled her out to the front entrance, the door broken and twisted, the sea strong enough to sweep them off their feet. It was a miracle they made it down to the track and to the base of the cliff just twenty yards from the back of the building.

He stripped off his borrowed coat and let the sea take it before boosting her up the first few feet. A difficult climb even in good conditions, dead brambles and gorse bushes scratching hands and faces, the rocks loose and crumbling. Even as they climbed the sea rose beneath them, tearing at the rocks in its desperation but they gained height, inch by inch, until they were both clinging to a tiny ledge several feet above the roiling surface.

The wall of rock gave them little protection from the wind and he edged his way until he was standing beside her, one arm around her waist, his body shielding her from the gale and the spray, pressing her against the rock face and hoping his strength was sufficient. He clung to the rock, aware of Fiona's exhaustion and the cold wind sapping their strength. He was sick of being cold. If he got out of this alive he would spend a whole day in a hot tub. Maybe two days.

And then it came: a roar louder than the sea, a downward draught stronger than the wind from behind, a light brilliant enough to scare away any night-time demons – a rescue helicopter hovering above the top of the cliff, its searchlight fixed on them as he hunched over to protect her from the downdraft.

And then she slipped. Not far, not really, but enough for her jacket to snag on a rock and the pocket rip open, the plastic bag snatched away by the wind and thrown into the thorny branches of a stunted bush a few yards away on the other side of a near vertical slab of rock. He would have to drop to the base of the cliff and make his way through the deep, swirling water before clambering up again.

He was a strong swimmer. He could do it. Someone shouted and he looked up, seeing an orange-clad crewman begin his descent on the end of the winch line.

Only a few minutes left before it was too late. He let go of the rock, lowered himself down a couple of feet to a wider ledge, water sucking at his legs.

"Leave it." She was leaning down, grabbing his shoulder, calling to him, her voice barely audible above the roar of rotors and the crash of waves.

"I can get it."

"No. I won't let you. It's not worth it."

"You need it. At least let me try."

And then she was sliding down towards him, slithering in the mud and muck to come to rest beside him. "Let it go, Peter. It's not important. I'd rather lose the Hall and everything else, than let you risk yourself." She pulled him closer to kiss his lips. A quick, hard contact, the taste of salt and longing and love, his body shuddering in response. "I can live without it."

A figure dropped down beside them, holding out the harness. Peter managed one last look at the gap but her hand stopped him. "It's not worth it. Trust me." And then she was in the harness and moving away from him and when he turned back, the plastic bag was nowhere to be seen and he could only stand there and wait for his turn.

It was a frightening experience and yet exhilarating: the helicopter huge and deafening above him, the harness tight under his arms, his rescuer silent and holding him so firmly that he had no fear of falling, but even so he was relieved when he was finally over the edge of the doorway and strapped into a seat beside Fiona. The noise was thunderous, the swaying motion enough to make him nauseous but they were both alive and he grabbed her hand and squeezed and then she pointed to the door where the winchman was kneeling. The crewman who had plucked them from death's reach was pointing down at the water before being lowered once more and he saw the heat-seeking camera, the blurry white image of something in the water.

Not a human, surely. It couldn't be Duncan, not out there, and Ben was not strong enough to survive. Her fingernails dug into his hand. A long wait, the winch man watching intently, holding the line and speaking to someone. Fiona was leaning forward as well, one hand pressed against her mouth. And then a helmeted head appeared and the crewman was dragged in, his hands full of something that looked like …

A dog. A tangle of sodden black fur with no sign of movement, eyes closed and its jaws clamped around a tangled mess of seaweed. The long tail thumped once on the floor.

"All clear!" The winch man slid the door shut before turning his attention to Fiona and Peter. Headphones and radio, an emergency blanket for each of them. The crewman hunkered down beside them.

"Lucky for you two we were already in the air. Is there somewhere close by we can drop you where you'll be safe? This is a bad one and we need to go straight out again."

"The headland in front of the Hall. We'll be safe there." Peter stretched forward to hold her hand. "And the dog as well. She belongs to…" He had no idea. Did Bess belong to the Hall, or perhaps it was the other way round. Without the dog he would never have found this place or Fiona, and Richard's body would have lain undiscovered, maybe even for eternity.

"Hang on." The chopper tilted, changed direction and

then they were moving, over the shattered remnants of the cabins, over Duncan's gatehouse just safe above the water line, over the courtyard where Duncan and Ben and the Wilsons were standing and waving, and then they were dropping down to hover a couple of feet above the level stretch of grazed grass on the top of the headland.

He kept hold of Fiona's hand until the crewman opened the door and even then it was hard to let go. Bess had not moved, other than a low growl when one of the crewmen attempted to take the seaweed from between her jaws, but he knew in his heart she would be fine. After all, what could possibly harm a ghost?

The helicopter hovered, the gentlest of movements, the door opened and they were escorted out, dropping down to the ground and running hunched over until they were away from the rotors and turning round to watch as Bess launched herself from the doorway and raced towards them coming to a halt in front of Peter.

He bent down to the dog, putting his hand out and she looked at him with dark eyes full of intelligence and trust. She took a step closer, dropping the clump of seaweed – and with it the sealed bag containing Richard's last will and testament – into his hands, just as a child started singing in the shadows of the Hall. A soft growl of welcome, and she was gone.

CHAPTER 29

The road seemed to go on forever, the landscape flat and formless, nothing but a series of gentle rises and falls, the fields on either side beginning to turn green with new growth. He was high about sea level, the ocean visible in the distance on his right, sparkling in the bright May sunshine. It had rained earlier, but only a brief shower, and he drove on confident of his destination.

His retriever pup, all legs and huge paws and floppy ears, was sound asleep in her harness on the passenger seat, undisturbed by the jolting of the SUV as it turned down the narrow track and headed for the inlet hidden from sight. A lurch as the vehicle bounced over the new bridge with its steel girders and railings and deck. A wider bridge as well, though he mourned the loss of its predecessor. The stones had come from this land, had been shaped by men from this land, and although many of the blocks had been recovered, the old bridge was gone forever.

The small bay opened up ahead of him: Black Dog Hall

half-hidden under scaffolding and plastic sheeting, the ruined quayside where last year there had been cabins, and before that, stone cottages. Circles of scorched earth where bonfires had burned the broken timbers, a new ditch dug and lined for the utilities and cables, concrete foundations laid out for the lodges to arrive. And then the real work would begin.

Duncan was driving one of the new quad bikes along the quayside, Ben – on his half-term holiday – no doubt somewhere out on the hills watching wildlife or taking photographs. The boy had talent and was already planning his future. Peter's birthday present to the lad – a new camera lens – was in the back along with the rest of his belongings. Everything packed away and waiting for the go-ahead for him to work from home instead of driving into Coupersons every day from the rented studio flat in Aberdeen. Home. The word sounded good.

Fiona wasn't expecting him. He'd thought about telling her last night when they talked, but she'd looked tired and he still hadn't been sure he could make it. An easy journey this time. No floods or diversions or accidents. Over the last five months he'd learned the short cuts and the places to avoid, although he couldn't resist stopping for a pasty if the van was there.

He'd miss those. Not as much as he had missed Fiona though. And he would still have to drive back to Aberdeen every couple of months to keep up with the board meetings and conferences and put his designs in for the latest submissions. The first ones had done better than anyone could have imagined. Four award-winning lodges, individually designed to fit in with their surroundings, construction on the first due to start next week. They were going to call them The Fitzwilliam Lodges.

The puppy raised her head as they approached the gatehouse, as if she'd been waiting for that very moment.

"Keira, lie down. Good girl." Her fur was soft under his fingers and he gave a gentle tug to one black ear. Twelve weeks old and already walking to heel. He wondered how she would get on with Sock and Mitt, although from Duncan's last letter, it was likely that there'd be a few more pets in the gatehouse for Ben to look after.

The courtyard was busy with white vans and trucks and workmen unloading more supplies: bags of cement and sand, wooden joists and reclaimed oak floorboards. It would be autumn before the basic structural restoration was complete, but he could see the Hall coming to life again. Fiona's new Land Rover was over by the store-rooms and he parked and got out to find her.

"Peter? You didn't say you were coming today."

She was running towards him, heedless of the bags and wires and wheelbarrows and he went to meet her, holding his arms out to lift her up and spin her round. Someone cheered, he heard the roar of the quad bike and the clatter of shovels but nothing mattered, only her weight in his arms and her face pressed against his. Warm breath and stifled sobs in his ear. "Please tell me it's for more than a week this time?"

A long kiss, not as long as either would have liked – the audience was vocal in its approval – but enough to send a flush of heat through his body.

"This time?" He brushed a strand of her hair away from his forehead and glanced up at the windows above. Two young girls and a black dog looking down on him from one of the upper windows, an elderly man standing behind them, nodding his approval. As he watched, they faded out of sight, and he turned back to her, smiling. "This time, Fiona Cameron, I've come home to you for good."

ABOUT THE AUTHOR

Leona Grace is the author of two classic western trilogies as well as several works in other genres, including ghost stories, wartime romances, crime thrillers and SF and modern horror. She lives in the northwest of England and, since retiring from a career teaching in specialist educational settings, devotes much of her time to writing.

Printed in Great Britain
by Amazon

78267415R00194